THE SPOUT SPRING

&

(AS A BONUS)
TOO POOR TO PAINT
TOO PROUD TO WHITEWASH

THE SPOUT SPRING
&
(AS A BONUS)
TOO POOR TO PAINT
TOO PROUD TO
WHITEWASH

The Early Years

A Book of Fiction by Mark W. Royston

iUniverse, Inc.

New York Lincoln Shanghai

The Spout Spring & (As a Bonus) Too Poor to Paint Too Proud to Whitewash
The Early Years

iUniverse, Inc.

For information address:
iUniverse, Inc.
2021 Pine Lake Road, Suite 100
Lincoln, NE 68512
www.iuniverse.com

ISBN: 0-595-30187-8

Printed in the United States of America

"To the thirsty I will give from the spring of life-giving water."

Revelation 21:6

CONTENTS

▼

THE SPOUT SPRING

TOO POOR TO PAINT TOO PROUD TO WHITEWASH

THE
SPOUT
SPRING

A
Book
of
Fiction

by
Mark W.
Royston

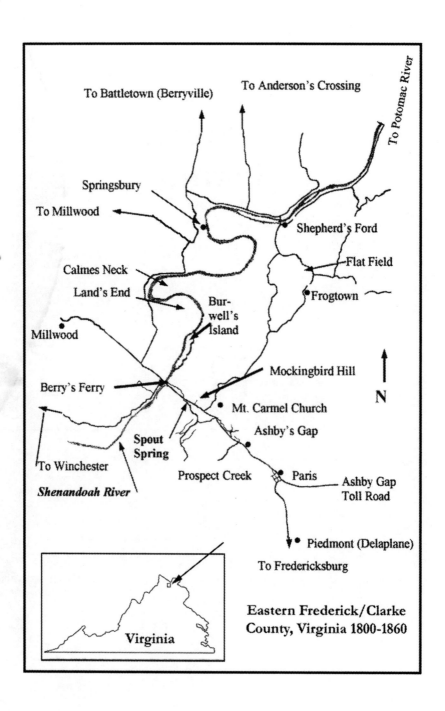

To Battletown (Berryville)

To Anderson's Crossing

To Potomac River

Springsbury

To Millwood

Shepherd's Ford

Flat Field

Calmes Neck

Land's End

Frogtown

Bur-
well's
Island

Millwood

Mockingbird Hill

Berry's Ferry

N

Mt. Carmel Church

Spout
Spring

Ashby's Gap

To Winchester

Prospect Creek

Paris

Ashby Gap
Toll Road

Shenandoah River

Piedmont (Delaplane)

To Fredericksburg

Eastern Frederick/Clarke
County, Virginia 1800-1860

Virginia

PREFACE

Today, you can walk right by it and never suspect that a spring of life-giving fluid once came from the mountain; that it flowed through a 'spring house' and meandered through a small meadow as it leisurely made its way to Prospect Creek. The meadow is now a marsh, which the mountaineers call a 'dreen.' Where the water enters the creek is hard to discern as there is mostly seepage. The wooden bridge that spanned the creek is gone. Though near a small highway, the invasion of the forest and the deer ticks helps keep it remote.

But this was not always so. The spring once flowed from the side of the mountain and down to a pool where it collected and then fell another three or four feet and began its meandering toward the creek. The water seemed to spout from the mountain, as in time the pool became hidden behind the forest growth. Later, someone inserted a pipe about 2" in diameter into the mountain pool, which gave even more of an appearance of a spouting spring as it made its last traverse out of the mountain. Along the way a spring house was built which was used to keep things like milk and butter cool, even on the hottest summer days.

The spring was ever flowing and it supplied water primarily for the nearest neighbors, but in drought times buggies and wagons, and later, cars and trucks lined up to await their turn to collect water in large vats. Most of the time the large containers were left on the vehicle and the water was toted across the creek in buckets.

Waiting for the buckets to fill was a rewarding time, as there was no way to hurry the flow. On a hot summer day there was no better way to work than to relax and watch the water spill into the bucket. Two large white oak trees stood sentinel over the spring and provided a backrest to those who waited. The spring was of such value that it was a part of the deeds that transferred the adjoining land to insure that ownership was maintained.

How to tell the story of the spring and the mountain people who depended on it? Their births, deaths, and marriage dates only tell a small part of the story. It would be nice to contemplate the way they might have lived in the early days of our country's history. Why not a work of fiction? The aura of the spring and its surroundings make it possible. So, read my story.

Note

The names of the persons are all actually people who lived during those days. The stories about them and the connections are fiction. It is the writer's way of telling how the mountain people might have lived in the early days of our country's history. The births, deaths, inventions, and the historical events are accurate for the most part.

PROLOGUE

It was early in the morning and Mathew braced himself against the hard driving rain and sleet, quickly slamming the door on his way outside. He glanced across the toll road toward what was left of a burned out house. Forever his father's screams at the death of little Louisa would be with him. Louisa was the first to be buried in the family graveyard on the hill. They lost her at the age of six.

But right now he was looking for the old man. He glanced up and down the toll road. "Why I am looking here, I do not know. He is never here. He is always at the Spout Spring," he muttered. No one in his right mind would leave the house on a December day like today, but then the old man was maybe just a little out of his mind. Ever since he turned eighty, it was more difficult to keep track of him. And it was in the early morning that he often slipped out of the house and made his way a few yards up Wildcat Hollow and across the creek to the Spout Spring.

In the summertime when the heat swept across the Shenandoah and pushed its way into the foothills, it was understandable why one would beat a retreat to the coolness of the spring. It flowed down out of a rock crevice, bounced its way to the foot of the mountain, and with one last effort to release itself from the hills, came through a formation of rocks that formed a natural spout, just high enough to allow space for a bucket. It meandered some 50 yards, before joining Prospect Creek, which drained the mountain area known as Wildcat Hollow. Along the way it formed pools that became natural places for a spring box. White Oak trees had sprung up and prospered as their roots sank into the moist soil.

Mathew apologized for waking his sister as he passed her bedroom before making the trek toward the Spout Spring. The creek was swollen from the downpour that was now into its third day, and gingerly he crossed the creek on the recently built wooden bridge. As he neared the spring he could see the hunched figure of his father leaning between two of the larger white oaks. "Hey, Pa," he called, "it is time for breakfast. Come on back to the house. You will catch your death of cold in this weather." Receiving no response he reached out and poked the old man and repeated the words. Not a movement. Touching him, his hand naturally recoiled as he felt the skin of a person who was no longer alive. "Damn," he gasped, "the old man is dead."

His mind raced as he muttered the first thoughts that came to his mind. "Serves him right, he should know that no one could survive long sitting here in this weather." He stood for a moment and watched a rivulet of water run off the wedge formed by the tilted tricorn hat, a constant part of the old man's attire, as he realized the stupidity of these thoughts.

The real problem now is how to get the old man straightened out, because if rigor mortis sets in we will have to bury him in a sitting position. His thoughts were a jumble as he continued his mental journey. *We should have made the old man lose some weight. He is well over six feet and his girth, well, he was a typical Royston. This is going to be a real problem. I had better get some help.*

Across the creek and back to the old house he sped. Once again, he woke his sister, Mollie, and told her where and how he had found the old man. Always the practical one, she shed no tears, only asking, "Are you sure?"

"Damn right. I am sure," he retorted. "Wake James, for we have some work that needs to be done quickly."

Shortly her husband James came into the kitchen, pulling up his pants and sliding on his suspenders. Mathew explained how he had found the old man, staring at the Spout Spring through unseeing eyes. "I think the best thing to do is to take a blanket and lay it on top of the spring box. We can lay the old man on that and wait for more help to carry him back to the house. It is going to be hell getting him across that creek, even with the bridge."

Mathew was still soaked and he hated leaving the fireplace that was producing heat sufficient to bring steam out of his clothes. But if the old man was not moved now, it would complicate the burying task, and who knew how long this blasted rain would last. James followed Mathew as they made their way to the Spout Spring.

Maybe I was just imagining things. Maybe I dreamt it, Mathew thought. *But if so, this wetness seems very real.* No, there was the old man, still in that crouched position staring at the spring. Together he and James spread the blanket over the wooden slats of the spring box and began to lift and tug and shove the remains in a journey from the white oaks to the top of the spring box.

James looked at Mathew as they struggled at their chore and mused, "Maybe we should just dig a grave here to bury the old man. After all, you know how much he loved this spot."

Mathew thought for a minute. "No," he said, "as much as the old man liked it, Ma hates it, particularly the dampness. She has a place picked out up on the hill next to Louisa and there, in time, we will have to bury them both."

The task was finally completed and sweat and weariness replaced the wetness of the rain. Mathew now faced a more difficult task. *Ma has to be told,* he thought. Mathew and Minerva had lived with the old man and Ann since their house burned. It was a chore that fell naturally to Mathew, as he was the only one of the boys who remained on property near the home place. Entering the house, he called out for his wife, "Min, awake yourself, there is a problem."

"Awake your own self," was a reply from the kitchen. "You know I cannot sleep with you up and about."

"Min, the old man is dead. I found him at his usual place, leaning against the white oaks and staring at the spring."

"Somehow that does not surprise me," Minerva replied. "Certainly that is where he would want to be at the time to go."

"But, damnit, he could have waited for better weather. It is raining and sleeting like I have never seen," Mathew cursed.

"What is that infernal talk all about?" came a question from a bedroom just off the kitchen.

Better face it straight up, Mathew thought. "Ma, the Constable is dead. We found him over at the Spout Spring."

"Does not surprise me," Ann answered without a hint of shock. It was just like she was talking about a neighbor 'leaving for higher ground,' as she always called it. "I have been expecting it. Where did you put him?"

"Jim and I laid him out on the spring box lid," Mathew answered as he went toward his mother.

She shrugged off the attempted hug as she always did and began to talk of the necessary steps to bury the old man. "We will bury the Constable up on the hill across the creek toward the river," she began, as if talking to herself. "We picked out a spot when we buried Louisa and now he will be the second one there, although, I should not be very far behind him."

"Ma, do not talk like that," Mathew protested.

"Well, it is true. I will be buried beside him, but if he had his way and if it were possible, he would want to have that consarned spring buried with him. Well, it is true," she repeated. "I have competed with that Jezebel for over fifty years. He would never tell me anything, but you could see his mouth moving as he would sit and talk to that spring."

"It is going to take some work to get Dad across the creek. I do not think that two of us can handle it," he reverted to the practicality of the moment.

"No hurry, he will be better off out in the cold until we can get all the kids here," Ann murmured. "We just have to make sure that he is not disturbed by the varmints before the boys get home and can help you tote him across the branch. After that, we will take him up the hill and bury him. Uriah Blue can do the talking. He is the oldest and is pretty good at it. He should have been a preacher," she talked non-stop.

She is talking way too much, Mathew thought. Normally getting this much conversation out of his mother would be like prying those wildcats out of the den up the hollow. A few strides and he brushed aside her protest and took her in his arms, probably the first time since he had left home to marry Minerva.

"I loved him so," she sobbed. "Why did he have to go?"

"Ma, you know I do not have the answer to that. Only God knows those things," Mathew said in a futile attempt to answer the unanswerable.

She snapped back and continued to voice her thoughts just like she was making a list. "Get a hold of the boys first. There is Uriah. I think you can still get across the Shenandoah to Millwood. Get him first, as the river may get too high. Then there is Joseph over in Fauquier and where's P.K.? Get P.K. right now."

"P.K. is just across the river, Ma. He is farming the Lindsay place," Mathew interrupted, knowing full well that his mother knew exactly where Peter Kemp was.

"Well, if he came around more often, I would know where he was," she said of her youngest boy.

"The girls," Mathew posed, "what about the girls?"

"They will be here. Girls know when these things happen," Ann replied in a tone that left no room for questions. By now Mollie had come into the kitchen and the three women talked of things that needed to be said by women at such times. It was time to get wet again.

Mathew went to the shed and saddled up the old dappled mare. She was the favorite of the Constable and would be the one that would make this run to Millwood. *If the river is crossable, it should not take much longer than an hour there and an hour back,* he thought as he headed west toward the Shenandoah.

"I can not take you across," came the soft sound of a black voice. "Massa Berry says it is too dangerous to make any more trips."

"I need to get across and tell brother Uriah that Pa is dead."

"Well, in that case, ride that mare aboard. Mister Peter is dead?" came the question from the Jo Anderson, an old black man with the same name as Mathew's mother's family.

Jo mused, "I remember I was just a young'n when Massa Peter talked Massa Berry into letting him farm that bottom land. He convinced Massa Berry that the rent money would buy him some new ferry boats." The boat's nose was turned slightly into the strong current, which helped propel the boat across the river and deposit them on the other side.

"Hang around. Uriah and I will be back within two hours, I promise."

"Do not know about that, maybe Massa Berry will not like it," Jo answered.

"I am counting on you," Mathew shouted, as he mounted and turned the mare toward Millwood.

He could hear the sound of the mill grinding as he neared the small town. There were two mills, both on the same creek about three-quarters of a mile apart. The one in Millwood was the largest and even in this terrible weather, it was running. Probably not grinding any wheat, he thought as he passed by. Weather is way too wet to make flour. A few minutes later, he turned up the hill that headed toward Berryville and topped the hill as he turned into Uriah's lane.

The sight of Uriah always startled him, as he was a dead ringer for the Constable. He was a bit smaller, but was sure to fill out as he grew toward the old man's age.

"Why are you here in such weather, little brother?" was Uriah's greeting.

On another day, that would have brought a retort as the 'little brother' was the subtle greeting that Uriah used to remind Mathew who was the elder of the family. "Pa is dead," Mathew did not know any other way to say it.

For a few minutes they talked of the morning's events and Mathew waited for the barb that never came. He was waiting for, "Why did you let the old man wander off?"

The retort would have been, "Of course, you could have had him stay with you," as he knew full well that the son living the nearest the Spout Spring was the son who would be responsible for taking care of the old man.

"Have you told P.K. or Joseph? Are you hungry? Can we get back across the river?"

A negative reply to the first two and "I think so, if we hurry," decided their course of action. Food would wait until the river was crossed. Uriah had a fresh horse and would find Peter Kemp as they headed back toward the river.

The three met at the west bank and after a passionate plea, Jo Anderson, the black ferryman, took them across to the Blue Ridge side. It was the last ferryboat to cross for seven days, as the river went on the worse rampage anyone could remember.

"Worse than the flood of '22," one old timer muttered.

Peter Kemp got the chore of riding on to Fauquier County to tell Joseph. By late afternoon, the four boys were planning the burial of Constable Peter Royston, age 81, resident of Clarke County, Virginia, a county that was only twenty years old in 1856. One by one, the daughters arrived as Ma said they would. Somehow the mountain communication chain did its job. Families from all through the mountains came to pay their respects to one of the elders of the Blue Ridge, who had lived there some thirty-five years.

They volunteered to stay near the body at the spring until it was time to bring him across the creek for burying. A couple reported hearing voices during the early hours of the morning, but that was assumed to be related to the mountain elixir which seemed to be a necessity to see them through the never ceasing rain. "Sure sounded female to me," one reported.

"And it sounded like she was talking to the Constable," another said. Both were practical men and this was mentioned only after the Constable was buried on the hill.

The grave was being dug by some of the local mountaineers and while the weather raged, each would pass the chore to another for a turn and then make his way back across the creek to the warmth of a fireplace.

Two days later the remains of the Constable were placed in a rough wooden box and brought across the branch to the house. In full procession family and friends went across the creek as it turned to cross the toll road. Taking a winding path up the hill, the Constable was laid to rest alongside his granddaughter, Louisa. Uriah said many words, none of which anyone remembered.

Dirt and mud were thrown over the box, and Constable Peter Royston had made his last physical visit to the spring. P.K., the youngest son and one with an artistic flair, fashioned a cross that had the words, "Constable Peter Royston, born 1776, died 1856. May there always be a spring in his step."

All smiled at his attempt at whimsy, but none brought up the question that was on everyone's mind. What are we going to do with the silver dipper? It has not been out of his sight since Uriah had given it to him some thirty years ago for a Christmas present.

Ann reached out and picked up the dipper that had been brought to the burial ground. "Maybe I will keep it myself to remember my husband."

Later, when all the neighbors had said their farewell, it was the brash Peter Kemp who finally brought it up. "Why did Pa love the Spout Spring so much? Where did Pa come from?" They all looked at Ann, wife of Peter and mother of nine. She smiled and said, "It is too late to ask him and if he did not want to tell you when he was alive, how can I tell you now?" With that the book was closed.

PRE–1800

1777

"Consul Holker, you have an unannounced visitor," intoned an aide.

"As long as he is not British, show him in," responded John Holker, consul from France, but at the moment far from Paris. A soldier in a Revolutionary War uniform strode into the room and was greeted by Holker. "Peter Kemp, excuse me, Captain Peter Kemp, what brings you to this city of brotherly love on this first anniversary of the signing of your Declaration of Independence?"

Captain Kemp jibed, "I haven't seen you since you passed through Gloucester County and moved to the frontier, and here you are a French official. What county is that you moved to? Berkeley? Have the Indians burned down the cabin yet?"

The reference to the cabin brought a wry smile to Holker's lips, as both knew the 'cabin' was a large mansion on a plantation in one of the westernmost counties of Northern Virginia. "While I have a small cabin there, I am thinking of talking to Fielding Lewis about obtaining some land in Frederick County, abutting the Shenandoah River and extending for a few thousand acres to the west. Maybe when this revolution is over, you can come up and help fend off the Indians and help me build a bigger cabin there," Holker continued. "It is real pretty country and it needs citizens like you."

"Looks like I am stuck in Gloucester, but I have somebody that I will send you in about twenty-five years. And I guarantee that he will be better than anybody you could ever have to run that farm, 'cause I will teach him myself."

"And who might this person be who holds such esteem in your eyes?" Holker asked. "And what is his background?"

"Right now he is only one year old, and his father is keeping a wary eye out for any authorities that might want to return the family to the blacksmith where his father was apprenticed." Kemp knew this would whet the appetite of his friend, the consul.

"Now how could a blacksmith's son be any good to me in running a thousand acre farm?" Holker asked.

"He is not just any blacksmith's son. His grandfather on his father's side once had some 15,000 to 20,000 acres down around the headwaters of the Rappahannock."

"Well, I never," Holker snorted, knowing full well who Peter Kemp was talking about. "So he did end up marrying your daughter. Just to make sure I know this stripling when and if he shows up, what name will he be carrying?"

Peter Kemp laughed. "I guarantee you will recognize him when he arrives."

He ended the short visit by saying he had to return to his army duties as a quartermaster for Washington. "The General is interested in an area called Valley Forge, and I am supposed to give him a report on it. Meanwhile, make sure those Frenchmen recognize us as a country and you may get a free trip to France for your efforts." Captain Kemp knew well that France's recognition was vital to the colonies and their efforts to be independent. "If they do not recognize us we may all be spending our time beyond the frontier. In fact, if the troops cannot handle the Redcoats, they may be here in Philadelphia one of these days."

1800–1810

December 31, 1799

What a way to see out the last day of the century, Peter mused. The youth unsaddled his horse and tethered him with a long rope, allowing him to forage in the dead winter grass growing plentifully along a branch the locals named Goose Creek. He could see the lights of Piedmont, a small town nearby, but he felt it best to stay away from any town that might have ties to the Piedmont section of Virginia. His father had warned him that the 'sins' of the father might just creep into the second generation as long as the blacksmith was alive. It was almost a balmy evening for the season, and he felt good as he and his tinderbox coaxed a small fire into warming some food for his meal.

"Tomorrow, I will climb the Blue Ridge and be in a new world," he said. When he was alone he tended to talk aloud as he had spent a lot of time in his own company. The horse gave a snort as if to agree with him. Both settled down to an early New Year's Eve. He was awakened at midnight by the sound of gunfire from the nearby village as they celebrated the dawn of a new century.

Early in the morning the horse foraging nearby awakened him. Over some coffee, left over beans and corn bread, he planned his day. He remembered the directions he had been given. After you leave Piedmont, the next recognizable town is Paris, which sits at the foot of Ashby's Gap on the eastern slope of the Blue Ridge. Turn left there as it meets the Toll Road and cross the mountain at the Gap. If you need more directions, wait until you clear the Gap. There is one house, just over the crest and that is about it until you reach the river. The Orear family is well known in the area and they can help with any questions. Since you will probably never see the city for which Paris is named, take a look back as you reach the crest to see an attempt to lay out a town to look like its namesake.

Peter saddled his horse and tied his meager belongings to the rear of the saddle. He swung a leg over the horse's back with practiced ease and headed the horse to the west across Goose Creek. A smaller creek joined Goose Creek at that point and he followed this meandering creek. *This creek changes course more times than Dad did as he kept out of sight of the blacksmith,* he mused. *I am glad the weather is nice, as fording this creek in rainy times would wear out even the best of horses.*

By mid-morning he had reached Paris, made his way up the Blue Ridge and pausing at Ashby's Gap, he took a look back at the Piedmont section of Virginia and the town of Paris. By now civilization had come to this area of Virginia and brought with it a patchwork of alternating fields and forest. Streams that were tree lined could be traced as they worked their way toward the tidewater section of the state.

State, he thought. He had only known Virginia as a state, while his father always referred to Virginia as a colony. What a difference twenty-five years could make in the life of a person. (Or for that matter, how about one hundred.) A hundred years before, his family had everything. The panic of '55 had greased the skids and loyalty to the crown had done the rest.

He brought his mind back to the present and looked down on Paris. On that mild New Year's Day the town proper could be seen as one main street with a 'Y' in the road. Emanating from the central area were double sets of stone fences that delineated where the future streets of a city would be.

With one last look he turned his attention to his new surroundings. To the west, the vastness of the Shenandoah Valley stretched out before him. Straight ahead was a road that had signs of being maintained and which was, he supposed, the continuation of the Ashby's Gap Toll Road. There was a wooden barrier, but no attendant on this January first, 1800. He worked his way past the gate and started down the mountain. To the left, he saw a well-worn but rutted road that headed into the forest. *Must go to the Orear's,* he thought. As he neared the turn-off he noticed a solitary figure on horseback. "Hallo," he greeted. "Is this the way to Springsbury Farm?"

"Every way is the way to every place, if you know which turns to take," was the reply.

Now here's a fellow I could enjoy talking to, Peter thought. "I am Peter Royston and you must be Mr. Orear," he answered. "Can you tell me the best way to Springsbury?"

"You want to cross the Shenandoah at Berry's Ferry and take the first road to your right," he said. "But you will not get there today unless you want to ford the river. The Ferryman Berry and Toll Man Ashby have taken the day off, as this day comes around once in a hundred years, though I believe both of them think they will be here for the turn of the next century."

Peter pondered how much Orear had told him about the men in so few words.

"And the best way to get to Berry's Ferry, when the ferry is running?" Peter questioned.

"Well, the fastest way is to go straight down the mountain on the Toll Road, past the Meeting House and over Fox Trap Hill," he advised. "It might even be faster if your horse slips on the loose shale as you descend the Fox Trap."

"There is another way?"

"Yes, this time of year the way I take is to turn left where the branch crosses the Toll Road. Follow the trail along the creek until it joins Prospect Creek at the Wildcat Den. Follow the creek until you leave the mountain. Berry's Ferry is straight ahead. Ask the ferryman the best way to get to Springsbury. Are you intending to work there? They need no help. I talked to a fellow the other day. Nobody is hiring in the Valley," Orear concluded.

This man is telling me more than I wanted to know, Peter thought as he said good-bye and started down the mountain a bit downhearted.

He could hear the rippling of the branch to his right as he rode down the Toll Road. As he followed the road past a sharp turn around an outcropping of granite, he saw the creek crossing, so Peter took the path to the left that followed the creek. Soon he was deep in a forest of hardwoods that had never seen a woodsman's axe. He was overcome by the beauty of the moment. He paused to watch squirrels scamper among the rocks as the sun filtered through the trees. He slowed the horse's canter to a trot, then to a walk, as Peter could not take in enough of the beauty. Finally, the creek joined a larger branch and he followed it to the right. He could see the sun break through a clearing ahead when his attention was drawn to a small stream coming into the creek from the south.

Getting down off the horse, he worked his way across the creek and cupping his hands, he captured some of the water that was joining the creek. Never had he tasted water so good. While the day was almost warm, the water was cool, and he could not seem to get enough. He had to find the source of this water. On foot, he followed the stream as it seeped through a small marsh and ended at a pool near some small white oaks. The water came spouting out of a crevice and dropped some four feet into the pool.

"Now this is heaven," he murmured aloud.

And he then heard a very feminine voice, "You do not know how true that is."

He jumped back and looked for the source of the voice. There was only the trickle of the spring as it made its final descent from the pool. "I must be imagining things," he said aloud.

"You are not imagining things. I am the spirit of the spring and for eons I have waited for someone who could hear my voice. I have talked to so many, but all they hear is the sound of the water falling."

"I do not believe what I am hearing,"

"Oh, yes, you do. You just are not ready to admit it. Let me tell you about yourself, so that you will understand this moment in your life. I am Maria and your name is Peter and you are twenty-four years old. Your father has you afraid of professing who you are, lest you be arrested. Is what I am saying true so far?"

Peter thought, *could I be talking to myself? Only I know my thoughts and this beautiful voice is telling me things that only I tell myself.*

"Do not lose me," the beautiful voice begged. "I have waited so long for someone to talk to. I cannot touch you, but I will be a part of you forever. Now I tell you, do not cross the river tonight. Stay here with me and cross tomorrow. And tomorrow you will meet the girl that you will marry. She does not know that I exist, but she will be affected by our relationship."

"How will I recognize her?" Peter questioned. "I may meet more than one."

"You will know from the sound of her voice, and her name will be the same as my mother's," responded this most memorable voice.

"Let me bring my horse across the creek and I will camp here tonight," Peter said as if assuring himself that he had been talking to himself.

The voice laughed, "I have already taken care of that. Look behind you."

Peter turned, and there was his horse looking not at him, but at the spring. He unsaddled the horse and began to reach for the tether. "Do not worry," said the voice. "The horse will not stray. I will keep him here. See how good the grass is, even in December."

Peter left the horse to roam, sure that he would have to make a search tomorrow before he could head out. Evening came and he built a small fire between some rocks. The intimacy of the evening as he talked to the voice in the spring became overpowering. Finally he drifted off and the night was filled with so many dreams that he had trouble separating dreams from reality. And why not? It had been a full day.

The morning dawned. Surely yesterday was a dream and he would look at the spring and wonder if he would ever hear that beautiful voice again.

"Already up? It is time to get moving," came the answer to his question.

"This voice is real," he practically screamed for joy. "How can I leave here, knowing that you are real?"

"You will leave, but you will return. You are entering a new part of your life where you will no longer fear the past. There is not room here at the spring for a home, but a few yards yonder where the creek turns to cross the road, there is a house owned by a less than likable old man that you will someday occupy. Then you can come and talk to me anytime."

"How will I buy this house and land? I have barely enough to pay the ferryman to make my way to Springsbury. And now I have heard that there is no work in the Valley."

"There will be work for you at Springsbury, and you will still have your ferry toll in your pocket once you are on the other side. Hurry now and come back to visit me soon."

Peter reluctantly saddled his horse and once again loaded his belongings. He crossed the branch and made his way to where the creek crossed the Toll Road. *So this is the house I am supposed to buy?* he wondered. It was a perfect spot. A delta formed as the branch made its turn to cross the road. From the east, the Toll Road came down from the area Mr. Orear called Fox Trap Hill. It dropped down to an almost level area and then took a straight route toward the river. The branch had been worked so that crossing it would be easy during most weather conditions.

Peter gave a sigh as he left his newfound home, albeit owned by someone unknown at the moment. *If only there was a way to buy it…,* he dreamed. He turned the horse west to locate the ferry. This would take the last of his money and he hoped that the fishing was good, as he might have to try his hand at it, if the job did not work out. He laughed that hearty laugh for which he was known. *And where will I get the fishing line?* A few minutes of riding brought him to the ferry. There were three or four boats tied up on the west bank that were guarded by a solitary black youth who could not have been over fifteen.

"I need a ride across," Peter called. "How much for me and my horse?"

"This is your lucky day, Massa" the youth answered. "Massa Berry said it would be good luck to give the first rider of the New Year a free pass, and you are it. He did not say anything about your horse, so I may be in trouble later." He grinned.

The horse and rider went aboard for the short ferry ride, and as they crossed Peter looked up and down the river. *Located so close to the mountains, it must be a wild one when the rains come,* he thought.

As if reading his thoughts, the black youth said, "Sometimes we have to fish the boats out of Burls' Island." Peter heard the accent so familiar to his ears and logged in the name 'Burwell' as the probable owner of the small spit of land that was so generously called an island. He guessed it qualified, since the water seemed to go on all sides.

Landing on the other side, Peter thanked the lad for his generosity, and his mind jumped back to last night. No way could he have known about the free trip. Had it been just a figment of his imagination? "Which way is it to Springs-bury Farm?" he asked the youth.

"Go up the road a piece and take the first turn to your right. Go past the first bend in the river, that be owned by Massa Calmes. Go past the tilt hammer mill, then look for the biggest house you done ever seen. That will be Springsbury."

Peter swung into the saddle and followed the instructions, all the while jin-gling the coins in his pocket to reassure himself of the events of the past two days. As he came to the bend in the river, he thought, *how dirty I must appear.* Travel-ing for four days can leave one pretty grubby. The river seemed very clear so he dismounted and washed up as best he could. *This will have to do. Maybe I will sneak into the barn at Springsbury and find a place to do better.*

Soon the main trail turned sharply from the course of the river and in front of him was the entrance to a farm. It showed signs of grandeur, but looked like the fence rows could use some trimming. This must be the main entrance to Spring-sbury, he thought, not realizing that he was entering through one of the side roads. Shortly, the road was joined by a larger one from the north and on a nearby hill stood a house that could truly be called a mansion. *I wonder if that is how my grandpa's house used to look before the crash.*

His reverie was interrupted by the sounds of a racing horse and buggy with the occupant screaming at the top of her lungs. The rig swept by him in a moment, but he reacted instantly and kicked his horse into a gallop. He overtook the buggy and grabbing the reins, he brought the snorting horse to a halt. He could see the horse shiver as the sweat ran down its haunches, and he kept a firm grip on the bridle until the horse settled down.

He turned to the driver and saw before him the most beautiful girl he had ever seen. Her long blond hair was swirled about her face, which was crimson with excitement. "Good day, Miss," he said in his best Piedmont accent.

"And a good day to you," she responded.

Peter's heart leapt. The voice was the same as the one at the spring. How could this be? he wanted to shout. The next words came out in a blurt. "Will you marry me?"

She laughed as if that was the normal conversation from someone she just met. "Probably," she teased, "but we will have to get to know each other better. Right now I am off to visit my friend at Springsbury."

She took control of the reins and Peter let her precede him as she drove in front of the large house and tossing the reins to an attendant, rushed through the door with the flair of someone who was comfortable with her surroundings. Peter turned his attention to the task at hand, that of finding Mister Holker. He talked to the attendant who by now was wiping down the girl's horse. *My bride to be,* he thought, *maybe that spring lady is only a spirit, but she can really predict the future.*

"Where can I find Mr. Holker?" he queried.

The black man looked at Peter's attire and considered his answer. "If he will see you, his office is just through that door." He indicated the main entrance.

Peter strode toward the entrance and the attendant beat him to the door and opened it for him. "To the left, sir, you will find him." Peter thanked him and knocked on the closed door.

"Enter," boomed a voice. Peter opened the door and walked into an office that was bare of any adornment except for a French flag hanging alongside an American flag adorned with the original thirteen stars and thirteen stripes.

Peter started to say, "I am Peter…"

John Holker interrupted, "You are Peter Kemp's grandson, and you have come to be my savior."

Peter stared at him. *How could he know who I am?*

Holker continued, "I have been waiting for you for a long time. Your grandfather said he would send you to me when last we met in '77 and Peter Kemp always keeps his word. How is my old friend, by the way?"

Peter dropped his eyes. "He died a few months ago, just after he pronounced that I was now capable to be the man you wanted."

Holker's eyes showed the disappointment at the distance that kept the old friends apart for so many years. "I saw him last when he was with General Washington at Valley Forge. We were friends for many years. What a leader he was! Did he tell you our agreement that you would be my overseer? I do not need to ask if you are capable. Peter Kemp would not have sent you, if you were not. It looks like you could use some grooming. I will have my man give you an advance and you can go to Battletown and talk to my tailor. He will know what style bests suits an overseer at Springsbury. There is a good room off the slaves' quarters. It will be suitable. You can clean up there."

Peter rejoiced at the moment. He would have to work extra hard to live up to his grandfather's promises.

As he turned to leave, Holker asked, "Are you still a single man?"

Peter answered, "Yes, but I just met the girl that I am going to marry."

Holker said, "You just arrived. Who could that be?"

Peter explained the encounter on the way in and Holker let out a roar. "You mean Ann Anderson! She and my step-daughter are the best of friends. If you can tame her, you will be lucky indeed, and I will be the best man at your wedding."

"That is a deal," Peter responded, "and I will be a proud man to have you." It was mutual friendship at first meeting.

Peter found the room that was given him and began to clean up. He heard a rap at the door and a black slave entered. "I will have some hot water ready shortly. I will bring in the tub."

Peter thought of the past days pronouncements and wondered how he could have dreamed all these things. *Were his wishes coming true? Was there really a lady at the spring who knew the future?* Already he was anxious to return and visit the place he wanted to call home.

Peter Royston, Overseer! Peter leaned forward and let the reins of the bay drop as the horse nibbled at the grass. Looking out across the many acres of Springsbury toward the Shenandoah, he reveled in the thought of his position. Less than twenty-five years old and he was given such responsibilities. Here only a few months, and already John Holker was giving him his head in running the plantation.

Holker was a man of many interests, which took him from Springsbury much of the time. Collecting on debts owed him from France and his duties in the Revolutionary War were taking more and more of his time. The plantation was largely self-contained. Blacksmiths were the heart of the system that made the plantation largely independent. Much of the seed crop was grown on the land, calves were born, and horses, too. There was even iron ore available from across the river with the tilt hammer mill busy crushing the rock that contained the ore.

As Peter looked across the river, he could just make out the depression and the stream that showed the entrance to what he learned was called Wildcat Hollow. *Had he really talked to a spirit?* The ache to return and know for sure occupied more and more of his thoughts, it almost pushing aside the image of the flaxen-haired beauty he had rescued when he first arrived.

He reached down and pulled on the reins of the bay to head back toward the manor house. John Holker was due back at any moment and it would not do to find his next in command daydreaming. Peter reached the house just as the dust was rising from the road entering Springsbury. John Holker was back and with him a large man who greeted Peter with a laugh and a Dutch accent.

"I hear you saved my daughter a few months ago when her horse started," he said. Holker interrupted and introduced Peter to Joseph Anderson.

"Not only that," Anderson continued, "now she says she is going to marry you. Now I am here to put an end to that foolishness. What makes you think you are good enough for my daughter?"

Peter carefully considered these words. *It was obvious that Ann Anderson must have taken a liking to him or she would not be telling her father such things.* Emboldened by his thoughts, he rejoined, "Yes, I do want to marry your daughter. I was just going to ask Mr. Holker for directions to your house, so that I could ask permission to court your daughter."

"Hurrumph" snorted Anderson. "Lot of good it would do me to refuse. Ann has a mind of her own, and while I claim to be in charge, it is she who does the deciding. Come on over and do your courting and we will see what happens." With that Anderson put a spur to his horse and galloped off to the north.

John Holker laughed. "That is the first time I have seen old Joe at a loss for words. Why not follow up this weekend and go visiting to Anderson's Crossing?"

"Before I do that," Peter stated, "I need to make a quick trip over to the mountains. I need to check on a spring over there that might be a source of water in drought times."

"Well, since that sounds like business to me, why not ride over this afternoon and do your checking?"

Riding south past the tilt hammer mill, he considered the foolishness of his actions. While it was true the spring did appear to be one that would survive the droughts, it was unlikely that the springs on the plantation would go dry. He wondered if Holker believed his reasons for wanting a trip to the mountains.

Riding up to the area, known as Berry's Ferry, Peter again saw the young black man that gave him free passage on January 2, 1800. "Since I will be making this trip across the Shenandoah from time to time," Peter pointed out, "I should probably know your name."

"It is Jo Anderson," the youth replied.

"And who owns you?" Peter inquired.

You could see the face change as the word 'owns' came out. "I belong to Mister McCormick who lives some ways up the Valley. I was sent down the Valley to be with some more McCormicks, and Massa Berry is my boss right now. I am on loan while Massa Berry needs me."

Peter noted the ease with which Jo Anderson moved from slave talk to more precise English. *There is more to this darkie than meets the eye,* he mused silently. "If you work for Mr. Berry and are owned by Mr. McCormick, where do you get the name of Anderson?" Peter asked.

"Well, my mother was owned by Mr. Joseph Anderson up at Anderson's Crossing and we took his name. I like to fiddle with things, so Massa Anderson asked if I wanted to help with the machinery at Mister McCormick's place. I said I did and there I was. That is, until Massa Berry needed some help with the boats. Now I mostly help with the boats when the harvesting is over. We're working on a machine that will cut the grain and tie it in a bundle, all at the same time," he confided. "Now ain't that something? We still got lotsa problems, and I think that Massa Mac is about ready to give up. But I ain't 'guine to let him. I think we can make it work."

The boat had long touched shore on the east side of the river, but Peter was enjoying the conversation. Springsbury spent much time on harvesting and a mechanical method would surely be a help. He could see the end of the cheap labor made available through the slaves.

"I will be back in a few hours," Peter told Jo Anderson and he rode toward the entrance of Prospect Creek into Wildcat Hollow. Arriving at the freshet that led to the spring, he paused. "This is the silliest thing I have ever done," he said aloud. "There is no way I should be crossing this creek and trying to talk to a spring. I must be out of my mind."

His self-argument was interrupted as he saw a man carrying out two buckets of water. "Hello," he said. "My name is Peter Royston and who might you be?"

"Philip Earheart," was the response. "And I live in that place there where the creek crosses the road." It was the house that Peter had seen some months before as he had left the hollow.

"Own it?" Peter questioned, in his abrupt way.

"No, none of us own anything here in the mountain. It is all owned by Rawleigh Colston, who lives over in Western Virginia, though he also owns much land in Kentucky and Ohio territories. We just rent from him."

"Well, if you ever want to move out, let me know. I like the area. Mind if I go over and get some water from the spring?" Peter wondered what he would do if Philip Earheart said no.

"Help yourself," was the response, as he stared at the Peter's empty hands, "Although I do not know how you can carry any water off."

Peter almost blushed. "I just wanted to clear the dirt out of my throat and to sit a spell." Philip Earheart went on his way and Peter crossed the creek, following the small but visible water trail back to where it dropped out of the mountain.

The lilting sound of the water falling quickly brought him back to his first visit some months ago. It was now April and the flowers were beginning to grow. And while it was still cold on this shady side of the mountain, the sun filtering through the leaves of the white oaks had a strange warming effect. "I have been waiting for your return," sang that same voice that he had heard from only two sources. "What took you so long?"

Looking around to make sure that Philip Earheart had not returned, Peter answered truthfully, "I thought I had been dreaming."

"How could you think you dreamt about such things? Did you not meet the person you will marry?" the voice persisted.

"I did meet someone with a voice like yours; how could you know all these things?"

The response came back as a query, "Did I know it was going to happen or did I make it happen?"

Peter thought he would let that remark slide. "I came back because I could not stay away and if you knew so much, you know that I would come." Then the thought of others being at the spring brought out a question, "Do you talk to that man, Philip Earheart?"

"Why, I think you are jealous," the voice teased. "That man can hear only the noises of his intestines. Tell me of your work and your life."

Peter told the voice of his successes and his shortcomings, of his desires and how much he would rather just stay here near the spring.

"It is not for me to take you from the world, but for you to take my words out to the world. The peace I give you must be passed on to others. Now, tell me how you are going to court this girl, and how you plan to get her to marry you?"

Peter admitted that he had little to offer this girl who seemed to have all the beaus she wanted. "I told her I wanted to marry her the first time I saw her, but I haven't seen her since."

"Do you expect her to come and court you?" the voice asked. "Get on your horse and go see her and do not come back here until you have her promise."

With that, Peter looked up to find the sun had begun to fall behind the mountain. "I must go," he said.

"I am waiting for your return," the spring bubbled in an enticing way. "But remember, court the girl and win her hand, before you return."

Peter swung a leg over the saddle and began his way back to the river. "If I wait too long Jo Anderson might decide to go home. He appears to be overly independent for a slave," Peter mused aloud. "Maybe I will have to cross at Burwell's Island." The horse snorted as if to let him know how it felt about a cold swim on this April afternoon. Luck was with him and he found Jo Anderson tinkering with one of the cables that held the boat. He prevailed upon the slave to give him passage across the river. As Peter rode west and then north, he heard the distinctive sound of the tilt hammer mill guiding him toward the south entrance of Springsbury.

The sounds of the evening were always a pleasure. The laughter of the slaves could be heard as they came in from the fields and looked forward to evening time when they were almost free. As supper was being prepared, shy but admiring females looked on as the males doffed their shirts and washed in the large trough. The trough water not only served as their bath, but also as water for the animals. Protecting the animals meant no soap was allowed.

The smell of food was different here as it was segregated from the main house, the white workers and the slaves. The best quality food went to the manor house and the slaves ate the coarser of the meats, fruits and vegetables. Peter thought the slaves' food was superior in taste even to that served in the manor house. The slaves learned to season well to hide the inferior quality of the available food. They served to their own a fare that was, in many cases, superior to the more bland diet enjoyed by the master of the house.

The Shenandoah Valley is a world of its own, Peter thought as he became familiar with more and more of the territory. In the northern sector, the river ran just under the mountains, making it susceptible to rapid flooding when sudden storms attacked the unmovable mountains, and finding them impenetrable, took their revenge on the valley below. It caused flooding beyond imagination.

The beauty and richness of the flat lands or bottom lands, which were created by the floods of the past, enticed owners to build in the area. Then the owners would need to be thankful for the generosity of the higher ground neighbor in flood times.

To the west was Winchester, a sizeable city and the political center of the northern Shenandoah Valley. While a land grant in the last century had given Lord Fairfax ownership and control of all the land between the Rappahannock and the Potomac River from the Chesapeake to their headwaters, the colonial governors had encouraged the settlement of the Shenandoah Valley against the wishes of the Lord.

When the war was over, the rights of the English lords were protected by the Jay Treaty. It was obvious that settlers around Winchester were 'different' from those living in the eastern part of the county known as Frederick. The county was divided into two distinct areas, conveniently separated by a creek running to the north that made its way through the Valley to the Potomac River. Western Frederick was heavily populated, Eastern Frederick was not. The divisions were severe. Eastern Frederick County was peopled by those with ties to the Piedmont and Tidewater parts of Virginia. Western Frederick had ties to Pennsylvania and Delaware.

To those living to the east of the Opequon Creek, derision was the weapon against those of lesser 'breeding' who lived on the west side of the creek. Those on the west fell back on their overwhelming numbers and the Courts that centered near the area of denser population. When court dates had to be kept, it was a difficult for the Easterners to make the trip over terrain that resisted attempts at road building.

There was raft traffic along the Shenandoah and some movement of grain to the mills and markets of Baltimore. Baltimore was the source of the manufactured goods that moved up the Potomac River to the Shenandoah junction. From there it was moved by wagon to Battletown and Millwood, as the Shenandoah River was much more accommodating to its outbound cargo than to its return.

Peter learned the political divisions and sided with those of his employer and his ancestry. Eastern Frederick was becoming more independent, as two grinding mills had been built in and near the town of Millwood. Just a bit less than a crossroads, it was blessed with a fast running stream that worked its way toward the Shenandoah, dropping sufficiently at that spot to make a mill possible. A few hundred yards out of the town, the creek dropped again to allow the building of a second mill. Roads changed to accept these new ventures, and grain was hauled by wagons to Millwood to be made into flour, and then returned to the consumers in the area, without the long trip to Baltimore.

While the iron ore supplying the tilt hammer mill was not of the best quality, it was sufficient to be forged into tools to keep the plantations going. Peter thus learned to meet needs, if at all possible, by using locally supplied materials.

The local ladies depended on Baltimore for their finery and orders from the merchants of Battletown always included the ladies' wishes in their annual purchases.

Persistence paid off, Peter thought. He was about ready to give up, and almost missed the words when they finally came. He ended his Sunday visit with Ann and as usual gave his customary goodbye ending with, "Will you marry me?"

Starting to mount his horse, he spun around at the quiet but resolute, "Yes."

Jumping back from the horse with such gusto that the bay took off on its own, Peter ran back to Ann and asked the question again, "Will you marry me?"

"Sounds like you are losing your hearing," she murmured. "Yes, I said, yes, and if you do not hear it this time it is NO forever."

On the way back to Springsbury, he exulted, "I have found myself a bride, I have found myself a bride." He picked up the pace as he entered the main gate and spurred the bay into a gallop. Chickens and pigs flew from the slave quarter's area and the commotion brought out John Holker.

"What is all the confounded noise?" he wanted to know.

"She is going to marry me, she is going to marry me," he kept repeating.

"Maybe that is a surprise to you," Holker said. "Everybody else in eastern Frederick wants to know, what took you so long? Looks like I had better get my new suit pressed if I am still to be best man. Where's the wedding going to be, at that Church of England Chapel?"

He knew that would be enough to set Peter off. Falling for the bait, Peter rejoined, "It is the Episcopal Church, not the Church of England and probably yes, that is where it will be."

"When?" Holker pursued.

"In June, most likely. I do not get to pick such things. Just be sure you do not make any plans to head for France or New England or anyplace else."

The word spread rapidly through Springsbury and Peter spent much time repeating himself, as everyone wanted to hear the news straight from him. And all the time he was thinking, *there is only one that I really want to tell this to.*

Late one afternoon found him crossing the Shenandoah and telling Jo Anderson of his great fortune. By now the two were friends so that some teasing went back and forth. Jo pushed it a bit by saying, "So you are going to marry an Anderson. It looks like we are going to be relatives."

Peter thought, *there are a lot of people who would make worse relatives.* Aloud, he retorted, "I do not need any darkie relatives, especially ones who do not know their place."

"My place is in the boat," said Jo Anderson and Peter let the conversation drift to other things.

"I am going to go up to Rockbridge and spend some time with Massa McCormick," Jo added, "so do not count on me being 'round here to take you cross the river every time you get the idea. 'Sides, it looks like you want to spend more time in the mountains. If you keep it up, wonder how you ever get any work done."

Peter flushed a bit, wondering what Jo might say if he knew what his real reason was for crossing the river.

Peter mounted the bay and made his way up the Toll Road to Wildcat Hollow, and seeing Phillip Earheart sitting on the porch of his log house, he stopped to visit a bit. "When are you going to move out and let me take over this house?" Peter asked.

"Well, you never know," Earheart answered, commenting that he saw Peter in the mountains quite a bit. "Just exactly what business does Holker have in this area?" Earheart wanted to know, thinking that Peter was here because John Holker had sent him.

Let him think that is why I come, thought Peter and aloud he said, "Now you know I could not talk about such things, if there was a reason he was sending me here. John Holker knows Rawleigh Colston quite well, and I am sure if he had any thing of importance he needed to know he would talk to Colston himself."

"That is, if he could ever find Colston in the area," Earheart mused.

Tiring of the conversation, Peter made some excuse and headed up Wildcat Hollow, and with a glance back toward the Earheart place, he turned toward the spring. It was a late fall day and the leaves were turning, making the place even more enchanting.

"It is about time you came to see me," the voice began.

"Now, do not start nagging me." Peter responded. "And here I am with the news that you have been waiting for."

"Do not tell me that she finally said yes," the voice questioned, "and have you set a date?"

"Not yet, probably in June."

"June is such a pretty time here at the spring. She will love getting married here," said the voice.

"Married here? Married here! Now you know there is no way that is going to happen."

"And why not?" the voice wanted to know. "I haven't attended a wedding for thousands of years, and you would surely want my blessings on that day. The last wedding I was involved in was a long time ago, but one that everyone will remember forever."

What a strange way she has of putting things, thought Peter. Then aloud he said, "Do you really think that she would marry me here and not insist on a church wedding?"

"Now, how could a church compete with the beauty that is here at the spring?" she wanted to know. "All you have to do is present it to her properly. I will guarantee such a beautiful day for a wedding that it will be the only thing talked about for years."

"Well, I have to think that over," Peter ventured.

"Phillip Earheart thinks there is something of value here at the spring. He sees you turn off from the road and comes over here to poke around. In fact, he is probably watching you right now to see why you keep coming here. Every time he comes over for water it looks like he is trying to find the treasure you have hidden here."

"He'll never know what the treasure is," Peter responded, for the first time admitting that he was attracted to the voice in the strangest way. The water seemed to increase in volume and the sounds of it falling were sweet music to him.

"I wish you could visit without him sneaking around trying to find out your business. Why not bring Ann here? That way she can see how beautiful the spring is, and Earheart will think she is the reason you come here."

Night was falling when Peter left the spring and passed by Earheart's house. He could see the flickering of a candle and the dropping of a curtain that signaled a watchful eye from within. Once across the river he urged the bay toward Springsbury, hurrying to be home before the slaves quit serving supper.

Once it is decided that a wedding will take place, it is best that the man stay out from underfoot. The girls giggle and plan, the mothers compare notes and outline the map of things to come. It seemed like Peter was not even welcome to visit. What more do you need of a male after the question has been asked and the answer given? It was almost like the seed of conception had been planted, so what more could a male offer? This brought up the problem that could change all the details.

It was the wedding location. How could he bring to question the location and then shift the location to the spring? It was indeed a challenge. Maybe he could get the females to do the job for him. Riding in from Springsbury on a Saturday, he greeted his bride-to-be' with, "Got time to ride over to the chapel and make sure it will be the right place for the wedding?"

"Ride?" Ann responded. "We can see the church from here."

"Oh, I must get married in the Anglican Church," Peter said. "That is the only one for me."

"Why not the Dutch Church?" Ann questioned. "And besides, I have never thought of you as one who cared for the insides of any church."

"When it comes to marriage, it is the man's choice," Peter insisted. "Why, if we can not get married in the Anglican Church, I would just as soon get married right outside in the open, in fact, I'd rather."

"Get married outside? Now that is a new one. Where would we get someone to marry us outside?"

"Oh, I have friends in high places," Peter laughed. "And I even have a place that is prettier than the insides of any church."

"And where is that?" Ann wanted to know.

"How many times have you been across the Shenandoah?" Peter asked.

"Only once," Ann said, "and I almost drowned."

"What happened?" Peter asked.

"My horse shied and I was thrown out of the boat, but a darkie that used to belong to my dad saved me."

"A darkie? What was his name?"

"Jo Anderson, he calls himself," Ann remembered.

"Well, if you want to see the prettiest spot in the world, you might get to see him again as we go across the river at Berry's Ferry."

An hour later the two were heading for Berry's Ferry and the spring. Peter told Ann about the beautiful spot, but could not bring himself to mention the lady that lived in the spring who talked to him. The river was on the high side, but presented no danger as they crossed. Jo Anderson acknowledged Ann's presence, but as was the practice, talked only to Peter. Ann seemed a bit embarrassed by seeing him. Remounting, they made their way to the Wildcat Hollow entrance and the creek that had to be crossed before finding the path to the spring. Peter wondered to himself, *what would happen if the spring started to talk to him while he was with Ann?* He could be in a peck of trouble.

The spring area was beautiful. It was almost like someone was expecting company and had gone to great lengths to make a spectacular display. Ann was moved by the beauty of the spot and dismounting, said to Peter, "Truly, this is a most beautiful spot. I can see why you want us to get married here." The spring gurgled her pleasure, but said not a word.

With a glance toward the spring, Peter took Ann in his arms and said, "I love you and this spring and the land around it not only will be our wedding site, but will be ours to live on in the future."

Ann gave a look at the area and remembering the house at the turnoff to the hollow, murmured, "It looks like someone already lives there."

"Do not worry about him," Peter answered. "I do not think he likes the mountains, and he does not own it anyway."

They stood and made wedding plans, and as they finally turned to leave, Ann said, "Now I will have to convince my mother that this is the place to have the wedding. I will leave it up to you to convince my father."

I will need to convince him and the bishop and John Holker and all the other people that will be involved, Peter thought.

"Peter, I never saw a churchman so perplexed," exclaimed John Holker. "'By God and all that is Holy, I have never held a wedding outside the church and I am not about to start now,' were his exact words. I explained to him that the other choice was the Dutch Reformed Church or maybe the Holy Mother Church of my own," he chuckled. "Guess what? You have old Bishop Meade doing the ceremony, though he is probably going to be over there with his censer beforehand, trying to stink up the place with incense."

Peter retorted, "He can try to stink up the place all he wants, but it is way more sacred than any cathedral he has ever seen."

"What does everyone else think of your wedding location?" Holker wanted to know. "I need to get this wedding over, so that we can get back to the business of my plantation."

"Well, old man Anderson thought it was pretty funny from the beginning. Mother Anderson is going along with it, but she is having a tizzy about how to get there. Ann has all her girlfriends wanting to dress like Greek goddesses and strew flowers all over the place."

Holker nodded, "All in all, I think it is going to be a great success, even though we are going to have it on a Tuesday."

"Tuesday, Tuesday," Peter exclaimed. "Why on God's green earth does it have to be a Tuesday? This is going to cost you a fortune if we invite anybody else from Springsbury."

"Hell, invite them all! Let them tromp up the place. I will leave it up to you to recover the lost work time, but the Bishop says he can only do it on a Tuesday."

"Tuesday it is, in July," said Peter. "And I will leave it up to Ann to pick the exact Tuesday."

"Hannah Blue, you are the most contrary woman I have ever seen," snorted Joseph Anderson. "Daughter Annie is getting married and you are all tied up about the route you want to take to get there."

"Say what you want, but there is no way I am going to go across the river in a boat with him," Ann's mother answered. "There are too many people who want to point a finger and laugh. So I will just find my way across at Shepherd's Ford and you can go anyway you want, and I know which way that will be."

"Well, you and Ann and the ladies go across at Shepherd's Ford and we men will cross at Berry's Ferry. Besides, the bride and groom are not supposed to see each other on the day of the wedding before the ceremony."

"That is excuse enough, Joseph Anderson, though we both know why you want to cross at the Ferry."

"Ma, you know good and well that it is only you that I love," Joseph Anderson implored.

On the day of the wedding, all found their way to the spring, with most of the men crossing the river at Berry's Ferry. The bride, her mother, and the rest of the ladies, trying to stay as dry as possible, crossed at Shepherd's Ford.

"We are gathered together to witness the joining of hands in Holy Matrimony," the Bishop intoned, trying to be as bishopric as possible with his makeshift altar between the two white oak trees. It was a truly beautiful day, as the Lady of the Spring had promised. The birds flitted, the dampness of the grotto-like spring surroundings cooled the air. There was a gentle breeze that made that Tuesday, July 14, 1801, a very special day. The ladies tried to make sure that their gowns stayed dry and the men walked as lightly as possible, as though inside a church. The spell of the spring captured them all.

"I do," said Peter.

"I will," responded Ann and the wedding of Peter Royston and Ann Anderson was over. The spring seemed to murmur its own blessing and once or twice, Peter was sure he heard the Lady of the Spring saying her own "Amen" during the procedure. When they turned to leave, there in the rear, partially hidden by the bushes, was the brown shape of Jo Anderson, who disappeared just as suddenly as he had appeared.

By the time the couple reached the ferry, there was Jo Anderson waiting to take them back as they returned to Springsbury to begin married life together. There was a look on Jo Anderson's face that seemed to be more than one who was wishing a friend well on his wedding day. Ann seem to take special care not to face him directly, and as was in keeping with the customs of the time, his eyes lowered when there was any chance that she might look at him.

On the valley side of the river, there was a carriage awaiting the bride and groom, and they waved to the others on the east side of the river as they rode off toward Springsbury. Jo would take his time getting the boat back across the river to continue ferrying the rest of the wedding party.

The last to cross were Joseph and Hannah Anderson, along with Bishop Meade. Hannah had finally agreed to cross at the Ferry after Joseph told her that people would talk if she insisted on returning home by way of Shepherd's Ford. He was careful not to engage Jo Anderson in any conversation as the short trip was made.

"I have got a bit of a problem," Peter observed.

"And what is that?" said the voice from the spring.

"Ann is heavy with child and I should be there for the birthing."

"That is true," said the voice, "and why will not you be there?"

"Mister Holker wants me to accompany him to Baltimore to pick up a stallion that is arriving by ship within the fortnight," Peter said.

"Why you and not someone else?" the voice questioned.

"He feels that only I have the strength to keep the stallion in check and my bay is the strongest horse on the plantation. Also," he confided, "I would truly like to see the Port at Baltimore Town. I hear it is quite a sight."

"You men," the Lady sighed. "What shall we do with you? Well, it is all right for you to go if Ann permits it. I will tell you now that I will make sure my son looks in on Ann, should the time come and make sure the child arrives just fine."

"I did not know you had a son and that he was a doctor. Does he live in the Valley close by?"

"Yes," she said softly, "he is in the Valley, and one of the finest of doctors."

"What is his name, so that I can tell Ann this news?"

"Do not worry about his name, if he is needed, he will be there, I assure you. Now to other things," she said softly. "What are you going to name the child?"

"If it is a boy, most likely he will have his grandfather's name, that is, if Ann has her way."

"Do you think it will be a boy?" the voice questioned.

"Most likely, if the Royston blood continues as it has in the past," Peter said, with a bit of bragging in his tone.

"And what is that name?" she persisted.

"Uriah Blue."

"Uriah Blue Royston," she rolled the name over. "Uriah, I understand, but Blue?" she questioned.

"Ann's grandfather's surname was Blue, although it probably started out as 'Blew,'" Peter mumbled, trying to remember the Dutch spelling.

"Well, Uriah was a great general and he lived before my time. It will be a name your son will be proud of," the voice continued.

"I really would like to be around when my first is born, but Holker has that stallion scheduled to be on a boat very soon," Peter added.

"If that is the problem, maybe I will have the ship miss its sailing, and we can have the baby now in October, and then bring in the horse next year. Besides, your John Holker does not know it yet, but bringing a horse across the ocean in October is most dangerous, and he could most likely lose his fancy horse," the voice said in a most resolute way.

"My lady, we have a baby, a boy and we named him Uriah Blue."

"How's Ann?" the Lady in the Spring wanted to know.

"She is doing fine, except a bit confused from the birthing."

"Confused?" the voice asked.

"Yes, the midwife said that Ann kept insisting that a doctor helped deliver the baby. He was there plain as day. Ann was sure. Yet the midwife says there was not a man within earshot and that included the father."

"Well, sometimes one can get confused at such a time, but you never know."

"I think there may be things that you aren't telling me," retorted Peter, a bit vexed by his lack of the understanding of feminine mind.

"What about your plans to take a trip? Tell me the way you will be going," the Lady asked.

"The usual route to Baltimore is through Battletown, then down along the Shenandoah to Harpers Ferry where it meets the Potomac, then through Frederick in Maryland and on to Baltimore," Peter answered.

"As you go along the Shenandoah and the Potomac, will you look for me in the water?" the Lady questioned.

In his pragmatic way, Peter asked, "Why should I look for you in the river? You are here in the spring, awaiting my visits."

"Oh, you are the selfish one," she accused. "Only a few buckets of my water are used here. The rest? I cannot keep myself from flowing from here to the creek and then on to the river and then on to the ocean. Life giving water cannot be contained and kept to one's self. Take what you need, but do not try and dam it so that it cannot be used by others. Pass it on, and let it be used as it flows into the ocean and must wait for the clouds to return it to the mountains. All of life's blessings should be considered to be flowing streams, never to be polluted or kept from others."

Peter left to return across the river to Springsbury more confused than ever.

As he boarded the ferry, he noticed a jauntiness in Jo Anderson that he had not seen before. "And why are you so happy?" Peter wanted to know.

"I got my freedom, anytime I want it, anytime I want it," he repeated as if singing a song.

They were close enough that Peter knew he could learn the details whenever he took the time to inquire. Right now he felt an overwhelming urge to be with Ann and his Uriah Blue.

1803

"Stand still, so I can get this confounded saddle on," Peter cursed the bay. While the horse was the best mount that could be had, she did not like early rising. Her shying and shivering let Peter know her feelings about the early morning call. "If we do not get an early start, we will not make Harpers Ferry before late night, and you may have to go back to sleeping in the grass. I know you are getting spoiled," he coaxed the horse.

John Holker was in the saddle awaiting Peter's final touches on the bay. He still was not happy with having to wait six months to get his new horse. How it came to be that the ship that was supposed to be carrying the stallion last fall would be called into service as a privateer was beyond him. "Oh well," he thought. "It will not be long now even though it is well into 1803."

Peter swung out of the main yard of Springsbury, and as he did a bag of food was tossed to him by a darkie. With a deft touch he divided the load so that it balanced over both sides of the saddle.

"That will get us to Harpers Ferry, even though there is some mighty fine eatings in Battletown and Charles Town," John Holker noted as he too balanced a load of food on his saddle. "It has been a while since I have taken a trip this long without a wagon along," Holker murmured. "It seems like the wife always needs more than a man can carry on a saddle horse. Speaking of wives, how is Ann doing?" he asked, knowing that he often created a certain amount of tension in the Royston household.

"Well, the baby is four months old and Ann still hasn't forgiven me for thinking about leaving last fall. What the devil," he uttered, as he kicked the horse into a canter, "You certainly do not need a man around at those times anyway."

Battletown was a bustling town on that early May morning of 1803. There was talk of changing the name to that of a developer who wanted to build some town homes and sell them to those who supported the farms and plantations nearby.

"Look over there," Holker cried. "There is Battletown Inn. Seems like just yesterday the old Wagoner, Dan Morgan, was proving who had the hardest fists and the hardest head in the Valley, as he fought all comers in the Inn. And now, just last July, he has just been laid to rest up at Mount Hebron Cemetery. What it must have been to see him at his finest! They will probably change the name of Battletown, just because it is getting too genteel," he complained. A quick stop for the horses to drink, and for both Peter and Holker to swig down a cup of coffee, and soon they were on their way north towards Harpers Ferry.

"What is all that dust up ahead?" Holker asked. "If we have to follow that all the way to Harpers Ferry, it is going to be a long day."

"Maybe we will have some luck and they will stop at Charles Town. It is only eight or ten miles away," Peter hoped. "The easiest way to find out is to catch up with them and see where they are heading." They stepped up the pace and soon found themselves amid a small caravan of men, wagons and animals. "Where away?" asked Peter.

"Harpers Ferry," came the answer. "Why not join us?"

"And who do I have the honor of addressing?" Holker asked of the leader.

"Meriwether Lewis," was the response, "from Albemarle County, although lately I have roved the country doing my soldier's duty."

"You say you are from Albemarle County and you are a soldier, but it seems that I recall that name from somewhere else," Holker pressed.

"You must keep up on the news of politics," Lewis responded. "I am the personal secretary to our President, Tom Jefferson."

"Why would the personal secretary of President Jefferson be going to Harpers Ferry?" Holker wanted to know. "With a fair army of men, not to mention some dogs and wagons."

"I am going to obtain a load of guns from the National Armory in Harpers Ferry," Lewis answered with a smile.

"Now, you have really got my interest piqued. It is strange enough that you are where you are, but why in the world would you be needing wagonloads of guns?" Holker persisted in his questions as he slowed his horse's gait to match that of the Lewis group. "Are you going to start a war?" he asked in a jesting manner.

"Not a war, but an expedition," Lewis confided. "Tom Jefferson has wanted the west explored since back in 1793, and it is just now that the expedition has been approved. We need the best guns made in the nation, all of one caliber and as interchangeable as possible. This will allow us to carry the least amount of lead and surplus weapons."

"How far is this expedition going?" Peter wanted to know. "And how many people are you taking with you?" Peter's tone suggested that maybe Meriwether Lewis was not quite mature enough for the job, as he appeared to be about Peter's age or maybe a year or so older.

"We are going all the way to the other ocean by land and claiming territory as we go," he replied and then added, "In case you think that I am not of age, I implored Thomas Jefferson to send me when I was only nineteen."

Peter blushed. "I hope that France and Spain do not have other ideas."

"We will be going as far as possible along routes that have been discovered by the Mountain Men, who take their canoes as far as possible and then hike into the country searching for furs. Their knowledge of the Indians and the Indians' ways makes us want to recruit them as a part of our team."

The time passed swiftly as Lewis outlined his proposed journey into the unknown. A town loomed ahead and for a moment Peter thought it must be Harpers Ferry.

"No," laughed Holker, "this is Charles Town, still a ways off from the Ferry." John Holker had owned much acreage in Berkeley County, Virginia and knew the town named after Charles Washington very well.

Peter, too, knew of the town as he had grown up in the shadows of other Washingtons in Fredericksburg. George was off leading the fight for independence as Peter was just beginning to mature, and he feasted on the stories of George, who had grown up just across the Rappahannock from the Royston Plantation. George's brother-in-law, Fielding Lewis, was the one who owned Springsbury before Holker.

He was a bit tentative going through Charles Town, wondering if he would see someone who was from Fredericksburg. He noted that the street of the town were named after other brothers of Charles Washington. As they passed through Charles Town, first he spotted Lawrence, then George, Charles, and Samuel, all streets named by Charles Washington after himself and his brothers.

"Let us pass through Charles Town and stop for the noon repast," suggested Meriwether Lewis. "Join us for what simple fare we brought." Soon a green field and some shade trees beckoned and the aides with Lewis set about preparing food. Peter and John Holker contributed out of their saddlebag and the meal was soon prepared. "I have never tasted such biscuits," Lewis announced. "Who has the recipe?"

Peter had to own up that they were prepared by the slaves to be put on their own tables. Even Holker was amazed.

"The slaves are eating better than we are," he muttered. "How can this be?"

Peter explained that the best food went to the master's table and the slaves were used to doing what they could to improve the taste of the inferior food assigned to them. "They have learned the secret of seasonings that are a bit spicy for the palate of the master," Peter laughed.

"Well, when we get back, we will have to try some of their cuisine," Holker suggested.

The meal over, they saddled the horses and moved toward Harpers Ferry. There were some simple signs along the way, pointing to farms and small villages. Later in the afternoon as they neared Harpers Ferry, Lewis kept taking out a scrap of writing with what appeared to be a map on it.

"And what may I ask are you looking for?" said Holker.

"The path to Tom Jefferson's rock," responded Lewis. Soon, he appeared satisfied with his map reading and muttered, "I have always had a way with maps." He rode off up a faint trail toward the top of an outcropping.

First to astound Peter was the panorama before them. Even though the forest covered much, through the clearings he could see both the Shenandoah and the Potomac. They had falls that cascaded some sixty to eighty feet as they rushed toward each other.

To the west the sun was starting to set and the light glistening off the Potomac made a surreal setting. Never would he forget this beautiful sight. "Now there is a sight that God made that no man can destroy," he thought out loud.

"Well, they built an arms factory that would probably make him a bit unhappy," retorted Holker as he interrupted Peter's thoughts.

"Why would George Washington build a gun factory here," Peter wanted to know, "with all the factories available up north?"

"It is the falls," Holker explained. "I have been all over the world and never have I seen the power available like where these two rivers meet."

Once Peter had taken in as much as he could of the distant view, he looked at the closer features of the area and was again amazed at a giant flat rock that seemed precariously perched on a point.

Following Peter's eyes, Lewis explained, "That is 'Tom Jefferson's' rock."

"How did it get that name?" Peter wanted to know.

Lewis pulled the scrap of paper from his pocket and read aloud the words of Thomas Jefferson as he first viewed this sight in 1783. "This large slab of shale is so balanced on a its narrow stone base, that a man can sway the rock by himself,"

Lewis asked, "Want to give it a try?"

"Not me," Peter declined, as Lewis jumped on the rock and with a rocking motion, started the rock swaying. "That is why you are going exploring into the unknown and I will be happy watching the wheat grow," Peter admitted.

"I hate to break up this party, but it is going to be dark soon," Holker enjoined. "As for me, I would like to sleep with a roof over my head and not have to count the stars as I try to sleep. Let us go find an ordinary and enjoy a taste of ale before we settle down for the evening."

The next morning, Peter and John Holker said farewell to the Meriwether Lewis group and made their way to the ferry that crossed the Potomac. As they and their horses were pulled across, Peter thought of Berry's Ferry and his love for the nearby Wildcat Hollow.

"I am glad the spring rains were gentle. I think this spot would be boiling in wet times," he suggested to Holker. "Right now, it seems no more of a crossing than at Berry's Ferry."

"Both can make your heart quiver if you catch them at their worst," said Holker. "A good rain in the Blue Ridge can make the Shenandoah a treacherous crossing if you are not cautious," Holker mused. "Of course not every ferry has Jo Anderson at the helm. That darkie is a wonder," Holker continued. For some reason, Holker wanted to pursue the subject. As they cleared the ferry and worked their way along the north side of the Potomac, he began again. "What do you know about Jo Anderson?"

"Not much," said Peter. "I know his mother was once owned by Ann's family and shortly after he was born, she was given to the McCormicks with the agreement that she would be freed at a certain time. Jo Anderson is as smart as any white man that I have ever known," said Peter, as he admitted to many conversations with him when he crossed the Shenandoah.

"But why should you be asking about a darkie," Peter wanted to know. "Are you thinking about buying him for whatever time he has before he is freed?"

"No, though one could certainly use his talents. I understand he is working on a mechanical wheat reaper when no one is looking, and that is a device that would revolutionize the farming world. Now they tell me he is going to be freed and I was curious about it. It was his mother that was a part of the agreement, not Jo. There has to be a story there."

"There is," Peter agreed. "As I understand it, Jo Anderson learned to count and would go around counting everything he could find. One of his discoveries was that each ear of corn had an even number of rows. This intrigued him. He counted so many rows in the ears of corn that Old Man McCormick thought he was lazy and not doing his work. As he was being reprimanded, Jo Anderson told his master of his discovery.

"Mr. McCormick laughed and said that was the way of nature. Every ear of corn has an even number of rows. 'In fact, if you can find an ear of corn with uneven rows, I will give you your freedom.' The very next year during harvest, Jo Anderson showed up with an ear of corn that was beautiful in every way, except that it had an uneven number of rows. Confronted with this miracle and finding nothing amiss in the ear's growth, Jo Anderson was offered his freedom."

Peter continued, "In response to this, Jo pressed on, 'Is that a fact, Massa McCormick, your word and no taking it back?'

'My word and no taking it back,' said McCormick as he felt that he maybe did not have all the facts and Jo Anderson had fooled him greatly.

'Massa McCormick, I accept my freedom, but I want to stay with my mama until she is free. And I did fool you. I went out to the cornfield last spring, just when the ears were setting. I took great care and dug out one of the rows and put the cornhusk back over it. I memorized where the ear was and waited for it to grow and ripen. I was feared that the row would grow back and I would not have an ear of corn with odd rows. But it did not and I brung it to you.'

McCormick let out a roar, 'I have been bamboozled,' he laughed. "Anybody as smart as you should not be a slave anyway. You can have your freedom and I'd be curious to what you are going to do with it.'

'I like working on the ferry but I have a hankering to do more. I hear that your cousin up the Valley is working on a grain reaper, and in time I would like to go work, not for him, but side of him. I have some ideas, but I want to stay with my mama until she is free.'"

"That is a great story," Holker laughed. "Do you think it is true?"

"I know so as it was told to me not only by Jo Anderson himself, but by Ann's father, Joseph Anderson."

The trail to Baltimore took them through the Town of Frederick. As they neared the town, houses began to appear and Peter commented on the quality and neatness of each one.

"Frederick is a German town, settled mostly by Pennsylvanians. Many are artisans. I intend to replenish my supply of gloves from one of them," Holker added.

John Holker kept looking for a particular place and finally he nodded to himself and beckoned Peter toward a combination dwelling and shop. Going in, the smell of leather of all varieties was overwhelming. A bell lay on a small counter and Holker rang it loudly. In a moment or two, a middle-aged man came from the rear of the shop and in English with only the hint of a German accent, asked of their pleasure.

"Gloves, my good man, I need gloves. Bring me out your stock for I need a goodly supply to be ready for my return trip in a few days."

"My gloves are made to order, there is no stock. I have much stock of leather just waiting to be turned into gloves, but no finished product."

"How long would it take to make me ten pair from your finest leather?"

"That would take weeks," the leatherworker explained. "Maybe I could have them delivered to you."

Peter could see that this was going to take some time. He let his eyes take in the shop and noticed the gold leafed name on the window, reading backwards through the window, 'John C. Frietschie, Glove Maker.' Inside the shop, one detected some attempt at keeping the leather stock in order but without success.

Across the street was another sign announcing the office of an attorney, Francis Scott Key. Peter interrupted the conversation between John Holker and John Frietschie, and nodding toward the lawyer's sign across the street, said, "Maybe you should ask Mr. Frietschie about that attorney. I remember you said you needed a good one to collect those debts owed you from France."

Mr. Frietschie snorted. "That fellow is a better poet than a lawyer. I have been trying to get him to make out papers for me to go to Pennsylvania and make an offering to Miss Barbara Hauer for her to be my bride. It is taken so long that I will probably be dead before he gets the first line written." His German accent was more pronounced as he became more animated in his conversation.

John Holker stopped the direction of the conversation with the comment, "I think I will stick with my Philadelphia lawyers. They seem to speak pretty good French."

Peter, again drawn to the outside of the shop, said, "Where did you get the flag? He counted seventeen stars and seventeen stripes. It is the first one I have seen since we added Ohio to the Union."

"Shame on you," Frietschie chided. "It is been since early March that Ohio is a state. You should have seen a flag by now, it is been almost two months."

"Well, on the plantation we do not go in much for flags, we have crops to grow and harvest."

Warming to the subject, Frietschie exclaimed, "You are never too busy to pay attention to our country's flag. My intended loves the flag so much that she always makes me a new one whenever a new state enters the Union. She made that one within a week of Ohio becoming a state. I will have her make you one and it will be delivered along with the gloves, if you promise to fly it every day. Very few flags are flown, only where the Federal government has buildings, but I fly the flag and always will. You people do not know what it is to live in a country where freedom is not permitted."

"Yes, I do," responded Holker. "I lived in hiding in France and England before I came to America in 1777."

Frietschie nodded, "Mr. Holker, you are well known in the region for your activity on behalf of the country during the War. We all know of your love for America. It is an honor to be working for you."

"Peter, I think I will rename the horse," John Holker mused. It had been some months since the new stallion was pastured in the area near the mansion. Holker could be seen observing the horse as it tried to escape its surroundings, galloping at full speed toward the fence, only to slide to a halt just before running into the wall. It was small as stallions go, but very determined in its mien.

"And just what do you want to name it?" Peter asked.

"I am thinking of Napoleon" Holker said. "The horse reminds me of Napoleon."

"Why is that?" Peter wanted to know.

"He is small but feisty and never seems content." Warming to the subject of Napoleon, Holker continued, "My correspondents from France tell me that Napoleon just 'gave' America the entire French Territory west of the Mississippi for fifteen million dollars—for that pittance, I could have bought it myself. Do you think I would look good as an emperor?"

Peter gave a noncommittal nod and pursued the subject. "How do you know so much about the affairs of our country?"

"My contacts in France are well paid to keep me informed of events that affect my own affairs. You must remember that I am still trying to collect debts from France and from America for my Revolutionary War contributions. Now America just doubled in size and young Meriwether Lewis can travel freely through the French Territory without fear of any French soldiers. In fact, the French had their tails beaten in Haiti by the free blacks and malaria. That is why Napoleon lost his ardor to rebuild his empire in America. Just think of it, the United States doubled in size, thanks to little Haiti."

"Our country is changing." Peter commented to the Lady in the Spring. "And I am not a part of it. I see the country growing in size, I even met the man who may become famous for his expedition to map it."

"Are you disappointed?" the voice in the spring wanted to know.

"Not really, I guess that I am just seeing my life for what it is and will be. I am happily married, I have one child and there will be more. I know how to run a plantation…it is just that I see the country moving and I am standing still. I listen to John Holker and know that he is someone who helped bring our country to life. My grandfather fought in the war. My great grandfather owned the largest tobacco warehouse in the colonies. I guess I am envious sometimes, but I would not trade it all to be anywhere except just where I am at this moment. My Ann is the best in the world and I love my work. I do worry about John Holker and what I will do when he gives up the daily operation of the plantation. But that will be some years."

From the bubbling spring came the reassurance, "Do not worry about tomorrow. Just relax and enjoy the life you have."

1804

"Peter, I do not know what the world is coming to," groused John Holker.

Peter rested for a moment, leaning forward in the saddle. This introduction usually resulted in a long oration on the subject at hand.

Peter nodded and John Holker went on, "Just when the country is doing well and we are prospering from the Louisiana Purchase, wars are unheard of and what happens? That son-of-bitch Burr goes and kills the man who is needed to keep the country on a sound fiscal policy. On top of that, he will most likely continue as Vice President of these United States. Nobody knows for sure why it happened. They were law partners. There were arguments about the politics in New York, but why would a man who almost became the President of the United States be stupid enough to get into a duel? I guess it was because he also missed being elected Governor of New York and he blamed Hamilton for that. I know he blamed Hamilton for losing the presidency to Tom Jefferson in '01, after they tied in electoral votes." Holker raged on, getting more agitated as he did. Finally he ended with the real reason for his concern. "I will wager that the French who owe me money will use this as another reason to not make their payments. If I do not get some payments soon my life will surely have to change."

Peter looked around at the busy plantation and observed, "This place pays well and is quite profitable. Maybe if you would just concentrate on what you have here, you would not need to worry about debts that are owed to you from years past." Peter continued, "It is true that times are changing and those who are now slaves will someday have to be freed. In times past, there were few slaves and the world did not care whether they lived or died. Now I hear they are going to abolish the importation of slaves from other countries. When that happens, you will see changes in the system that will force us to look for labor saving devices. Why, if we could harvest wheat mechanically without the need for so many persons at harvest time, think of the money we would save."

John Holker nodded in agreement, "Maybe that darkie, Jo Anderson, will be our savior yet. I have heard he working on a mechanical reaper that will harvest grain."

"Actually, it is the McCormicks who are doing most of the work, but it seems like the ideas come from Jo. I fear they are a long way off. From what I hear, every time they try to get it running, something breaks down. The biggest problem is the difficulty in getting the wheat to stay near the cutters. I think they have the cutter designs pretty well worked out, though the shears that do the cutting work in a reciprocal motion, causing a lot of stress on the machinery." Peter said these words with an air of knowledge that he really did not have. He had listened to Jo so many times, he could repeat them word for word.

"Well, one of these days it will happen. Though I doubt that I will be around to cheer them on when it does," Holker muttered. "Right now all we have are slaves and we can only use what we have."

1807

"What a beautiful day!" Peter exclaimed to the Lady in the Spring. "You can tell that winter is coming and it will not be long before the first frost. The harvest on the plantation is over and only the butchering is left. Ann is soon to bring me a new child and I somehow know it will be a boy. She wonders if the doctor will be there that helped her with Uriah."

"Has she talked to that doctor?" the Lady wanted to know.

"How could she? She was the only one who saw him. You said he would be there and according to Ann, he was."

"Maybe the others weren't looking at the right time. Some doctors can be in and out of your life without anyone knowing it," the Lady asserted. "You tell Ann to talk to the doctor and even if she does not get an answer, he will hear her and be there when the birthing time comes."

"That is ridiculous!" Peter snorted. "How can she talk to someone who she can not even see?" Peter blushed when he realized what he had said. "Well," he stammered. "You are different. You are really there. It is just that other people cannot hear or see you."

"So my son is really there and she should talk to him. I promise he will be there for her at the time for your son to be born."

If the Lady thinks it is going to be a boy, then we can count on it, Peter thought. Getting to the practicality of the problem, Peter ventured, "How can we name this child without Ann wondering how I know it is going to be a boy?"

The voice continued as Peter stood there with that certain perplexed look, "You still haven't told Ann that you talk to me. What is wrong? Do you think she would be jealous of a voice in a spring?"

"No, one of these days I will do it. It is just hard to explain."

"Even to someone who sees a doctor that no one else sees," the voice teased. "Besides, the old tradition is to name the second boy after the father of the mother, with the middle name after someone who has impressed you."

"You are right, of course. It should be Joseph, after Ann's father and we will think about who has made the greatest impression on us."

The tilt hammer mill was especially noisy as Peter passed it on the way back to Springsbury. One of these days, he thought, I am going to spend some time learning how that machine works, although I could ask Jo Anderson. I am sure he knows what makes every machine work. Darkness was just falling when he entered the house and gave Ann a hug. She seemed especially sprightly as she cooked supper, all the while entertaining her first born.

He stooped to give her a kiss and jumped into a conversation, which was a continuation of the one he had been having with himself. "Let us name the new boy Joseph after your father. And what about Asbury for the middle name?"

Ann leaned forward as the baby gave a quick kick. "How do you know it is going to be a boy? I have been feeling that it is a girl that is kicking around in here."

"Somehow I am sure that it will be a boy," Peter answered, still not able to bring himself to talk of the Lady in the Spring.

"Well, I will surely agree with Joseph but why Asbury? That is not a likely middle name."

"I have heard that the second child is named after the mother's father with the middle name being after someone who impresses you. That preacher fellow, Bishop Asbury that preached at Mount Carmel up in the Blue Ridge sure impressed me."

"And me too," Ann added. "So it will be Joseph Asbury. That is, if it is a boy," she said, not sure how Peter could be so convinced of the gender of the unborn baby.

With Ann in such a receptive mood, Peter plowed on, "Have you seen that doctor that you said was here when Uriah was born?"

Ann answered, "How could I find him? I am the only one who saw him. And I have trouble remembering what he looked like."

"Well, if he was around for the first one, he would surely be around for the second one."

"Peter Royston, are you funning me?" Ann wanted to know. "You are not the one who usually talks of such things. Of all people, I would not think that you would be encouraging me to look for someone that nobody else can see."

Peter turned red. *If she only knew,* he thought. "Well, it would not hurt to talk to him just as if he were right here in front of you. You said that his presence made the delivery of Uriah so much easier."

Ann agreed, "Maybe you are right, but right now it is time for supper. Would you rather have me talk to the good doctor or serve you supper?"

"I would not have believed it," John Holker enthused. "We took a boat from New York City up the Hudson River to Albany in about 35 hours, and not a sail hoisted and nobody rowing. I do believe, I have seen it all."

"No sail, no oars?" Peter quizzed. "How did the boat move?"

"Some time ago, a Scotsman invented something called a steam engine that uses water and steam to produce power. They burn wood to heat water and when it boils, the steam is collected and is used to move a piston that has power to take the place of horses. A fellow named Robert Fulton bought a special steam engine and put it on a boat. He uses the power it generates to propel the ship."

This astounded Peter and he asked, "How does the power in the cylinder move the boat?"

"Well, I do not understand it all myself, but I know it happens. I was in Philadelphia and all the talk was about this great genius, Robert Fulton. It seems that he has been at it so long that his boat was called Fulton's Folly. But now everybody wants to ride on it. Just think, from New York City to Albany in 35 hours.

I just had to go and see for myself. It is a dirty process with all the smoke coming from the chimney, but it is worth the dirt to have the progress."

Peter just knew he would be confiding this information to Jo Anderson the next time he crossed on the ferry, and it would be best to have as many details as possible. "How does the steam in the engine move the boat? What do they put in the water to make it go?" he persisted.

"Well," Holker hedged, "as best I understand it, the piston goes back and forth and moves a wheel at one end. That wheel moves some other wheels and finally the last wheel turns a great big bunch of paddles out on the end of another wheel. The paddles push against the water and make it move. As one paddle is leaving the water, another is dipping into the water and keeps it going. One of these days they will have boats all over, though I understand that Fulton wants a patent, and it will be up to him to decide when and where the steamboats will be used. I hear that he has the rights to all the steamboats on the Mississippi River already, as well as many of our bays. I do not know where he going to get the money to do all that," Holker wondered. "I know that Robert Livingston helped with the early finances, and I think they are some sort of partners. You remember Livingston. He was the chap that Jefferson sent over to France to buy New Orleans and he came back with the entire French Territory. God, what I would give to be young again and be in the midst of all these changes," Holker exclaimed. "I would be exploring the west in a steamboat, I would."

While Peter always looked forward to the trips up Wildcat Hollow to visit his spring, this time he was more interested in Jo Anderson and the ferryboat ride. "It is going to put you out of business. We will not need a ferryboat man to pull the boat when the steam engine takes over," he chortled to Jo Anderson.

"And what makes you think that I enjoy this work?" Anderson questioned. "There are other things in life that I want to see and do, but what is going to take my place?"

"The steamboat, of course. Have you heard of the steamboat?" Peter wanted to know.

"Well, it seems, yes, I have. I talked to Massa McCormick the other day about my freedom, and he was telling me about some sort of boat that did not need a pole or an oar or a sail. Though I think he was just trying to get my attention away from my freedom. You see, Massa McCormick gets paid from Massa Berry for all the work I do here and he does not want to give that up. He will someday, but not just yet. But tell me how this boat works; I am always interested in how things work."

Peter explained as best he could and when he got to the details of the paddles that made the boat move, Jo's eyes came alive. "That is it!" he shouted. "That is it. You just made me a mechanical wheat harvester. The paddle wheels done solved a great big problem. There are others, but the biggest one will be solved by the paddles."

Peter did not know what Jo was talking about, but did not want to let on how little he understood about the whole situation. He nodded as if he understood and ventured, "Are you going to use the steam engine to harvest wheat? Get rid of the horses?"

"No, maybe the steam engine will come later, but now I am just going to use the paddle wheels to get the wheat forced into the cutters. Right now I am going to keep this to myself. I have things to do before I spend a lot of time on my reaper. At the moment, I have to get you across the river so that you can go sit by your spring and while away the afternoon."

Peter wondered why Jo was so pointed about the spring, taking liberties only a friend would take and certainly not one of his position. Jo continued, "I think you should spend as much time with Missus Ann as you do at the spring."

Peter defended himself as best he could, knowing that he enjoyed much the time he spent with his spring as his only companion.

"Do I spend too much time here?" Peter asked aloud to the spring. "Ann does not say anything about my trips over here, but she must wonder. We now have a second child named after Ann's father and for the circuit rider bishop who came up to Mount Carmel Church last year. Joseph Asbury is a wonderful little one just starting to crawl. Uriah Blue is just getting old enough to start learning. Ann has a slate board and some chalk so that he can write his letters. I guess she will be using the Bible to teach him to read. It is too bad that only the rich can afford hiring a teacher. Many children have parents who cannot read or write and cannot teach them, and they end up making a mark where their name is supposed to be."

"You should never spend time with me when you should be with your family. My only desire is to have you happy with your work and your family. Be off now and let me be at one with the nature that surrounds me."

Peter made his way across the river and headed back to Springsbury, knowing that he did spend too much time away from Ann. It seemed much easier to tell the Lady in the Spring his thoughts, dreams and ambitions than it was to try and get the time free with Ann and the children.

1808

"Peter, well, he did it again," Holker snorted. "There aren't enough lawyers in Philadelphia to get my money from France if that Thomas Jefferson continues handling the international affairs in this manner."

"Mr. Holker, you know that I am not a student of politics, and I have no idea what you are talking about," Peter responded. "What is happened now to get you so excited?"

"In December the government passed an embargo act that will kill all trade with other countries. We had the Non-Importation Act in '06 that forbade the importation of some goods from England. Now they are prohibiting all international goods from being imported. This nation lives off foreign trade. The shippers thought they could get around it by shipping to Canada for transshipment to other countries. Now they are talking about banning any commerce with Canada. It will not work, it will not work, it will not work," John Holker repeated. "I only ship some grain to France, but in New England they live off exportation. Of course, England and France fighting each other does not help my cause either. If we keep this up, we will be fighting England again or each other." Holker continued, "If we have a war, maybe you will have to go and help fight it. You are only thirty-two and have two children. During the Rebellion that would have been a prime age."

Peter gave that some thought and figured that Holker was teasing him. *I am not much of a fighter, but if I had to, I would go. I would do anything to keep from being a part of England again.*

On that cold January evening around the fire, Peter pulled Uriah close to his knees and held little Joseph in his arms. "I do not know why people want to fight," he murmured. "I hope and pray that none of my sons have to fight in a war. If we settle things with England, I see no other place where we could ever have a war."

The thought of her sons having to fight in some future war brought Ann into the circle. "You men," she chided, "the only way you know how to settle things is by fighting. I am going to teach these young ones not to fight. Speaking of teaching, we need a book that we can use to teach Uriah. He is starting to learn his letters and now he needs to begin putting letters into words and words into sentences."

"I will ask Mr. Holker if we can borrow some of his books. We could always use the Bible. That is the way I learned."

"The Bible is good for his moral life, but many of the words are no longer in use. We need to make sure they will learn the language of the future."

Uriah was a serious child and he knew he was the topic of conversation. "Mommy, Daddy, why are you talking about me?" he wanted to know.

"We are not talking about you," Peter assured him. "We are talking of your future."

"Future? What is future?" Uriah questioned.

"The future is tomorrow and the day after that and the day after that," Peter explained.

"Someday you will grow up and leave our house and have a home of your own," Ann told him. "But before that we have a lot to teach you so that you will be a good man when you leave."

"I like it here on Daddy's farm," Uriah said.

Peter laughed. "It is not my farm, it is Mr. Holker's farm, and it is not a farm, it is a plantation."

John Holker was in a political mood. "Well, that Tom Jefferson is trying to make everybody mad. He is got the New Englanders mad because of his embargo and now in 1808 he has barred the importation of slaves. We can raise our own or buy them, but we cannot import them. Not that I disagree with him. I never liked the idea of somebody owning somebody else anyway. But it is sure going to rile up those boat captains and the slave collectors in Africa, not to mention the slave owners who would rather teach a non-English speaking slave how to work on his plantation, than worry about the home grown ones who might get educated and rise up against him. Serves them right," Holker said finishing his thought and rebutting his own argument at the same time. "This slavery will be the end of us," he continued. "We cannot let it get much bigger and yet we have no way to pay for our help otherwise. The snowball is rolling down the hill and we will become a part of its destruction. Not that I will be around to see it happen, but it will happen, that I assure you."

"I do not know about the future of slavery, but you have a whole lot of years left before you meet your maker," Peter assured him. Peter turned and looked over the vast acreage in front of him. *I wonder what we would do without slaves,* he pondered. The entire idea of such a caste system overwhelmed his imagination. *While there is a tremendous gulf between the races, there are many bridges,* he thought. *Maybe I should talk it over with the Lady in the Spring. She knows all the answers before I pose the questions.* Peter suspected his trips to the spring bothered Ann, but for as many times as he had tried to tell her of the Lady, the words just would not come out of his mouth. There was no way that she would understand, though he ached to have Ann be with him at the spring and to bring Uriah and Joseph along. He wondered if they would be able to hear the Lady talk. When he was away from the spring, he thought he had imagined it all. Yet when he returned, he would always hear the fresh lilting voice that renewed his outlook on life.

"Yes, Peter, you are right. There is a tremendous gulf between races and colors. It has been so for thousands of years and has been the cause of much strife. It is hard for anyone to understand it. I suppose it goes to the heart of our soul. When we are born there are a lot of animal instincts in us. We think only of ourselves as we cry to be fed and clothed and changed. Parents are our first teachers. Without them, or someone taking their place, all the animal instincts would remain. Depending on the parent we become more or less civilized. We learn to love and we learn to hate. As time goes on, others become our teachers or we become their teachers. Many times, humans act like packs of animals. They do things together they would not do alone. Slavery has been on earth for time untold. Even if they were not slaves, we would find a reason to look down on others because they look different from the bulk of the people. That is a trait of an animal culture. It does not seem to matter how brilliant they are and how dumb the group in power, the minority group are still looked down on. What is more difficult to understand is when the races are intertwined, the offspring is still put in with those who are slaves. Slave owners who beget children of slave mothers, condemn their own children to be slaves. That I do not understand. It is probably because society and their own family members would condemn them in turn. Right now, it is going on in high places, and I am sure you can also see it much more closely. While you may not be able to change the system, you must treat others, no matter who they are, as you would want to be treated. And make sure you train your children to do the same."

1809

"Peter, where can we find a lot of pitch?" John Holker wanted to know.

"Pitch?" Peter queried. "What are you going to do? You are not going to go into the rafting business again to try to get grain down to Baltimore. You know that Morgan's Mill is running fine."

"No, I am going to prepare our vegetables for winter."

"Mr. Holker, sometimes I wonder what you are thinking. You know the only way to keep vegetables is to dry them in the August sun. What in the world has pitch got to with that?"

"Peter, do not think too much," Holker responded. "There is a new way to save vegetables for the winter that makes them taste just like fresh-off-the-vine, but we need pitch to seal the lids."

Peter said, "There are no stands of pines left on Springsbury, but there may be some in the mountains. Maybe I should ride over and look. Just how much do you think we need?"

"I do not know," said Holker. "My spies from France tell me that Napoleon paid out 12,000 francs to the man who invented the process. But secrets are hard to keep. By the time we get the vegetables ready for harvest and collect the pitch, I will have more details. But right now, find me plenty of pitch. If we do not have enough, all the vegetables that we try to preserve this way will be spoiled."

"We have a good crop this year. Why not save a part using the old drying process and only save some using the new—what is it called—process?" Peter suggested.

"Sounds like a good idea, and I do not know what it is called—maybe we will name it after Napoleon. The way he is fighting wars against everybody, that may be the only thing he is remembered for," Holker chuckled, letting Peter know how he truly felt about the great dictator. "I have to order in a supply of glass jars also. They should be in stock in Baltimore. I will need corks to match the openings."

Peter crossed the Shenandoah and made his way to the turnoff at Wildcat Hollow.

Seeing Earheart at his door, Peter greeted him with the usual, "When are you going to sell me your property?"

Earheart responded, "Any year now, I am thinking of moving to Kentucky. I hear the land is free there and you do not have to pay any quit-rents. What brings you across the river this time?"

"I am looking for some pine trees...know of any about?"

"Certainly, just up the Fox Trap Hill on your left, there is a great stand of pines. One of the few left in the mountains. Most have been cut to keep the coopers busy. Further up, on the Green place, are a lot of cedars if you want to make shake roofs. What are you looking for pines for? Is Holker going into the barrel business as well?"

Peter gave a noncommittal answer and saying a farewell, turned the bay toward the steep slope of Fox Trap Hill. A few hundred yards and the Toll Road leveled out, and then started a slight descent into a meadow area. *How I love these mountains!* Peter thought. There were squirrels running ahead of him and he could hear the whirring of a covey of grouse fly from cover. For a moment he forgot the reason for his trip and it was the smell of resin that brought him back to reality. *There must be a lot of pines to make this much stink,* Peter mused.

He pushed the bay across a steadily flowing spring dreen. To his left, there was an immense stand of pines. *Now if there is not enough pitch here to satisfy Mr. Holker, I do not know where he could find more.* The bay dropped his head and began forging on the ample grass growing in the marshy area.

Peter sat in the saddle for a while and then pulled the reins on the bay and began working his way up through the stand of enormous pines. Two or three hundred yards up the hill the pines gave way to a large meadow of grass that was belly high to the bay. To the west Peter could see all the way into the valley. "What a sight," Peter said aloud. "The more I see the mountains, the less I want to live in the valley, and the valley is about as pretty a place as one could find," he added.

Back at Springsbury, he reported his find of pines in the mountains to Holker. "What is there is good, but the mountains are mostly hardwoods. The pines are being taken over by the oaks, maples and hickories."

"Do you think there is enough to seal up a couple of hundred glass jars that have been corked?"

"Certainly enough for that," Peter assured him.

"Well, let us give it a try on the beans, the peas and maybe a few jars of corn. That will be funny. I have only seen corn eaten when it is first full kernelled. After that it is ground into meal or fed to the cattle and horses. I can never imagine having corn in the middle of winter. What is this world coming to, Peter? There are so many changes that I can scarcely take it in."

Both Peter and Holker watched the gardens and they were ready when the different crops became ripe. They supervised the cooking of the peas and corn and beans on the stove, simmering them slowly for almost six hours. In turn they had the bottles heated in an outside tub of water. The tub was taken off the fire and the vegetables swiftly poured into the jars.

Before the jars could cool, the corks were installed and the pitch smeared around the corks to make seals. "That is the way my spies say it is done by Napoleon. Now let us wait and see what happens. By the time we find out, Madison will probably have us in a war. Seems like all the talk from Washington is about fighting the English one more time."

Peter did not care much for the direction of the conversation. It seemed like Holker was much too concerned with fighting. From what Peter could figure, the only thing a war was good for was to kill a lot of people who did not want to be killed. Not that he knew anybody who really looked forward to being killed. *If a war has to be fought, maybe now's the time to do it, even though we do not have any big army to fight off the English, or anybody else for that matter.* Peter then realized that he was thinking only of himself and his small family. A war fought now would be over before little Uriah would be old enough to be a part of it.

Later that evening he sat by the fireplace and drew Uriah and Joseph close to him. Ann noticed that he appeared moody and came and sat beside them. "Winter seems to bring out your sad side, my husband. What are you thinking about?"

"War," Peter answered. "War. John Holker says we are going to have another war. We will be fighting the English again. I was thinking that if we have to have a war, have it now. I may have to go but Uriah and Joseph will not have to worry about it."

Ann winced, thinking of life without her taciturn, but loving husband. "Peter, you are thirty-three years old. I think any war would be fought without one as old as you."

"Maybe so," Peter answered, "but the ones who choose who goes to war are usually the ones who do not do the fighting. They can pick any group they want."

"Tell me again what this conflict is all about," Ann questioned. "Why are we going to have to fight?"

Peter answered, "I am not sure myself. It has to do with the English Navy. Seems like they want to impress Americans, who were once colonials in their Navy, and we may have to fight to tell them they cannot do it."

"Seems like an awful weak reason for going to war," Ann said with a woman's logic. "Why not settle it over a table?"

"That would be the sensible way to do it, but war seems to bring out the insensibility in people."

Ann stared at the fire, deciding that now was not the best time to talk of bringing another life into the world, even though she wanted to tell Peter that he would be a father again with the new year a-coming. Maybe this one would be a girl. Girls do not worry about wars. Maybe they should have girls running the country. Ann smiled, thinking of how little power was entrusted to women. "We do not even help decide who runs the county, let alone the state or nation. The best we can do is to raise our boys to be good citizens and hope they will make decisions that we would have made ourselves."

1810–1820

1810

"I think we are going to have another baby," Peter confided to the Lady in the Spring. "Ann hasn't said so outright, but she is sure acting that way."

"And you, Peter, do you want a girl or a boy this time?"

"Well, boys are a lot less complicated, but I think Ann wants a girl and so do I. The thought of war seems to bring us around to wanting girls. We hate to think of our children fighting in a war."

The Lady questioned, "Have you picked out a name?"

"How can we pick a name when we do not know what it will be?"

"Why not use a name that could be either a boy or a girl? There is a Saint named Francis that I particularly like, who has such a name. Maybe that is the one you should choose. If it is a girl, all you have to change is one letter."

"And will the doctor be with her this time?" Peter wanted to know. "She insists there has been a man in the bedroom that helped her deliver the babies and it sure was not me."

"Certainly, if she wants my son to be there again, he will be there," the voice murmured.

"Massa Peter, you can come in now and see your fine child," the soft voice of the slave midwife called. Peter rose from the chair outside the bedroom and started in to where Ann was. He had heard the wails of a newborn and knew the delivery was over. Uriah and Joseph knew they had a baby brother or sister coming, but the young eyes could not stay awake until the viewing. They would have to wait until tomorrow to see the new child who would compete for their affections.

Peter stared at this beautiful woman who was his wife and the mother of his children, as she wearily tried to keep her eyes open. She held closely to her the very tiny wisp of a person, so dainty that he did not have to ask. They had a girl. There was a slight stirring of the curtains, and a shadow seemed to pass through the closed window and disappear.

Peter knelt beside Ann and looked for a long time at both of them. Ann stirred, and Peter reached out to hold her hand and the tiny fingers of their newborn. How could life be any better than this?

Ann smiled and said, "We have our little Frances." She closed her eyes and slept the sleep of one who knew she had done a great thing.

1812

"Peter. It is happening. We are at war again. And here I am an old man." John Holker seemed to regret, not the war, but his inability to be a part of it. "Here I am almost seventy years old. I have seen a lot. I, and my father before me, fought the British so many times, it only seems proper that I do it again. Governor Barbour has called out the militia to defend Fort Norfolk. Although, I think that any British general worth his salt will sail right on by Norfolk and head for Washington. Now our government will regret locating their country's capital right on a waterway. Why, they can sail right up the Chesapeake and the Potomac and toss their anchor onto White House soil. That is the dumbest place in the world to have a capital. Someplace like Winchester or Frederick would have been better." Holker droned on as Peter thought only of the immediate effect of the war.

Later on that June evening, Peter gathered Ann and his growing family together, and they watched the sun set.

"It seems so peaceful," Ann said. "Why does someone have to come along and make storm clouds?"

"That I cannot tell you," Peter responded. "I am just glad that I do not belong to the militia. Maybe the war will be over in a short period, but I doubt it. Mr. Holker talks about the hawks in Washington who would like to have this country claim all of North America. Canada would then be a part of the United States. Mr. Holker says that Canada will fight that, with all their might. Many of the families of the Tories that wanted to stay a part of England moved to Canada when we won our independence."

Twilight seemed to hang on forever, and the family watched until it was so dark that supper was served by the flickering light of a Betty lamp lighting the dining room. "One of these days, we will have a better light, like the whale oil lamps at the manor house," Peter promised.

"I would settle for a way to light fires and lamps without the tinderbox," Ann wished.

"One of these years, someone will come up with something automatic that will light lamps," Peter surmised.

"Ann is pregnant again, and I think she is a bit tired. This time she seems so listless. She snaps at the young ones more."

The voice from the spring seemed to understand. "Maybe there is something going on inside that you do not know about. How is she physically?"

"She seems to be gaining a lot of weight. Other than that she seems to be doing well."

"Maybe you should pick out two names this time," the voice suggested.

"Two names, you do not mean twins?" Peter asked in a stunned voice.

"It has been known to happen," the voice assured. "Why not pick a boy's name and a girl's name, just to be sure?"

"Well, you were wrong for once," Peter started the conversation. "It was not twins, just a great big girl. We called her Mary, Mary Catherine, although Ann has already given her a nickname of Mollie."

"Oh, Mary, that is such a lovely name. Was it an easy time for her?"

"I do not think that any birth is an easy time," Peter, now the expert, said. "Her friend, the doctor, was there and that comforted her. Although, I sure wish I could meet him."

"So it was not twins," the voice mused. "What were you going to call the other one if it were a boy?" she wanted to know.

"The name of Mathew is from the New Testament and Whiting after an old friend from the next plantation."

"Maybe you had better hold on to that name. I have a feeling so strong about another boy."

"Peter, things are not going well," John Holker complained. "The British have blockaded the coast and every time we fight them on land, it is a disaster."

"Do you think England will win and take us over again?" Peter asked.

"I doubt that," Holker exclaimed. "England has her hands full just trying to be the Emperor of the Seven Seas. I think she would be happy to see us lose just so that she can brag about her Navy. But it is going to be her Navy that loses it for her. My spies have told me that time after time our Navy has beaten the British in one-on-one battles."

"Maybe we will get out of this thing after all," Peter said, in a hopeful voice.

"Well, I do not think you should be worrying too much about it. You have enough to worry about between Springsbury and your growing family. I hear that Ann is pregnant again. When are you going to name one after me?" Holker teased.

"Ann, John Holker was wondering why we haven't named a child after him," Peter mentioned to his wife.

"For some reason, an inner voice says this will be a boy, and if it is, we have settled on Mathew," Ann stated. "Mathew, I like."

Peter knew that the matter was settled when Ann spoke in such tones. While he admired and liked his employer, he was not particularly enthused about his name. Maybe if we have more, we can please him with a name that he likes."

1813

"We almost lost the both of them," Peter told the Lady. "The baby was premature and Ann was sick with the consumption. I thought we were going to lose them."

"How are they now?" the voice wanted to know.

"They are doing well. I must admit that I have not been much of a prayer, but I sure prayed hard and it seems that we had a miracle."

"Was my son there? Did you see him?"

"Ann says he was there and it was his touch that seemed to make the difference. I sure do not know how a doctor that only Ann sees could make a difference."

"One day you will understand," the voice said, "but right now the important thing is that they both are all right."

"The British are burning Washington," John Holker yelled as Peter saddled up the bay for the day's work around the plantation.

"That is less than one hundred miles away," Peter said. "Should we do anything to prepare ourselves here?"

"No more than what we have done. Watch the cattle and hogs carefully. We will need all the meat we can get to help feed those who are deserting Washington."

"What happened to the President?" Peter wanted to know. "Did he get captured?"

"No, the Navy came to the rescue with a young naval officer, Joshua Barney, I think his name is, who pulled the marines off his ship in the Patuxent and traveled by land to Bladensburg. He met the British before they got to the Capitol and the White House. Thanks to his delay tactics, the President and the Congress were able to escape north." John Holker loved the tactics of war and let people know that he understood the intricacies of battle.

"We have a baby girl! Hannah is her name." Peter said as he slid from the saddle.

"Why did you call her Hannah?" the voice wanted to know.

"Well, that is the name of the wife of John Holker and it is a beautiful Old Testament name," he added. "Ann is hoping this war will end soon, as she thinks that every time she hears war news she gets with child."

"You will have to watch the times you discuss war," came the teasing response.

1814

"Peter, I think that the glove maker from Fredericktown was right." John Holker paused for the effect of his words to settle in.

"What are you talking about, Mr. Holker?"

"Well, he said that lawyer lad, Francis Key, was a better poet than lawyer. It appears he was right. Everybody is talking about the poem Key wrote at Fort McHenry. They are starting to sing it like an anthem. We do not have one, you know. They have even come up with a tune, some old tavern song, I hear. Not that I have ever spent any time hanging around a tavern."

"I will be going up to Boston to be married," John Holker confided to Peter. "As you know, the marriage to Hannah was a matter of convenience and we were never man and wife. We only went through the ceremony to stop any talk. That has been dissolved and I will be marrying in the Church come January 15."

These details came out as casually as if Peter were always in the confidence of John Holker. Peter was not sure of his response and only said, "I will take good care of the place while you are gone, and we will have the manor ready for you and your bride when you return."

As they were talking young Uriah came out from the stable area with a span of horses ready to be hitched to a wagon. "It is hard to believe that Uriah is only twelve years old," Holker said in an astonished voice. "I would rather watch him work with draft horses than my grooms tend the thoroughbreds. He has a way with draft horses that I have never seen before. I do not know what he will do when he grows up, but his work should be with horses."

Peter looked at Uriah, almost six feet tall and agreed. "He handles the horses so well, you would never guess he was only twelve. I wonder what he will be like when he is a grown man?"

1815

"Glory be and Hallelujah, the war is over. Maybe we can go back to worrying about things that count, like running this plantation." John Holker was in a jovial mood. He had a new wife, one that spoke with the accent of a New Englander. She was bringing back some of the fire of his youth.

Peter looked about and could not see that the plantation suffered much during the war. In fact, it had done quite well. The war brought Springsbury prosperity that boom times bring. Peter could sense a coolness from Holker's new wife that made for serious thought about his future. While he had enjoyed the prestige of running a plantation, he had saved little. He lived in a superintendent's house and ate off the plates belonging to another. He began thinking of where he would go when the inevitable happened.

1816

"Peter, you think you are the only one having a baby around here," John Holker crowed. "I may be an old man but I have a beautiful baby girl. I am going to name her after the daughter who died many years ago."

"Congratulations," Peter said enthusiastically. "I think that Ann feels that if the war is over, the babies will stop coming."

"Peter, you have to tell her that war has nothing to do with it. She is a mighty fine lady. You may have many more."

1817

"Peter, we have a new president. And I might say the country seems to know what it is doing. We elected another Virginian, although it would be better if we elected one from the Valley. I wonder if we will ever have a president from the Valley?" he continued with his musings.

"Well, I am sure that if we ever do, you will have something to do with it," Peter opined.

"I doubt that," Holker added, but was pleased by the compliment. "Peter, I sense you have something you want to talk about but are reluctant to bring up."

"That is true," Peter said. "It appears to me that your son is showing a desire to be the operator of Springsbury, and I know that it will not be long before I will have to find something else to do. Guess I will have to try my hand at actual farming."

"It is true that I am depending on young John more and more, not only for the plantation, but for financial duties as well. He gets along with my wife well enough, even though he was of my first wife's womb. I doubt that he will ever recover any of the money owed me. Blood is thick, you know, and I would not disagree with you that it might be time for you to look for a change. If you want to be a farmer you will have to turn in your boots for shoes. Maybe between me and that father-in-law of yours we can come up with some land. What say you stay on and work with my son, John, until we find the best possible land for you? Any idea which direction you might want to head?" he queried.

Direction? Peter thought. *That sounds like he expects me to move out of the county or state.* Aloud, Peter said, "No direction at all, Mr. Holker, unless you consider just across the river a direction. The mountain land does not seem to be too good for farming, but if I could get my hands on some bottom land, and maybe live just above the flood line up around Wildcat Hollow."

"Wildcat Hollow?" Holker questioned. "That is on Rawleigh Colston's land. He owns all of the mountains except for the bottom land. All he will do is rent it to you. Of course, he cannot live forever, like I plan to. I know Rawleigh and if you want a particular place, maybe I can talk to him."

"There is a place, just as you enter Wildcat Hollow, that is leased to a man named Earheart,'" Peter continued. "Maybe I could take over his lease."

Holker suggested, "I will write and tell Rawleigh of your interest and make sure that he does not lease it to someone else. Meanwhile, teach young John all you can about this plantation."

1819

"Time seems to be catching up with me," Peter told the Lady in the Spring as he related the conversation with John Holker. "Ann is with child again and it will be the last one born at Springsbury."

"Beautiful Ann," the voice bubbled. "I have not seen her since her wedding day."

"Well, she has changed some but she is still beautiful," Peter answered.

"Maybe when you get closer, I will see her when she comes to get water. I might even get to talk to her. A woman needs to talk to other women, you know," the voice said.

Peter laughed at the thought of Ann talking to the spring. "I doubt that she will hear you, but I will encourage her to haul some of the water. I have to be the farmer, you know. I hope your son, the doctor, will be there as he has in all the past births. Ann will be thirty-eight or thirty-nine and I am concerned that she will be healthy for the birth," Peter pursued.

"I am sure he will be there as always and will provide for her, even though she'll be the only one to see him. What are you going to call the baby?"

"I will name him after my side of the family, if you are sure that it will be a 'him.' Peter Kemp will be his name, after my grandfather. He is the one who sent me to this country, you know."

"Massa Pete, you have a fine baby boy," the midwife announced.

Peter leapt up and said, "How is my wife?"

"She is doing fine, and she would like to have all her family come and see the new one who will change the entire family around." Peter and all the children crowded into the bedroom, and Ann looked at all she had brought into the world,

What a great responsibility God has given me, she thought. There was Uriah, now sixteen and a man; Joseph, turning twelve and who thinks he is a man; Frances, almost nine; Hannah, just six; Mathew, the one who always was close to her; and Mary Catherine, nicknamed Mollie, just going on five. *I teach them all I can, but wish there was a way to have them taught by a professional.* Thoughts ran through her head as she enjoyed watching the children as they reacted to the new intruder into their lives.

It was Joseph who brought the question to the surface, "Ma, where is he going to sleep?"

"Right now, right here with me."

"You know what I mean. When he grows up and wants a bed of his own."

"Well, that will not be for a little while and by that time we will have a house of our own. I think by fall, we will be living in another place."

This was the first any of the children had heard about moving. Their life was at Springsbury and each understood the relationship as much as their age allowed it. "Where are we going to move?" "When are we going to move?" and "Why are we going to move?" The last came from Mathew.

"We will talk about it later," Ann said tiredly, noticing the very somber look on Uriah's face.

Later Peter said to Ann, "We need to talk about moving. Mr. Holker has promised to help us find a place. Maybe your father has some ideas of a farm we could rent."

Ann said, "But you want to live across the Shenandoah and that narrows the search a bit. Remember that house over near the spring where we were married. I can see us in that house."

Peter could hardly contain his enthusiasm. "It sure would fit a family the size of ours. I have heard that the tenant, Phillip Earheart, wants to move to Kentucky."

"Why do not you look into it, Peter, and see if it is what you want," Ann suggested.

It was not long before Peter made the trip across the river to talk to Phillip Earheart. Jo Anderson noted something different in the way Peter acted and pried a bit. "What makes you so lively today, Mr. Royston?" He always started the greetings with Mister, always remembering his place, though the two were good friends.

Peter teased, "If everything goes right, I will not be subjected to all your questions in a few months. I am on my way to visit Phillip Earheart and hope to make an arrangement with him for what furnishings he has in the house. Mr. Colston said Earheart was moving to Kentucky and I could have his place. That means I will not be traveling across the Shenandoah very much."

"Well, and I will not be here to take you across. I am taking my freedom and going up Harrisonburg way to work on the reaper. We almost got it running, but there are a couple of major problems still bothering Mister McCormick. My mama is also getting her freedom, and I am talking to Mister Berry to see if I can build a small house over near where you are going. I think she can survive by working for the white folks around the ferry area. Maybe you can keep an eye out for her for me. Remember, she once was an Anderson slave."

"You can count on me," Peter assured him. "I hope to be farming Berry land."

Peter looked at the house where he could be living in a very short time. It was a two-story log house that appeared from the outside to not be very large. *Maybe I am making a mistake here,* he thought. *Trying to raise a family as large as ours here might be a bit rough. There are few houses in the area that would be large enough. Somehow we will make do.*

With that, he rapped on the door and shortly Phillip Earheart answered.

"I hear tell you are heading for Kentucky," Peter began.

"Yeah," Earheart muttered. "My brother lives there and tells me that land is mine for the asking."

"Are you taking anything with you? I am hoping to take your lease, and I can use any furnishings that you might want to leave. That is, if we can come to an agreement."

"I am not taking anymore than I can get into a small wagon. The roads over the Gap are not good, and they say it is easier to bring things down the Ohio than it is to haul over land. Come in and look around. I have a lot of farming equipment that you might want. I am assuming you are going to farm?"

"I have a deal with Mr. Berry and Rawleigh Colston says I can farm the upper part of this area near the meeting house," Peter responded.

"Come on in and let us make a deal. I am anxious to get started for Kentucky."

Entering the house Peter saw that it was larger than it appeared from the outside. *Maybe Ann might like it here after all. She has been used to pretty good living all her life,* Peter thought.

Earheart showed Peter the entire house and Peter tried to keep a mental count of all the personal property he was being shown.

"Why not write it down?" Earheart suggested. "You can write, I assume."

"That is a good idea, and if you have something to write on, I will do so. Do you have a pen and ink that I could use?"

Earheart blushed. "Ain't much for writing myself. Maybe you should bring back the missus and we can get it all down legal and proper."

"That is a good idea. How much money were you thinking of asking?"

"Well, before I tell you, let us look at the farm equipment and the stock. They are worth a lot, you know."

Peter said, "It may not be what they are worth but what I have to pay you. How much were you thinking?"

"I am thinking of $200. I will need that to get to Kentucky."

"Maybe you will need that, but that is way above what I can pay."

It took the better part of an hour and they settled on $150, to be paid at the time Earheart left the house. "I will bring my wife over to make sure she wants everything," Peter said. "We will make a list at that time."

Later that evening Peter told Ann of his trip and the deal with Earheart.

"That will take most of our money. I hope you did the right thing," Ann said.

Her tone left Peter a little worried about the agreement he had reached with Earheart. "It includes all the equipment and horses that we need to farm. We will need only enough for seed, and I believe that Mr. Holker will let me have enough seed corn, barley and wheat to get the first year started. It is a bit late to plant anything this year anyhow. We will just have to make do this first year. I was hoping that your father might have a hog or two on the pole for us to get by this year."

When she arrived to survey the house and finished looking at the inside, Ann looked at the list she had prepared and agreed that Peter had negotiated a good deal. "Here is what I have written," she told Peter. "Three feather beds, one cupboard, one bottle case, six Windsor chairs, household and kitchen furniture. And let us not forget a sorrel horse and a pied cow."

Peter began to tell the children where and when they were moving. All showed excitement except Uriah. He looked at Peter squarely and said, "Pa, I will not be going with you when you move. Mr. Castleman has offered me a job as a wagoner, and I told him I would take it."

"You are only sixteen and while you look like a man, are you sure you are up to handling a team of horses all day long?"

"And maybe all night, too," Uriah added. "I will be driving his long haul wagons, going all the way to Baltimore to pick up loads."

Peter knew that Uriah had made up his mind, and deep inside he knew he was doing the right thing. Uriah was a man and a handler of horses superior to most no matter what the age. "Let us tell your mother at the right time," Peter suggested. "You know how mothers are when the first one leaves home."

Peter also told Holker of his plans and Holker picked up on the doubt that Peter had for survival during the first year. "I think my son could use some more seasoning. Would you come back here after you move and help until the crops are put in next spring?"

Peter could scarcely contain his enthusiasm, but he countered, "I will need time to get my own crops in, but if that is all right with you, I will be glad to help here."

So it was on August 15, 1819, that Philip Earheart filled his wagon and headed west to Kentucky. The same day Peter and Ann Royston made their move across the river to Wildcat Hollow. Ann had taken the news of Uriah leaving home with more calmness than Peter expected. *I knew the time was coming, when I saw his face after Peter Kemp was born. That boy is not one to hang around the house,* she thought. *It is good that he will be doing what he likes to do. I am more concerned about my husband. Peter has never been a plowman. He has always put others to the plow.*

Peter seemed to read her mind. "I am looking forward to seeing my own seed pop from the ground. There is something about planting it yourself and waiting for the results. To make sure we get the best seed, we will buy from David Landreth over in Pennsylvania. They say he has the best seeds anywhere around. There is one thing for sure, I will be more concerned with the weather now than I was at Springsbury."

A thorough house cleaning was in order, and they and all the children who were able took to the task. Stopping for a rest, Peter stood on the back porch and looked past Prospect Creek toward the spring.

Ann, seeing his gaze, said, "Peter, you be the first to bring some water from the spring. I am sure you can find your way over to it."

Peter blushed, wondering why she had chosen such words, but picked up two buckets from the back porch and headed toward the spring and maybe a few words with the Lady.

It took some time to get a routine where he would get up early enough to cross the river and make his way to Springsbury. It took a bit longer to cross the river now that there was a new man on the boat.

Jo Anderson was still in the area as he labored to build a small log cabin for his mother. When he needed help to lift the logs, Peter would find time to work alongside him, and it was late September when Jo pronounced the cabin habitable for his mother. He thanked Peter for his help and said, "I will be leaving tomorrow for the South Valley. Some of her friends will help her move. Mr. McCormick has given them permission to help. But I want to thank you for what you have done."

Peter gave it some thought and said, "Jo, we have known each other for many a year. No matter how far I look I could find no one, white or colored, that is a better man. God speed to you and may you complete the contraption you call a reaper."

"And may you have a harvest large enough to need it," Jo retorted, unaccustomed to such praise.

"Be sure you make it small enough that we can get it across the river," Peter rejoined.

1820–1830

1820

"Peter, I am with child again," Ann announced in a somewhat tentative voice. "Here it is 1820 and I am still bearing children. I get so tired these days that I can hardly move. Joseph is with you most days in the field and Frances is only ten. She helps a lot though."

"We are starting to get our first crops off the bottom land and it will be a plentiful year. I have to admit it is a lot more work than I imagined. There is a big difference doing all the labor yourself. Joseph works hard, but his heart is not in farming," Peter answered to let Ann know that there was a lot of work to be done outside of the household. "As soon as it gets colder we will be butchering the hogs. Some of the neighbors in the mountains will help with that, and I will return the favor. We will give some to Jo Anderson's mother, Arissa, to help her through the winter."

Ann nodded. She had already accepted the presence of "Aunt Arissa" as the children called her. The animosity between Arissa and Ann's mother was still evident at her every visit. Whatever was between them was deep but was unspoken. Joseph Anderson very seldom came to visit and Ann was saddened by his absence.

Ann was beginning to share Peter's love for the mountains. There was something serene about the trees and streams. She and Peter were frequent attendees at Mount Carmel Methodist Church, although she mainly went for the chance to socialize with the mountain folks. The log structure was now some sixty to seventy years old. People came from many miles to hear the itinerant preachers who showed up to tell their stories. It was different from the church of her youth, and Peter seemed to enjoy it even though it was much simpler than the Episcopal Church that he had attended irregularly.

1821

It was early spring in 1821 when Ann called to Peter saying it was time for the arrival of their eighth child. Peter hurried to Arissa's cabin and told her that the time was nigh. Arissa had become midwife to those in the mountains, and even though she could not be accepted into their homes on a social basis, they were glad to have her at times like this. In what seemed like an eternity, the wails of a new baby filled the house and Peter was soon introduced to a new daughter.

"What are you going to call the baby?" the voice in the spring wanted to know.

Peter said, "We are going to name her after you and Ann and after John Holker's daughter. The name will be Anna Maria."

A bubbling sound of pleasure came from the falling water. "The child will be special and will bring both of you great pleasure, as does it me to have a namesake."

The summer of 1821 was full of long days and warm evenings. Word came from Springsbury that John Holker was in poor health and Peter found himself drawn to the manor house and to long visits with Mr. Holker. The booming voice was beginning to wane and he tired easily.

"Remember that Meriwether fellow that we met going to Harpers Ferry?" Holker wanted to know. "He sure made a name for himself. Traveled all the way to the Pacific Ocean and back, they tell me. Why, if he were English, the King would have knighted him." John Holker laughed at the thought of an American being knighted.

"And remember the time we preserved the vegetables? I do not think a single one lasted through the fall, let alone the winter. Why, you could hear the corks popping all the way to Millwood as they spoiled. We had to wait until that place opened up in Hagerstown that would take our vegetables and preserve them for us." John Holker continued his musings, "Peter, we have been through a lot together. You helped me put up the flagpole to fly the flag that we got from the glove maker, Frietschie, over in Fredericktown. Wonder if he ever married that Barbara girl he was courting. We came close to meeting Francis Scott Key—I would have if I hadn't insisted that those Philadelphia lawyers be the ones to get my money back. I will bet that Key fellow could have done the job for me."

Peter nodded, happy just to hear Holker talk of the old days. He decided that it was time to ask Holker a question that had bothered him from their first meeting. How did you know I was Peter Kemp's grandson? I gave you no hint."

"It was the hat that gave you away. I remembered precisely the tricorn hat that Captain Kemp wore and you were wearing his hat. I do not think I have ever seen it far from you."

Holker changed the subject. "We have seen some great changes, probably more than any other time in history. Why, up until a few years ago, the fastest one could go was the same speed that Jesus Christ traveled. Now look at us. We have steamboats that go at unheard of speeds. I hear tell that they will be having wagons traveling on rails powered by the same type of engine. Up in New York they are working on a canal that will go all the way from Lake Erie to Albany. Those steamboats will really be working to keep up with all the goods coming from the interior of these United States. I do not mind dying but, God, I would love to be around in the next thirty years. I'd be up there taking a ride on that New York Canal, that is for sure."

John Holker's wife came to the door and her look said that it was time to bring his visit to an end. Peter would be back another day. He hadn't even had time to tell Holker of the new baby and the name given to her.

Peter made his daily visits to the spring. He had buckets in hand and of all the chores doled out to the children, toting the water was the least of them. The spring was used for drinking water only, as the creek behind the house supplied all the wash water that was needed.

"I do not think that Mister Holker has long to live," he spoke to the spring. "The consumption just about has him. I am going to miss the old man. He is been like a father to me for over twenty years."

"For all of us, there comes a time to die. We are a part of humanity, but only a transitional one. We are born, become a part of the world, affect it small or great, and then pass on to another life," said the voice in a philosophical tone.

Peter broke in, "How about you? Why is your spirit here in the spring?" The idea of death had Peter bringing up things that he had only dared think about before.

"I was not always the voice of the spring. I had my human life and I, too, was a part of humanity and had my effect on the world. Even now, I am called to other places. Have you not come to the spring and found my voice missing?"

Peter considered his answer. "It is true that sometimes I search the waters for your voice and do not hear you. I thought it was me that could not hear you because of distractions. Where do you go?"

The voice answered, "Wherever I am sent is where I go. Sometimes I am gone for a short period, sometimes for a longer while."

"What do you do when you are gone?" asked Peter in a confused voice.

"Mostly I talk to people who are chosen to hear my voice. On rare occasions, they even see me as a person, but that is reserved for only a few."

"Will I ever be able to see you?" asked Peter.

"It will be when you are passing through from this life to another. But that will be many years in the future."

Peter pondered the words of the Lady in the Spring far into the evening. Ann's voice interrupted his thoughts. "What are you thinking of, my husband? You appear to be thousands of miles away."

"I was thinking of Mister Holker and the short time he has left on Earth. I guess also, I was thinking of us and what life has in store for us. I am sure we will never have the security you had on your father's farm. I, too, worry about your father and what your mother will do when he is gone. I worry about the children. I worry about Uriah and his many days and nights away, when he is hauling goods from Baltimore. I worry about our girls and who they will marry. I worry about Joseph, who does not want to be a farmer."

"Slow down, Peter, why worry about things you can not change? And if you could, you probably would not want to. Come sit by me and talk to little Anna Maria. She likes to hear your voice. Hold Peter Kemp on your knee and let him play horse with you. Think of the good things that God has given us. Think of us together. I know this is the first time you have faced the death of someone you are close to. It is times like this that bring out these worries."

The night began to turn unseasonably cool and Peter reached for the tinderbox to start a small fire in the fireplace. Turning his thoughts to the realities of life, he thought out loud, "I wonder when someone is going to invent a way to light a fire that does not involve striking a flint in a tinderbox. I am sure we have been lighting fires this way for generations. I will wager that Jo Anderson could come up with a way to light a fire, if he set his mind to it."

"It sounds like you are also worrying about that darkie," Ann interjected.

"It is true. I miss his voice and his pleasant ways. He should come and visit his mother. She is not getting any younger either."

Ann knew her husband, and at times like this, the only way to distract him was through the children. Anna Maria had a cooing voice that made him laugh and two-year-old Peter Kemp was going through a stage that taxed the energies of everyone. Peter bounced him on his knee and the sounds of "Giddy-up-bay" rang through the house. The world was right again.

Peter had been called to John Holker's side. He crossed the river in the rain, noting the rising waters. "If we are going to have a flood, it may as well be in the spring. Get it over with before planting time," he muttered. They had just said, "Mister Holker wants to talk."

As he entered the bedroom it was obvious that Holker had worsened. Between fits of coughing he managed to greet Peter. "Peter, it is good to see you. Come in and let us talk of the days when we were both able to fight the battles that came our way. They tell me that you had a daughter last year. Why did not you tell me before?"

Peter measured his answer. "We were so busy reliving the days of yore that it just never got out."

"And what did you call this daughter?"

Peter had a feeling that Holker knew the answer, but he responded, "Anna Maria, just like your daughter."

"Ah, that is a lovely name. Did I tell you that I had two daughters named Anna Maria? My first died before the turn of the century with the same disease that claimed my first wife. Oh, for better medicine. I might even wish for a bit of it for myself now. It seems so cold. Is it storming? I cannot see a thing from in here. Stoke up the fire a bit for me, will you, Peter?"

It is warm enough in here to be a summer day, Peter thought as he gave the burning embers a bit of a stir. He returned to Holker's bedside and it was clear that Holker knew his time was near. "I guess that Nancy will want me buried in Hallowed Ground," he muttered, "although, that would be all the way to Winchester, and frankly the Chapel is a lot nearer."

Peter was not too up on this Hallowed Ground subject, but knew it was a Roman Catholic thing. Being a Catholic in Eastern Frederick County was a very lonesome affair. The Chapel was from the Church of England and was the burial ground of most of the landed persons in the area. Peter had no answer for this and let it slide by.

"Where are you going to be buried, Peter, when it comes time? What church are you taken to?"

"I have not given it much thought," Peter replied. "Ann and I are real mountain people now and we mostly go to the church part way up the mountain called Mount Carmel. It is where the church-goers from the mountain get their religion. Mount Carmel has been around a long time although the church records are missing. Maybe they never kept any. The story is that Lord Fairfax gave the land to a Miss Ann Green for nursing him through an illness."

"It is a solid log church. It even has a loft for slaves to sit in, although there are no slaves on the east side of the river. Once in a while the darkie, Arissa, comes and sits all by herself in the loft. She seems so lonely with her son, Jo, gone up the Valley. She is a godsend to the women in the mountain at birthing time."

Holker muttered, "You talked a lot but still did not say where you wanted to be buried."

Peter answered, "Probably on top of that hill near our house, that is, if we own it by that time."

"Sure sounds like Hallowed Ground to me." Holker had seemed to want to say something about Arissa but was distracted by Peter's burial subject. He could not find the words and the conversation trailed off.

When it came time to go, Peter leaned forward to shake his hand, but Holker pulled him near and hugged him in an embrace that Peter knew would be final. "I thank God for your grandfather, Peter Kemp, and for him sending you to me. I find it even more pleasant to know you named your last boy after him." With that Holker turned toward the wall and asked, "Peter, will you please shake up the fire a bit for me on your way out?"

The ferry was still running when Peter approached the river and the new ferryman worked his way across and deposited Peter on the east side. "This will be my last trip until the rain stops and the river goes down," the ferryman announced.

Peter thought, *this would just be a shower for Jo Anderson.* He rode toward Wildcat Hollow and noticed Arissa standing in the doorway, apprehensively watching the rain come slicing down. It would be a long night for Arissa, as her cabin was just inside the flood plain of the river. It would not do to be caught inside, if the river rose too fast and cut her off.

Peter was drenched as he entered the house. "I know how Holker felt," he said. "Stoke up that fire so I can dry out."

Ann helped him pull off his coat and laid a blanket around his shoulders. "What a crazy man to be out in a storm like this," she murmured.

"Not only that, it may not be the last time I am to be out. I have to make sure the cows and pigs are protected as much as possible, and," he added almost as an afterthought, "I may have to check on Arissa. She may have flooding problems."

"Let her own take care of her. You will catch your death of cold," Ann reasoned.

Peter gently said, "Now Ann, you know we are her closest neighbor, and she has been more than a friend to us, even though she may not be considered one of us. Remember she has been midwife to your child and her son carries the Anderson name." Ann had no answer for that and turned to heating some soup on the hearth.

It was well into the early hours of the morning, but still dark when Ann heard Peter stirring. She knew what he was about. When he opened the door to go out, Ann was by his side, dressed as warmly as she could be and carrying some extra blankets with her.

"And where do you think you are going?" Peter wanted to know.

"Well, I would be awake worrying until you returned, so I may as well go with you."

The water was just beginning to run past Arissa's door as they neared her cabin. Peter could not see whether the flooding was from the river or from Prospect Creek. The land was much flatter as it neared the river and while there was no danger of the creek flooding their home, the same could not be said for Arissa's cabin.

They found Arissa standing in the doorway. "What in land's sake are you white folks doing here at this time of morning?" she asked.

Peter said, "Arissa, the river is rising. It is still storming. We will take a few minutes and lift your furniture as high as we can get it, and then you are coming to stay with us until this flood is over."

"Massa Peter, you know I can get into trouble living in the same house as white folk. I do not think it is wise for you to do this. I will just stay here and pray for the best."

"Arissa, you let us worry about what people say. You cannot stay here and risk drowning. You will come with us."

Arissa still was not convinced, "Missy Ann, are you sure? You know what your Mammy thinks of me."

"Arissa, I would not be here if I did not want what is best for a neighbor. We will worry about upsetting my mother some other time."

The fire in the fireplace was a welcome warmth as they returned to the house. The children were a buzz with the excitement of the storm and gathered around the three of them.

"Get some blankets and we will make a pallet here by the fire for Aunt Arissa," Ann ordered Frances, her oldest daughter, now twelve years old.

"Which ones?" asked Frances as she wanted to make sure of her mother's wishes.

"Get the ones that we use for company. You know the ones we have your grandmother use when she is here." Ann was not above some irony of her own.

The children soon settled back into their beds and Ann made Arissa lie down for what was left of the early morning. Arissa settled down on her pallet and little Peter Kemp crawled up next to her and snuggled close as they both drifted off.

"Peter, I hope we are doing the right thing," Ann said to her husband as they returned to their own bedroom.

"The right thing?" Peter snorted. "The only thing."

The storm went on for another four days. On the fifth day, the sun rose and its welcome warmth brought the family outside. The effects of the flood were evident all the way to Wildcat Hollow. "We are lucky the creek did not get into our house," Peter said as they surveyed the damage. A noise from up Ashby Gap Toll Road drew his attention, and he could see four or five men striding towards them.

"All of you get back into the house," Peter ordered. When he spoke this way there was no argument. They quickly went back into the house and Peter stood in the doorway, near the shotgun that was always there.

"Good morning, Mister Royston," began the leader.

"Mister Royston? You are very formal this morning, Mister Smallwood."

"Peter," the leader began anew, "the word is out that you have a colored living in your house."

"Why yes, Arissa is staying with us for a spell," Peter responded. "You know Arissa, she was the one who stayed at your house when your little Aaron was born."

"Tain't the same thing," John Smallwood answered. "And you know it."

"Well," Peter asserted, "I have been having such terrible stomach cramps, that I thought I was with child, and we wanted Arissa around just in case she was needed."

Laughter came from the other four cohorts and John Smallwood knew he was beaten. Noting that Peter had given him a way out, Smallwood jested, "From the size of your stomach, I could see how you could make that mistake."

The crowd that was surly a few minutes before, now roared with laughter. "Now that that is settled, let us thank the Lord for a beautiful morning. And since he has sent you down here, we need to survey Arissa's cabin and get it back into shape before she can return to it. I surely would appreciate your help. You know what an asset she is to our little community. We sure do not want her to have to go back across the river to live. What would you do for your next child?"

Smallwood nodded, "You can count on us. Let us get right at it."

Before the day was out, the cabin was mucked out of the mud that had entered through the door left open by Peter some five days before. Much of the mud had left on its own through the open back door.

"Royston, it was right smart of you to leave both doors open. I doubt that the cabin would have survived the force against the front without the door open."

"Well, you fellows that live up higher do not get a chance to be around floods like we bottom people do. Think maybe you are the smart ones," Peter joked.

John Smallwood said thoughtfully, "We are all living on land owned by Rawleigh Colston. Hear tell he is right sick. We do not know what is going to happen when he passes on." They talked as the cabin was cleaned out and soon the cabin was as clean as before the flood.

John Smallwood surveyed the cabin and said, "Peter, it is clean, but awfully damp. Maybe Arissa should stay another day or so at your place before she comes back to live here."

Peter chuckled at the turn around of the day's events. "You are right, besides I might get those stomach cramps again."

Later on that evening, Arissa said to Ann, "Missy Ann, you are married to one smooth man. I do not know what we would have done if he had not handled the situation that way."

"I did not know he was that smooth myself," Ann answered. "But in the end, everything turned out real good. Now you be sure to be in your usual place come Sunday, up at Mount Carmel. I think that is real important."

A few days later the river had returned to its banks and Peter surveyed the bottom land. There were cakes of mud that covered the entire farm area that were already beginning to split into a checkerboard design. "Got somebody's good farmland from up river," Peter surmised. "Maybe this year will bring a good crop. If it keeps drying out I can plow in a week or so." He continued toward the river and ended up near the ferry crossing. The ferry was in operation and Peter saw a familiar figure helping to bring the boat across. "Jo Anderson, as I live and breathe, it is good to see you."

"I had to come down as soon as I could to see how my mammy was doing. I hope she did not get flooded out. Wish I could have been here to take care of her."

"She has neighbors, you know," Peter said. "They will take care of her."

Jo replied, "But they could not get across the river while it was flooded and they are at least a mile away, just past Tilt Hammer Mill Road."

"Sometimes, the neighbors are not the ones you expect," Peter continued. "I am on my way to Millwood to make sure they will grind my wheat come fall. We will talk more when I return." Peter rode the bay onto the awaiting ferry boat and made his way toward Millwood. There, he was assured that he would have his wheat and corn ground at harvest time.

"By the way, we buried your old boss last week," said Hugh Nelson, who was standing near the door of the mill.

"You do not mean John Holker?" Peter exclaimed. "Why I was just with him just before the flood."

"Yes, they took him all the way to Winchester and buried him in some papist ceremony. Only a few of us went. I do not understand any of that Latin stuff."

It was a long slow ride back toward the river as Peter thought of the loss of someone who had meant so much to him.

Waiting for him as he exited the ferry boat was Jo Anderson. "Peter, my friend and neighbor, I do truly apologize for who I considered my mother's neighbors. She told me what happened and now the word neighbor has a new meaning."

"Would you not do the same thing for me, Jo Anderson? Just let it be known that we are neighbors to your mother." Peter added, "What are you doing with the reaper? Is it ready to cut my wheat, or do I still have to do that with a scythe, me, my wife and all the children, and sometimes, your mother?"

"I guess you are stuck with the scythe for a few more seasons," Jo answered. "The McCormicks are doing more fighting among themselves than they are working on the machine. I tell them that all they need to do is put in the paddles to bring the grain to the cutter, rather than worrying about bringing the cutter to the grain. The problem is, we can only test during the harvest season. When we find out that stuff will not work, we do not get it fixed until after harvest is over. Then we have to wait until next season."

"Peter, I am glad that we kept Arissa on this side of the river," Ann began.

"Why is that, my wife?" Peter wondered.

"Well, we will need her in a few months."

"For what? It will not be time for the harvesting to begin."

"No, it will be for her more traditional duties," Ann smiled.

Understanding came finally to Peter. "You mean we are going to have another child?"

"You catch on slowly, my husband," she teased. "Haven't you noticed my weight gain?"

He did not want to admit that he had noticed a bit of weight being added, but thought it was just being forty that did it. "Number nine," he said. "We are starting to have a real family now. Wonder if it will be a boy or a girl?" He could hardly wait to talk to the Lady of the Spring. Maybe she would tell him if it were going to be another boy.

Sunday morning found the entire family at Mount Carmel. In the slave loft, there was not one, but two, as Jo Anderson joined his mother for the service. There was little communication between the two races, but there was some nodding and acknowledgement from the others.

The mountain people had accepted Arissa, but only Peter was acquainted with Jo Anderson. The rest knew him only as the boy who used to run the ferry. Later, after Jo and Arissa began their walk down the Fox Trap Hill, there were some looks at Peter as if there might be an invasion of coloreds in the mountains.

Peter thought that they had enough exposure to this problem in the past week, and casually told them of Jo Anderson's work on the mechanical harvester. "He spends most of his time these days up around Harrisonburg at the McCormick place. He is a free man, you know, as is Arissa a free woman."

"Well, as long as he does not get too uppity, he'll be all right. He sure could handle those boats," they conceded as they said good-bye after church.

1823

With John Holker gone Peter lost his contact with the politics of the outside world. Little did he know, or care, of James Monroe and his Monroe Doctrine. The time came for Ann to have her baby, and it was a girl. They called her Sarah Catherine, after Ann's side of the family. The other girls could not have been happier. There was not much extra room in the house, but the eight children settled into two bedrooms. Once in a while Ann would find Peter Kemp sleeping by the fireplace, as if he were looking for Arissa. Three going on four was a wonderful time of learning and Peter Kemp knew how to bring out the best in everyone. No one could be unhappy around the lad, now known as P.K. "He has such a twinkle in his eyes," both Peter and Ann would say over and over.

Christmas Eve was a cold day, but not too cold with little wind off Fox Trap Hill. Ann busied herself with preparations for the next day. Uriah was going to join the family this Christmas, and she had a surprise for all of them. As she cooked she kept looking at a scrap of paper in her apron pocket.

"What you got there, Ma?" Joseph wanted to know. "Is it a love note from Pa?"

"It is not for you to mind, Joseph," she retorted. "You will find out soon enough." She continued to pull out the paper as if to study the words written there and commit them to memory.

Peter came stomping in the house about noon, pulling a freshly cut cedar tree. "Cedar trees are getting scarce. The best place to find a Christmas tree is up on the Green place, and even there they are getting scarce. People are coming all the way from Upperville to cut down a tree," he complained.

His demeanor changed when the young ones came screaming out into the living room. "Let us help you set it up so that Saint Nicholas will come and trim it for us," was the chorus from the ones old enough to know of Christmas, but young enough to believe in the tradition of Saint Nicholas.

Ann gave a half-hearted protest. "Saint Nicholas, it is not. It is Santa Claus." Santa Claus was the English version of the Dutch saint to which Christmas gift giving was attributed. She thought of the paper in her apron pocket and murmured to herself, "Though, from now on, it is going to be Saint Nicholas, if this poem catches on, as it appears that it will."

"We will let the Saint trim the tree, but remember that Christmas is the birthday of Christ, and we will continue with our tradition of reading the Nativity, first from the book of Matthew and then from Luke. Tonight, we will let Mathew do the first reading, and then Uriah will read from Luke. After that, all you children will be off to bed to sleep tight, until we call you at the dawning. Then you can come see if the Saint trimmed the tree," Peter pronounced.

Supper was a bit late and the children paid scant attention to the food. After eating, the fire seemed to draw them closer together. They were all ears to the stories told by Uriah as he recounted the many trips he had taken to Baltimore and his description of the various materials he hauled back to the Shenandoah Valley. Uriah was now twenty-two and as tall as his father, though not the same breadth.

Joseph would be eighteen the coming January. While there was a four years difference in their age, they were very close. Joseph was a bit more slight and showed little interest in farming or animals. He rode well, but his future would not be on the farm. Peter let these thoughts pass through his head as he watched his full family enjoy the shadows of the night. The only light came from the fire.

When it was time for the readings, he would light the Betty lamp, though it gave off scarce more light than a roaring fire.

"Pa, let us get at the readings," Ann urged as she watched the youngest one start to nod off. Peter reached to the mantel and brought down the family bible and opened it to the first chapter of Matthew, and passed it to his son. Mathew was thirteen and was adept at reading. He positioned the Bible to get the best light and began, "Now this is how the birth of Jesus Christ came about…"

Peter leaned back and his mind wandered to Christmases of years past, back to his own youth and the first time his father passed the Bible to him and said, "Peter, it is now your turn." He was scarcely aware of Mathew finishing, and as he came back to the present, he turned the pages to the second chapter of the Gospel of Luke.

He passed the book to Uriah and motioned for him to begin. "In those days Caesar Augustus published a decree…" Peter looked at his children and wondered if they, too, in years to come, would reach for the Bible and pass it to their own children to read the Nativity story.

Uriah finished his reading and closed the Bible. The youngest, Anna Maria, Sarah, and Peter Kemp were nodding, and Peter was about to announce the bedtime for at least the very youngest. Ann motioned to Peter and he waited for her to give the word he expected, when she said, "Now I have a story to read to you, but I want to make sure that everyone is awake to hear it."

She pulled the scrap of paper from her apron and said, "Now this is a poem that was in a paper I read. Nobody knows who wrote it, but it was in the New York papers last Christmas." She moved toward the fireplace, and settling down, began to recite with only an occasional glance at the paper. "'Twas the night before Christmas, when all through the house…"

Peter was not sure how to react. This certainly was not a poem about the Nativity. He started to say something, but as he started, he looked around at all the children and saw their rapt attention. Peter Kemp slid over close to the roaring fireplace and was trying to see up the chimney. Mollie, Sarah and Anna Maria were wide awake. Even Frances, Hannah and Mathew were entranced. Uriah and Joseph were hanging onto every word.

Well, Peter thought, *I am going to have to talk this over with Ann, but first I will visit the Lady in the Spring tomorrow.*

The poem over, Ann said, "Now to bed, all of you. The Saint is not going to come around here and trim this tree if you all stay up all night."

"In the poem Saint Nicholas brought presents to all the children. Besides trimming the tree, do you think that he will bring us a present?" Mollie asked.

Ann reddened a bit. Times had been slim in recent years. It was harder and harder to keep the farm going and have any cash left over. Any presents for the children were homemade clothes.

A snort from Uriah brought her attention to him pulling out a handkerchief from his pocket and elaborately blowing his nose. "I must be catching a cold. Too many long days on those wagons," he muttered.

All of the young children were put to bed, and Ann brought out the corn-popping pan and started it to heat in the fireplace. She brought out strings of bright red berries and some ornaments that came from her past Christmases. When the corn was popped, they began to string the kernels onto a long thread. All of this was used to trim the tree that Peter had finished putting up.

"It looks pretty good," Ann said to herself as she looked over at Peter staring into the fire. *I wonder what he is thinking,* she thought. She looked around and found Uriah standing near her.

"Well Ma, how about those presents for the children?"

"There is not much this year. It is been a long one."

"Sometimes that old Saint Nicholas comes in different ways." Uriah smiled. "Excuse me for a minute." He went outside to the stable where his horse was feeding and opening up his saddlebags, he began pulling out what seemed to be an unending string of Christmas presents. Bringing these into the house he placed them in front of Ann and said, "Maybe you had better figure out who gets these. I had some money left over when I was in Baltimore last time, and I just could not pass these up."

The tears were streaming from Ann's eyes as she hugged her oldest. "You are indeed a funny looking Saint Nicholas, but what a Christmas this is. I can hardly wait until tomorrow myself." She started finding some ribbons to wrap around the presents. There were beautiful combs for Frances, Hannah, and Mollie. There was a carved wooden horse and carriage for Mathew Whiting. There was a top for Peter Kemp and dolls for Sarah Catherine and Anna Maria.

There were three other presents that were in a sack that he did not open. "Those can wait for tomorrow," Uriah muttered.

Peter said little, and Ann was concerned for her husband's ego as he appeared to be supplanted as the Christmas provider. She slipped over to sit with Peter and she too stared into the fire. "The hardest part of watching our children grow is to let them become providers themselves. But remember, it is a long way from providing on a one time basis to that of providing full time, year after year."

Peter nodded. "It is indeed hard to understand the changes that are taking place. I am getting worse than John Holker ever was."

The night went slowly as Peter slept by the fire, awakening from time to time to throw some more logs on it. He would glance over at the tree that at times appeared to be an intruder and at others a live being, awaiting the yells of children rising with the dawn. The berries and popcorn glinted from the glow of the fireplace, and Peter found himself wondering about the other three presents that were lying in the sacks near the tree.

He was dozing when the squeals awoke him. Children were everywhere. They spotted the presents underneath the trimmed tree.

"There is a Saint Nicholas. I thought Ma was teasing," shouted Mollie as she tried out her comb. Dolls were hugged and P.K. knew instinctively how to make a top spin. Frances and Hannah traded off trying out the combs on each other's hair. When the hubbub died down there were Ann and Peter and the oldest two children left with no presents.

There was the sack of presents that was still unopened. Finally Uriah stepped forward and said to no one in particular, "I think Saint Nicholas must have been scared off last night. He left a sack of presents that aren't even opened. Let us see what we can find here." He reached in and pulled out another comb. "Let us see now, who did not get a comb?" The girls looked at each other. They all had combs.

Finally it dawned on Frances, "Ma, it is Ma, she did not get a comb."

"I think you are right and so this is for Ma. And with all you girls hogging up the mirrors, maybe she needs one of her own." He reached into the sack again and pulled out a silver plated hand mirror.

Ann could not hold back the tears. "What a Christmas! What a son to have!"

"Oh yes," Uriah continued. "I want to make a deal with my little brother, who wants to be the best shoemaker in the state, if not the nation. I have a problem getting shoes to fit my big feet. I found a 'last' that should make shoes to fit me. Here it is for my brother, if he will promise to not only use it for his customers, but use it to make me a pair of shoes from time to time."

Uriah could tell from the smile on Joseph's face that he had made a hit. "Remember this present is for the both of us," he continued, so that everyone knew he was included in the gift receivers. "Now, I think that Saint Nicholas has taken care of everybody, hasn't he?" Uriah asked.

"Papa, what about Papa?" Mollie said.

"Do you think that Saint Nicholas brings presents to papas?" Uriah asked. "Sure would not be much of a gift bringer if he forgot Pa, would he? Let me check that sack again. Yes, there appears to be something that is left." Uriah reached in and pulled out a present that told Peter that Uriah cared a lot for him.

"As much as you love our wonderful spring water, how could you not have a special water dipper of your very own?"

Peter stared mutely at the fanciest silver plated dipper he had ever seen. Finally, he stammered, "Uriah, you should not have, but I am glad you did."

Ann smiled. "Let us get some breakfast. It is been a merry Christmas for all of us."

Peter made his way to the spring with two empty buckets. In one you could see a handle of a dipper protruding. As he started dipping the water into a bucket, Maria's voice rang out. "Do I see a new dipper? Does it make dipping the water any easier?"

"Not really," Peter admitted, "but I just had to show you a Christmas present brought to me by Uriah. He brought presents for everyone. In fact, they were about the only presents we had this year."

"You sound like maybe you are sorry he brought the presents," Maria suggested.

"I guess maybe I am, a bit. It is the responsibility of the provider of the house to bring his family what they need."

The voice answered, "And you have, Peter, my friend. You provide food, shelter and clothing. Do they really need more?"

"They do not need more, but you should have seen their faces, and I am sure, even mine, when the gifts were given out."

"Did Uriah make much out of giving the presents?" Maria wanted to know.

"No, he made out that Saint Nicholas was the one who brought the gifts."

"Good for him," Maria exulted. "You have raised a good lad."

"Well, this Saint Nicholas is giving me a bit of a problem, also. There is a new poem that Ann read last night that is so good that it may replace our tradition of reading from the Bible. You could tell that the children were enthralled with the idea of someone bringing gifts. In years past, it was Saint Nicholas' chore just to trim the tree."

"Where did that concept come from—to have the Saint trim the tree? Is it common place?"

"No, it is a mountain tradition that came from the families that were too poor to give their children many gifts. In other areas, it is a common tradition for the good Saint to deliver the presents. In either case, I would prefer that the children spend more time thinking about whose feast day it is, and that they should be giving and not receiving."

"Peter, Peter," she admonished, "who had the most fun last night, Uriah, or the rest of the family?"

Peter thought for a moment, then admitted, "Why, I believe it was Uriah. I have never seen him so filled with life as when he was unloading those presents."

"That is the answer, my friend. In order to have a giver, you must have a receiver. Those who receive are happy for the gift, but it is the giver who is blessed."

Changing the subject, Peter asked, "Back when you were…back in your early days, did you celebrate Christmas?"

"Oh yes, Christmas was very special for me. In fact, my son, the doctor, was born on Christmas Day. We too, received unexpected gifts and I am sure, that made the givers very happy."

Peter made his way back across Prospect Creek with his two full buckets of water, not understanding the meaning of Christmas any better, but things just seemed to make more sense when the Lady talked. He felt strangely at peace whenever he talked to her.

1825

January of 1825 was as cold a month as anyone could remember. Ice formed so deep on the Shenandoah that wagons wore ruts in the ice as they crossed at Shepherd's Ford. Little could be done outside so Peter busied himself with inside chores. It was late in the day and late in the month when a knock at the door brought his activity to a halt. He crossed to open it, while at the same time glancing at his weapon that stood near the door. Why he did this he was not sure, since there was no one in the mountains that would want to hurt them.

"Nimrod," he called loud enough for Ann to hear. "Nimrod, what brings you across the river on such a cold day?"

By this time Ann also was there to greet her brother. "Come on in and warm yourself, you'll catch your death of cold."

Nimrod Anderson responded, "It is not my death I came to tell you about. It is Pa. He died this morning. Just fell over and died. No warning at all."

Ann gasped. Her dad was almost seventy-nine, but had been in good health. "You can not mean it," she said.

"I hate to say it, but I do. If they can get a grave dug he will be buried in the family graveyard come tomorrow." They sat and talked of their growing up and about their father. Nimrod was two years older than Ann and was always her protector. There was a bond between them that made it necessary that he be the one who brought the news.

"How is Mother taking it?" Ann asked.

"Good," answered Nimrod. "She is shocked, but it seems like she had a sense of foreboding that something was going to happen. Just last Sunday, she got out her special black dress and when someone asked if she was going to wear it to church, she said, 'not today.'"

It was agreed that Nimrod would spend the night and a pallet was made near the fire. Once again Peter Kemp came out and snuggled near Nimrod, close to the fire. "We will leave you two to keep the fire up tonight, and then tomorrow all of us will travel to the farm to bury Dad," Ann suggested.

Peter added, "It is best we try to get across at the Ferry, even though we could probably make it on the ice. I think the Ferry is safer."

They rose with the dawn, fed the cows, horses and pigs and hitched the wagon. "It might be a long trip. We want to bundle everyone up well so that no one gets frostbite." Peter gave a "giddy-up" to the horses and they started across the creek and made their way to the river, with Nimrod following on horseback. As they passed Arissa's cabin Peter got down and said, "Maybe I had better tell Arissa where we are going, just in case we get back too late to feed the animals tonight."

Ann agreed, even though she knew that the main reason was to tell Arissa of Joseph Anderson's death. In a few minutes he was back and said to no one in particular, "She is taking it pretty well."

Ann snorted. "Why should she not take it well? He was her master in her early slave years." Peter did not respond and shortly the ferry was reached. There were ice blocks floating down the river and the ferryman worked hard to make the crossing.

Once on the other side they started the six or seven mile trek to Anderson's Crossing. Passing the entrance to Springsbury Peter fought the impulse to turn in. While he liked being in his own house, there was something special about Springsbury. There was an ache in his heart as he thought of John Holker and now Joseph Anderson. His mind went to the first meeting when Anderson demanded he give up courting Ann. *The old man had a way about him that made you like him even when he was mad at you,* he thought.

In a bit over three hours they made it to the farm, and upon arriving they all went to the family graveyard. There, a grave had been dug, and the body of Joseph Anderson was laid to rest. The coffin was a simple wooden one, purchased the day before in Berryville. After the graveside services, all went back to the

Anderson farm, and the conversation was all about Joseph Anderson. He was a successful man, everybody decided, a man of strength and honor.

"He treated his slaves well," one said, bringing up a subject that was on the mind of most. "He actually gave freedom to some of them, even though he needed them on the farm. I am surprised that some of them were not at the services."

"Some were, but he only died two days ago. How could you think that many people, let alone former slaves, could be there?"

The following day Peter told Ann, "It is much warmer today. It looks like a warm spell is coming on. We should probably get going home before the ice starts to break up in the river. And also we need to feed the animals."

"Why do not you borrow one of Father's horses and ride home, leaving us here to visit with the family? This is a hard time for all of us, especially my mother. Come back and get us in a couple of days."

Peter agreed and taking the sorrel that belonged to Joseph Anderson made his way back to Wildcat Hollow. He saw the figure of Arissa watching as he passed her cabin. She did not come outside to greet him and moved back from the window as he passed by.

Before he fed the animals he went inside the house and used a tinderbox that was laying on the mantel to start a fire in the fireplace. Soon the chill in the house was replaced with a warm glow. *There is nothing like a good warm fire on a cold day,* he thought.

The next day continued to be warm and Peter made his way to the spring. He needed the help of the Lady to sort out his thoughts.

"Why do not you come and see me more often?" was her greeting. "Have you forgotten about me just because it is cold? See here how warm it is around the spring. No ice or frost at all."

Peter had to admit this that had always puzzled him, "Why is it not cold near the spring?"

"It is because I come from deep within the earth. My temperature is always the same, winter or summer. I can cool you in the summer and warm you in the winter," she continued. "I am like the God in Heaven. I am commissioned to bring solace to those who will stop and be near me."

Peter was now used to the voice and he talked freely with her. "Why do people have to die?" he wanted to know.

"You have asked me that before," she said. "There is a time for everything. Would you want to live forever? There is a much better place that you will find after you pass through this life. Imagine, no more worries about the crops or droughts or floods. You never will be cold or hot. You will never hurt."

"But I worry about my family," Peter said.

"And they about you. It is natural for humans to worry. That is because they have no faith in the after life. Talk to my son about it and he will tell you that many sicknesses come from worrying."

Peter responded, "It is only Ann that sees your son and then only when she is giving birth. If you would tell me where he practices I could go see him, though I admit, I am not much on doctors."

Peter thought the conversation was getting uncomfortable. He picked up the filled buckets and made his way across creek and into the house. *Imagine not worrying. Now that would be something,* he considered, stoking the fire.

The summer of 1825 showed a marked increase in traffic on the Ashby Gap Toll Road. The usual number of mountain people and an occasional paying customer became, first, a rivulet of Pilgrims, and then turned into a torrent of travelers.

The Royston house was at the downhill end of Fox Trap Hill, just where the Toll Road took a zigzag before turning toward the river. Peter worried that a runaway wagon could easily end up hitting the east end of the house. There were always moments of anxiety when the brake shoes began their squeal, and the snort of the horses told them that the horses were doing their best to hold back the load.

No wagon ever hit the house but there were a few instances where a wagon overturned as the driver turned the horses too quickly. At these times Mathew and Joseph were ready to lend a hand to help right and reload the wagon. In most cases all they got for their efforts was a "thank you" as the travelers tried to keep whatever cash they had for the unknown costs of the journey.

Most of the travelers were good people heading west to find a better life. An eagle eye was kept on the chickens and pigs, as those who would steal very seldom announced their intentions to the unwary.

Peter said to Ann, "It is lucky we have our barn, stable and pigpen across the creek. It is a natural barrier for those with bad intentions."

It was at the ferry that problems arose. Sometimes the ferry crossing would back up for four or five hours. The wagons would mill about and cause damage to the crops that Peter had planted in the area. Some people would start cooking fires, and there was always danger of a fire starting that could damage not only the adjacent wagons but also the crops in late season.

Finally a solution to the problem was reached that also created some cash in their pockets. Ann, Frances and Hannah set up a fire pit and a large iron kettle near the ferry crossing. In it a stew of sorts was prepared and sold to the wayfarers at such a cheap price they could not resist. Frances and Hannah would serve the stew while Ann kept the pot filled and boiling. The ferry added a man to direct the wagon parking and assign the traveler their turn on the ferry.

While Peter had lost the political input from John Holker, it was now Ann who would listen to the talk of the travelers. She began to pick up on the conversations that told of the goings-on in Washington and the eastern part of the state. She learned of the Monroe Doctrine and that was passed on to the children during their study time. Much was retold over the dinner table when all could absorb the details.

"Did you know we have a new president named John Quincy Adams? His father was the second president. How do you figure that they could look all over the country, and the only person they could find to be president was the son of another president? It sure beats me how those things work."

Peter added, "And if John Holker were around, he would be wondering how this would affect his loans out to France and our own government. He told me the United States owed him over four hundred thousand dollars. Now that is a lot of stew in the stew pot."

Ann retorted, "It does make our earnings look small. But we have it in cash, and he could not spend his notes." She continued, "A lot of the people heading west are upset at the election. In fact, that was the straw that pushed them towards the west. It seems that Old Hickory beat Adams in the general election. He got more votes from the people and more of the state votes. The representatives had to choose because no one had a majority, and they picked Adams over Jackson, and that has a lot of people mad."

Peter smiled. It was strange to him that Ann had much more political knowledge than he and yet she could not even vote.

"Pa, it was easy getting across the river, but I may have to swim back if I take too long to tell you why I came," Uriah said.

"In any case, it is good to see you my son. It seems that you do not have much time to spend away from your work."

"Pa, let us get Ma in here. That way I only say it once."

"Now what is so important that you need both of us?" Peter wanted to know as they waited for Ann.

When both were assembled Uriah, stumbling a bit, blurted out, "I am going to get married."

"Are you going to tell us the name of the lucky lady, or are we going to have to guess?"

"It is Hannah White from Millwood. You know the White family."

"Yes, a fine family. Have you set a date?"

"It will be next July if her parents approve."

"You mean you are telling us before you ask her parents? What are these modern children doing to tradition?" Peter asked.

"Shush, Peter, the next generation always does things differently. Why I remember you did not court me exactly according to tradition."

"Well, I was afraid of losing you, and if it weren't for my persistence, you would have married someone else," Peter teased.

Uriah smiled. He missed seeing the teasing that went on between his parents.

"How goes the wagonering?" Peter wanted to know. "You will need to be home with your bride come next July."

"It is still a lot of nights away from home, but we will live close to her family so that she is protected."

"There is no protection like a husband," Peter continued.

"Peter, stop lecturing him. He will have plenty of time to work those things out. It is the love that counts," Ann admonished her husband.

Uriah was wearing a strange overcoat and Peter could not help but comment on it. It had kind of a slick finish to it and was not of leather or wool.

"It is called a Macintosh, Pa. The material is made out of rubber and it does not let the rain get through. It is sticky in hot and cold weather, but it is a welcome when you get caught in the rain on a long haul with no place to stop."

"Macintosh?" Peter questioned. "Why in the world would they call it a Macintosh?"

"It was named after the Scotsman who invented it, Pa. It is been around for four or five years over in England."

As Uriah prepared to return to Millwood, Peter said slyly, "I would not wait too long to get married. I would not be surprised if Joseph Asbury does not beat you to it. He is traveling across Ashby's Gap every day to learn shoe making, and I see him eyeing that Glascock gal every time she comes over from Paris to Mount Carmel for preaching services. We used to never see her there, but now she is there most every Sunday."

"Pa, Joseph's just a lad. Any marrying for him will be a long time off," Uriah answered.

"Do not be too sure about that. He has a steady job and he is almost nineteen. One thing for sure, people will always need shoes," Peter said.

"And they will always need freight hauled." Uriah lifted the reins of his horse and headed toward the Shenandoah.

The stream of travelers continued. Peter asked one why he did not go through Manassas Gap past Front Royal. The gap was about the same height but the east slope was much less steep.

"It is the cost. We can cross Ashby's Gap and pay the ferryman half of what it costs to go through Manassas Gap. Only the rich man can afford Manassas. Besides, even though the hill may be steeper, the team can manage it, and it cuts off miles if you are going into western Virginia or Ohio. It is about a tie if you are heading for Cumberland Gap."

"I knew it would be coming, but this farming does not lend itself to saving money," Peter confided to Ann.

"And what are you talking about, my husband?" Ann wanted to know.

"Well, it has been almost six years since Rawleigh Colston died, and we had no place to send the quit rents. The lawyer talked to Uriah about it last week. Says we owe a bit over four hundred dollars. I guess the only way is to borrow some money to pay it off. Uriah says that the lawyer will get someone named Joseph Stephenson to lend us the money if we put up all our personal property and get somebody to sign with us."

"Who do you have in mind to co-sign? It seems awfully hard to borrow money and never see it," Ann mused.

"Uriah said he would sign and he talked to your brother Joe about being an additional signer."

"I do not care much for everybody knowing our troubles," Ann muttered.

"Well, the entire mountain has the problem. Nobody has been paying the quit rent and it is going to be a hardship on many. They are getting ready to survey all the land that Colston owned and divide it between his heirs. I do not know who is going to own the land we are on. It may take a number of years before we find out anything."

"Ma, making shoes is the best job in the world," Joseph said to his mother. "It only takes a half hour to go over the Gap to Paris to go to work, and I do not have to worry about floods."

"Joseph, I think there may be other things to draw you to Paris," Ann teased.

"Ma, Harriett is a mighty pretty girl, and I think I am about ready to ask her to marry me. But even that aside, I love making shoes. One of these days the shoe industry will eliminate the shoemaker from making new shoes. All he will be able to do is repair factory made shoes. Right now only the wealthy can afford to get shoes made by a cobbler. Otherwise, factory made shoes take a lot of breaking in."

When Joseph Asbury gets to talking shoes you are in for a long day, his mother thought.

Joseph continued, "We are seeing a lot of requests for Wellington boots, although they probably do not look like what the Duke wore when he defeated Napoleon. We still only have a straight last and the pair have to be made as if a man had a straight foot, and everybody knows that is wrong. We are experimenting with making our lasts in pairs, so that there will be a right foot and a left one. Since there are a number of last sizes, it will be expensive. Maybe we will make up for it by having the planters from around Upperville and Piedmont come and buy from us."

In an effort to get Joseph away from shoes, Ann said, "And when are you thinking of getting married?"

"If she will have me, maybe it will be next July. That will be three years after Uriah was married. Actually, I should get married on Saint Crispin's Feast Day. You know that Saint Crispin is the patron saint of shoemakers, but that is October 25th and I really do not want to wait that long."

"And Harriet would not like to be wedded on a shoemaker's holiday. I do not think that would be the way to start off a marriage," was his mother's sage advice.

"Well, the people got their wish," Ann mentioned at suppertime. "Mr. Adams only had one term and Old Hickory beat him soundly this time."

"Where are you hearing this news?" Peter wanted to know.

"Mr. Lloyd was talking about it at Mount Carmel last Sunday. He does a lot of cattle trading and many of his customers in the Valley are talking about it," Ann responded. "That separator down the middle of the pews at Mount Carmel may keep the women on one side and the men on the other, but they haven't figured out how to stop the sounds from traveling from one side to the other. They probably would if they could."

Peter wondered who she meant by 'they.' She always looked at him every time she had something to say about the 'Man's World.'

Mollie approached Ann, "Ma, I want to tell you and maybe you can tell Pa. I want to get married in July. James and I have been seeing each other for a while now, and he has asked me to marry him."

"Mollie, you know you do not need my permission to marry. I suppose Peter will want to have his say, but you know what his answer will be. James is a good mountain boy and we know the Dorans well. See them every Sunday at Mount Carmel."

1830–1840

1830

"Ma, I have some news for you," Frances confided to her mother. "Tom Grubbs and I are getting married in two months."

"Well," Ann responded. "It does not surprise me. Ever since Mollie got married last year I have been watching your progress with Tom. He is a fine person and I know you will be happy together."

"Well, here I am fifty-five today. Four of my children are married, and I think another is thinking about it, and the grandchildren are coming faster than I can count. I am feeling awfully old today," Peter complained to the Lady.

"But is it not a beautiful day!" the Lady exclaimed. "It seems quieter lately. What happened to the crowds? Many used to come here for a drink of water when the wagons backed up."

Peter explained, "The people are still going west but they have found different routes. I hear many are using the Erie Canal, and go to some place called Buffalo. They dropped the toll price at Manassas Gap and many are going that way. We made some cash money feeding the travelers, but I am really glad to wake up in the morning and not hear the sounds of teams coming down Fox Trap Hill."

The wind was biting as Peter hunched down near the base of the white oak tree near the spring. "Ash Wednesday is early this year of 1832." He spoke to the Lady in the Spring, wondering if the weather meant anything to her.

"Are you planning on a special atonement for the next forty days?" the Lady asked.

"Not really. It seems like the past few years have been one continuous time of atonement. I did find some good sedge over on Burwell's Island that I could burn into ashes. I think it is important for all of us to remember the need for fasting before the Easter season, and I always put the ashes on the foreheads of all in the household."

"Where will you be on Easter Sunday morning?" the Lady wanted to know.

"Mount Carmel begins its year the week after Lent starts and we will most likely be there for Easter. It closes for the winter months, as there is no heat in the church."

"Even though Easter will be early, why not talk to everyone and plan to have an outdoor Easter at sunrise among the rocks at the church? Remember it was at sunrise that we found the risen Lord on that first Easter Sunday."

"You sound like you were there at the time," Peter suggested in a questioning voice.

"Do I?" the voice answered. "It is possible that I have been to many, many places and seen many, many places that we haven't talked about. But it is true that the boulders around Mount Carmel are very similar to those where He was buried for those three days."

"And how do you know about the boulders at Mount Carmel? Have you been there too?" Peter wanted to know.

"If you think I could have been present at the Son's death and resurrection, why could I not be at Mount Carmel also?" she stated with a conviction that left Peter with no more questions.

Why am I so confused when I leave her, but so glad I came? he pondered as he made his way through the snow across Prospect Creek to the warmth of his house.

Anne watched Peter as he settled down in front of the fireplace, seeing the smudge of the ashes on his forehead. *Why do I begrudge him his time at the spring?* she wondered. *He never talks to me about things that are on his mind. It is almost like he works things out over there.* There was a certain bit of jealously over the time he spent at the spring.

The Lent of 1832 seemed to bring up many thoughts as Peter pondered his future in the mountains. The surveyor, George Love, must have completed his work by now as he had surveyed the mountains last summer. Rawleigh Colston has been dead now almost ten years. *Everybody in the mountains needs to know which of the heirs will own the property they are leasing. What kind of arrangements will we be able to make with the new owner? Will they be selling it, or want us to continue leasing?* These thoughts gnawed at him as the winter lost its grip and the days turned warmer. It would soon be time for plowing again. The harness was mended and even the horses seemed to be looking forward to the coming work-load.

Sunday, April 27, 1832 was a day to know there was a Risen Lord. The mountains had been alerted that the Easter services would start outside Mount Carmel just as the sun rose over Ashby's Gap. Peter and all his family were among the first to arrive. They left the horse and buggy and the extra horses ridden by the boys near the cemetery rail fence.

There would hardly be room for the people near the church. The dew on the grass and boulders kept the men on their feet. The ladies laid out comforters and hoped they would stay dry enough to keep their Easter finery from absorbing the moisture from the ground. Peter watched the crowd gather as they made their way up the hill to the church.

The mountains are becoming more populated, Peter thought, as he began a silent roll call. There were the Dermonts, the Tripletts, the Shacklets, the Flemmings, and the Lanhams. The Thompsons, the Grimes and the Johnsons came from near the top of the mountain. There were the Morgan, Strother, and Fitzhugh families, the Dorans that Mollie had recently married into, and the Grubbs. Missing were some notables such as the Smallwoods, but then Peter remembered that they were probably at the recently opened Baptist Church out past Flat Field near Morgan's Mill.

It is a shame that Bishop Asbury is not alive to see what his circuit riding preaching had helped bring to fruition in the mountain community, Peter thought. There were many from nearby Paris and even from across the river. By the time the service was called to order, and the opening hymn sung, many of the men and their tired legs were searching out the most comfortable boulder they could find. The granite was rough and ground into the trousers, but it was better than standing throughout the service.

The preacher seemed to love the sound of his own voice and showed little signs of letting the Lord loose so that he could start off for Emmaus. Peter began to doubt whether his promoting the daybreak outdoor service was such a good idea after all. First the children, then the men, and finally the ladies began to fidget, then to squirm, and finally to alternately stand and sit as the preacher droned on.

The enterprising voice of the impromptu choir leader, Mollie Doran, finally seized on an exhortation of the preacher as he cried out, "Just to have been there that morning to be able to walk closely with Jesus," and began the closing hymn, 'O, For a Closer Walk With God.'

Well, the idea of an outdoor service was good, Peter thought as they headed back down Fox Trap Hill. *I wonder what they would have said if they knew where I got the idea for this type of service?*

It was a memorable Easter. The ladies busied themselves with the makings of a fine Easter dinner, while the men gathered near the creek and enjoyed, first, the shade, then the sunlight as a itinerant wisp of a breeze made the moment run hot or cold. Besides his own boys there were the new additions, Sam and Tom Grubbs and James Doran.

Uriah was telling some outlandish stories from his wagonering adventures. "Why, you will not believe what they are doing over in Baltimore," he began. "They have something called a railroad that has two steel tracks set just so far apart and a big wagon with wheels that fit onto that track. They have tried a number of ways to pull the wagon. First there were horses out in front but that did not work very well. Then they tried horses walking on a platform that moved under their hooves when they walked. The platform was tied to the wagon wheels and the whole thing rolled down the track."

Uriah had the natural ability of a storyteller and all waited intently for the coming words. "The company that is doing this is called The Baltimore and Ohio Railroad and they intend to lay down these rails all the way to the Ohio River. That way they can send people and freight to the Ohio, to be transported down the Ohio."

"I would like to see what those horses looked like after walking all that way on a platform," Joseph Asbury commented.

"That is not the end of the story," Uriah continued. "Now they have something called a 'Tom Thumb,' which is a steam engine that seems to really work. The engine is just like the one that powers the boats on the Hudson. Why, they have hauled up to thirty passengers at speeds up to eighteen miles an hour."

"Uriah, we need to check the supply of the peach brandy," Mathew exclaimed. "There is no way anything can travel that fast."

"Well, maybe that is a slight exaggeration," Uriah backed down, "They did have a stage driver's horse that outran the engine in a race. But carrying passengers is not the place where the railroad is going to shine. It is in the freight hauling business. They have tracks all the way out to Ellicott's Mill, and Frederick is just a few months away. They have hauled fifty tons in a single load on that big wagon."

"Why, I was one of the haulers of part of that first shipment," Uriah continued. "I did not have to drive the team all the way to Baltimore to get a load. They say it only took a ton of hard coal to push that load forty miles and they did it in less than three hours. One of these days, the tracks will be all the way to Harpers Ferry, and we will just have to haul the freight from there up the Valley."

"What is that going to do to your freight business?" Joseph wanted to know. "Maybe you might want that last back and you can learn how to be a cobbler."

"No way, my little brother," Uriah countered. "Once you are a teamster, there is no other trade to consider. All in all, it will be a good thing. The freight will cost less and the people will be able to buy more. That should increase the amount of freight I can haul from wherever the railroad is. Besides, there is no way the train will get any closer than Harpers Ferry. They can never build a bridge strong enough to carry those big railroad engines across the Potomac. We will still have to ferry the freight wagons across the river."

Mathew nodded toward P.K, now thirteen years old. "Me and P.K. will stick it out here in the mountains. You can have all these modern inventions. Give me the good feel of dirt underfoot and the eyes to watch the grain grow and the seasons change. There is no place like the Blue Ridge."

P.K. grinned the grin of a thirteen year old who had been included in an adult conversation. "I do not believe all those stories Uriah is telling anyway," he added to the conversation.

Peter leaned back against the warm logs of the sunny side of the house. *It just does not get any better than this,* he thought. Maybe if they knew about the Lady who lived in the spring, the whole world would be a bit less complicated. The thought of passing on what they would surely believe to be a fantasy faded, and he agreed with Mathew Whiting, "Give me the Blue Ridge."

1833

"Pa, we finally know who owns the land around here. Some lady from Baltimore named Mary Ann Nicholson. She was one of Rawleigh Colston's heirs and she got some 2,500 acres," Mathew passed the word on to his father.

"Finally," Peter muttered. "I wonder if she will be selling it or renting it."

"Renting it at the moment," said the young Mathew Whiting. "But Will Benson and I have made an offer on part of it, which has been accepted."

"Which part?" Peter wanted to know.

"Slatey Ridge and the land just across the road from us all the way up to Mount Carmel," responded Mathew.

"Why on earth would you want Slatey Ridge?" Peter pursued. "It is only good for growing rattlesnakes."

"It is Slatey Ridge that is going to pay for the whole lot of it," Mathew confided. "Slatey Ridge is full of iron ore and we are going to keep that tilt hammer mill humming. Of course, we cannot do much with it until she agrees to sell it to us, but that should only be a short time. Meanwhile we will farm it. Besides, there is a cave exit on top of one hill that might bring some more surprises."

Peter interjected, "Mathew, I think you might be dreaming, but I want to continue farming a part of it, unless you want to charge me too much for it."

"Pa, you know I would not do that. Even though it will have my name and Will Benson on the lease, it is yours for the farming," Mathew said, sensing that his father was not happy about not being a part of the deal.

"How do you know there is iron ore on Slatey Ridge? All I ever saw was a big slate pile that keeps tumbling down the mountain," Peter wanted to know.

"Will Benson found the ore when he was hunting over on the ridge. Snuck some out and had it assayed. Not real good ore, but a lot of it," Mathew answered.

"When will you take possession?" Peter asked.

"Somewhere around the middle of May," Mathew said.

"When that happens, maybe we can take a ride over and look at it together. I always wanted to know what iron ore looks like. Meanwhile, we got a lot of plowing to do."

The spring dreen area at the spring was awash with a fusillade of popping flowers. Each type seemed to try and outdo the others in sending their seed to the outermost areas. Even the honeybees that scoured for nectar were affected by the explosions of the poppy tops. Peter took in the scene as he came to visit the spring. On most days this would have created a feeling of exultation as he witnessed nature at its best. Today he was not having any of it. His mind was preoccupied with the words of Mathew and he needed to talk to the Lady about it. "Iron ore," he muttered. "Iron ore. There is not enough iron ore on Slatey Ridge to fill a tinker's dam. How do I go about telling him he is sending smoke up the wrong chimney?"

"Sounds like you have a lot on your mind, Peter," the voice said. "Why are you so wrought with anxiety?"

Peter related the conversation and the voice came back with, "Are you sure it is Slatey Ridge and its iron ore? Could it be something else?"

"Well, he could have asked my advice before he jumped into something so important," Peter admitted.

"Peter, Peter, you must let the young ones grow up and take their place in the world. Mathew is nigh twenty and as I recall you were not much older when we first met, and you were sure you were capable of running a plantation."

"Five years is a long time at that age," Peter groused, not wanting to give up his dour spirits.

"Peter, this decision by your son may cause you a lot of early grief, but as usual you will persevere and you will be the best for it. Enjoy what you can when you can, and let one with more power than you take care of the details." The voice sounded a bit more somber than usual.

Peter returned across Prospect Creek more confused than ever. He was not sure how Mathew Whiting could cause him trouble. The one good thing about making a mistake in your youth was the time left to repair it. Peter was now fifty-six. He certainly had not amassed an amount that would give him comfort in his old age. He knew he would be dependent on the children as he entered the years of decline. But right now, he needed to keep the farm going. It was Mathew Whiting and P.K. who were still at home to help him. One good thing, they did not seem to want to leave home for some distant place.

"Ma, I hope it does not shock you too much, but Sam and I are getting married."

"Well, Hannah, I thought Sam Grubbs was just coming to see us because Fanny married his brother Tom," Ann teased. "It is getting more difficult to tell your father of all our girls leaving home. It seems it is just one after the other."

"There is a movement afoot to create a new county," Ann told Peter. "I talked to Uriah as I returned from Berryville and he tells me he signed a petition to form a new county, breaking off from Frederick."

"It is about time," Peter commented. "The distance between Eastern Frederick and Western Frederick is more than the miles to Winchester, even though that is a far piece, as there are no good roads to make the trip. Eastern Frederick is made up of Piedmont people. Western Frederick is Pennsylvania and Delaware. It is tradesmen and artisans. John Holker predicted this would come many years ago. No doubt he not only would be signing the petition, but would be circulating it by horseback."

"I also heard that the darkie, Jo Anderson, is over on the Lakeview farm with the noisiest contraption you have ever heard," Ann continued.

"You suppose that he has brought down the thing he calls a reaper?" Peter questioned. "Maybe I will work my way across the Shenandoah tomorrow and see what he has."

"I am sure he brought it here to be near Arissa. Her health is not good and it is right he should be near her."

As Peter passed by Arissa's small cabin, he saw her standing near the door. He greeted her and asked if Jo was at Lakeview Farm.

"Yes," she replied. "He was by yesterday evening for some vittles. It was good to have him home."

"I hear you have been ailing, Arissa. I hope it is nothing serious."

"Serious? I should say not. It is just a mild case of feeling sorry for being alone and growing old. The best I calculate, I am sixty-six. That is still young enough to birth a bunch of mountain kids," she said. "Maybe a whole new generation."

Peter said, "I am on my way to Lakeview Farm to see that contraption that Jo brought down from Harrisonburg. Why he brought it this far to test it, I do not know. It seems like they grow plenty of wheat up in that area. Do you know what part of Lakeview he is working? It might make it easier to find him if I knew what section he is in."

Arissa laughed that soft laugh that everyone enjoyed. "Mr. Royston, if you listen real well, you can hear him from here. I do not think you are going to need any guidance from me."

Peter crossed the Shenandoah and headed south, turning at the small spit of a lake that gave the farm the name. The lake had been formed by a magnificent flood in the past and was fed by a small spring that offset the evaporation. Peter thought for a moment that maybe he could hear the Lady's voice at this spring also. He shook his head and muttered something to the effect that he must be going crazy if he thought every bit of water around contained the Lady's voice.

The racket of a thousand knives hitting together brought him back to reality. Following the sound he pushed the bay towards the far end of the farm and ahead of him was a sight to behold. Four horses were hitched to a machine that had more mechanical motions than one could imagine. Near the ground were a series of scissors that raced back and forth. Above this was a large horizontal wheel made of paddles just like the ones he had imagined driving the steamboat on the Hudson. The entire machine was balanced on two wheels, with a man in the middle. There was another man riding the lead horse.

As the horses pulled the machine, the wheels turned, and through some sort of gear, it drove both the paddle and the mechanical scissors back and forth. As he watched the reaper moved into action. The wheel rotated and went through the standing wheat bending it toward the scissors. The scissors cut the wheat and it fell onto a small track that pushed it to the side. There were workers at the end picking up the cut stalks of grain and binding them into bundles. They stood the bundles against each other in the normal shocks and left them to dry.

Peter saw the familiar figure of Jo Anderson standing to one side and headed the horse toward him. "What a sight to see, my friend," Peter said as he dismounted and shook Jo's hand. "It looks like you finally did it. My guess is that this machine can do the work of twenty men."

Jo laughed. "Maybe a lot more than that if we can figure out how to tie off the wheat into sheaves automatically. I hear there is a man by the name of Howe who has a sewing machine. Maybe some of his ideas can be used to solve that problem."

"Tell me," Peter questioned, "Why did you bring that machine all the way down from Harrisonburg to test it here?"

"Those McCormicks are fighting among themselves so much with every one of them making unworkable suggestions, so the only way to get something done was to get it out of their sight." Jo Anderson continued, "There is going to be a big family fight over who claims the credit for this. I think that Mr. Cyrus will win out, as he is the biggest talker of all of them. I may finish off these tests and take it back to them and give up working with the reaper. I know that all I will ever get out of it is my own sense of pride. I just may come back and run the ferry. I am forty-six now and my mammy is sixty-six. She can use my help also."

The days were getting shorter as Peter made his way to the spring. Harvesting was almost over. He paused as he looked at the area that was always a solace for him. 1832 was quite a year. Uriah had a baby boy and Joseph a baby girl. Mollie had a baby girl. Hannah was marrying Sam Grubbs right after Christmas. He had heard about railroads and had seen something that might revolutionize farming. They were talking of traveling at the unheard of speeds of fifteen to twenty miles an hour. *Why, one could get to Winchester in an hour. That is, if someone wanted to go to Winchester,* Peter thought.

He considered that there was an election in Washington and there was a new Vice President, someone called Martin Van Buren from New York. *One of these days it would be nice to know more about the people running the country,* he thought. About the only way to get any news was to make a trip to Winchester and that involved going through White Post to Double Toll Gate, then north along the Valley Pike by horseback. There was no way to get to Winchester without spending the night there. It was way too expensive just to vote.

1836

The door rattled from Joseph's knocking assault. "Ma, Ma, where are you?"

"Give me a minute, son," Ann answered as she opened the door. "What brings you on this side of the ridge?"

"I had to deliver some boots over in Millwood. Tried to stop in and see Uriah, but he was off to Hagerstown, hauling some goods. But I am the one with the surprise this time. It is usually Uriah bringing back the unusual materials, but this time it is me." He paused, waiting for his mother to ask about his surprise.

"It cannot be very big, 'cause I do not see any large package," Ann said.

"Well, sometimes big surprises come in small packages," he said as he reached into his vest pocket and pulled out a small tin.

Land sakes, Ann thought, *what in the world could be in that little tin that could be so surprising?*

Reaching into the tin he pulled out what appeared to be a small twig of white wood with a globule on one end. "Look at this, Ma," he exulted. "What do you think of this?"

"I think you have been smelling too much of that leather tanning solution," Ann countered. "What am I suppose to think of a little stick of wood?"

Joseph Asbury turned the tin on its side exposing a roughened surface. He took the stick and deliberately pulled the end with the coating across the rough side of the tin. The wood flared up and began to burn.

Ann shrank back, saying, "What in Heaven's name is that?"

"It is called a match stick, Ma, although I do not know where the name came from. Seems like it should be called a scratch stick because that is how you light it. From now on, you do not have to depend on a tinderbox. There is a company that does nothing but to make these matchsticks. As long as you keep them dry they will start a fire anytime you want to. Think of it, no more keeping the flames going all the hot day, just so you would have a fire in the cool evening." Joseph Asbury continued, "I bought this tin for you. Surprise Pa with it, when he comes in from the field tonight."

"I thought the railroad and the steam engine were the greatest inventions of our lifetime," Peter said to the Lady, "but those matchsticks have to be the best invention ever for the ordinary man."

"Tell me again how they work," the Lady wanted to know.

"Well, I am not sure how they work, but there is some material on the end of a little stick that turns into flames when you pull it across something rough."

"You mean anybody who has the stick can make a fire?"

"Why, sure, anyone with a grain of sense could do it," Peter responded.

There was a pause as if the Lady had a sense of foreboding, "I hope that you keep them safely put away at all times."

1840–1850

1842

"Ma, Pa, as you know I have been courting Minerva Carpenter for some time now and we think it is time to get married. If it is all right with you we would like to make it in the fall, with the preferred time being in September."

"Mathew, it is sure all right with us," Ann said. "Your father and I were just talking about it the other day. But why did you pick that date?"

"As you know Minerva's grandparents were Calmes and they have a few ideas of their own about where and when we should get married. First, they want us to get married in the Church and second, they have a grandson coming in at that time from the Navy."

"And who might that be that you would plan a wedding around his visit?" Peter asked.

"His name is Commander Perry and he fought at the battle of Lake Erie way back in the Second War with the British."

A light glimmered. "I remember a Perry who won the Battle of Lake Erie. I seem to recall Mr. Holker talking about it," Peter said.

"That is not the one. This one is younger, about our age or a little older. He was just a young officer in 1812. The word is he wants to open the Pacific to American trade."

"Do not know why we are talking about it," said Peter wearying of a subject of which he knew little or cared less. "Have the wedding where and when you want, and we will be there."

"Where are you going to live?" Ann questioned, already knowing what the answer would be.

"Well, this is our land and we would want to continue to live here," Mathew answered.

Turning to Peter, Mathew teased, "Now that you are the Constable, you may want to do the honors along with the priest."

Peter snorted. "If I had my way, you would be married over by the spring, where your mother and I were married."

Mathew Whiting retorted, "I do not think so, Pa. There is no one else that feels the way you do about that spring."

Peter, thinking back through the year he had been Constable, thought, *I cannot see much to this Constable job. It does not pay anything except when I witness somebody signing something, and in the mountains, there is a long time between seeing those 'X's.*

Out loud, he pressed an idea to Mathew Whiting. "Why not try hard to get a Post Office here at Berry's Ferry? As it is, most mountain people pick up their mail here at the house. Someone brings it over from Millwood and gives it to Jo Anderson. He does not know what to do with it, so he gives it to me."

"There is a problem with the mail that needs fixing, Pa. You know that a lot of the mail comes in without having been paid for. You have to pay the post costs and then collect from the person on this end," Mathew Whiting cautioned.

"I already have that problem," Peter grouched. "I have worked out a deal where I know who pays, and who does not. If they do not pay, I do not pick it up and they have to go to Millwood to get it. I tell Jo Anderson which mail I am good for. Besides, I hear that they are coming out with stamps that attach to the mail assuring that the postage has been paid, and while they can still send it without postage, it will not be long before you will have to prepay the costs before they will handle it."

"That sounds like a good idea to me," Mathew Whiting considered. "And while you are at it, why not set up a little store, and then there will be no reason for the mountain people to cross the Shenandoah at all."

"They would even save the ferry fare. Not a bad idea, my son" said Peter, warming to the idea. "Maybe we can get Uriah to buy things for us wholesale in Maryland and our profit will be better."

Quickly the talk changed from weddings to a way of bringing in some cash. Mathew was just as happy, as he was not sure that Peter understood what being married in the Church meant.

Just as the talk of one wedding settled down, in came Anna Maria. "I want to get married in September," she confided to her parents.

This came as a complete surprise to both Peter and Ann. "Who in the world would you be marrying?" Peter asked. "I did not know you had a steady beau."

"It would be Washington," Anna Maria said, blushing.

"Do you mean Washington Anderson, your first cousin?" Peter thundered, "Why, I will not have it, marrying your own first cousin. There are too many dangers there!"

"Pa, Washington and I have talked over these problems with a doctor and we are assured that everything will be all right."

"When did you have in mind to do this?" Ann asked. "As you know, Mathew Whiting is being married the first week in September."

"Would the end of September be satisfactory? We were thinking of getting married at the Anderson house. As you know, Grandma Hannah Blue is not doing too well and it is hard for her to travel."

There are too many things happening, Peter thought. *I need to talk to the Lady about all these new plans.* He made his way across the creek, which now had a log bridge spanning it. He stopped to sway back and forth, using his action to transfer a rhythmic motion to the bridge itself. *This is a nice bridge, if I do say so myself,* he thought as he left the bridge and moved toward the spring.

It was an extremely warm summer day and he leaned back into the white oak's protection from the sun and told his concerns to the Lady in the Spring. The water falling seemed to murmur encouragement as he continued.

Finally he slowed down enough for the Lady to pose a question. "What do you intend to do about all these concerns?"

Peter thought for a long moment. "Why, not much, if they happen, they happen."

"Then, why are you worrying about something that you will do nothing about. It is enough to worry of those things you can control. Clear your mind and think of the beautiful life you and Ann have had together, the children that are raised and gone or are going, and the two you will have left at the house."

"Four," Peter asserted, "if you count Mathew not leaving and his new bride coming to live with us." As always, he felt better as the filled buckets were carried across the creek. This time there was no time to get the bridge swaying, and besides he might spill the water.

Mathew's wedding was over and the newlyweds returned to the house from Winchester. Peter, Ann, Anna Maria, Sarah Catherine and P.K. followed some discreet time later using the new road that had been created from Winchester, down through Carper's Valley across the Opequon and through Boyce. *It was sure shorter than the road through Double Toll Gate and White Post, but a lot more hills to pull,* Peter thought.

Finally they arrived at the ferry and Jo Anderson poked and plodded and took hours to get them across the river. "What is taking so long? He seems to have lost his touch." Peter complained.

Ann smiled, remembering the day some forty years ago that she and Peter made that same trip in reverse. *Jo Anderson did them the same favor that time, so long ago,* she thought. She looked at Jo and saw in him the person that Peter had seen almost from the beginning. No longer did she think of him as someone of another color and inherently inferior. As his accomplishments came to mind, she totaled them and thought there are only few persons alive with his capabilities. And just to have Arissa around, when there was birthing to be done, fear left when she arrived. It was almost like she had taken the elusive doctor's place in the room.

The September sun beat down and Peter decided to quit harvesting an hour or so early. Making his way past the creek, he doused himself with the coolness of the rushing water. *It would be a nice time to sit and visit at the spring,* he thought, but something drew him toward the back door. As he entered, there sat Ann in the rocking chair, crying silently as she rocked back and forth.

He rushed to her and knelt before her, wanting to know what was the matter. Quietly she handed him a note in Mary Catherine's handwriting. "Ma, Pa, there are so many things going on and with two weddings this month. I did not think you could take another one. Lewis and I have run away to Hagerstown to be married. No church thing, just a Justice of the Peace. We understand that Uriah will be in Hagerstown picking up some freight, and we will get him to stand up for us."

Peter took Ann in his arms and just sat there with no fine words, no answers. Finally the crying subsided and Ann stood up, wiped the tears from her face with her apron and began supper. She was a practical woman and realized that little could be done to change what was happening and why should she? Lewis Bennett was a fine boy and would make a good husband. The only regret she had was having missed seeing the love in her daughter's eyes when vows were said.

1846

A warm spring brought the decision to open Mount Carmel Church a bit early. Ann could not help but note that P.K. seemed downright anxious to get back to church.

"Ma, I think I will go up early and make sure everything is cleaned up and ready for church," P.K. volunteered.

Even Peter noticed. "Now there is something going on that I do not know about."

"I think it has something to do with a certain girl from over around Paris," Ann suggested. "He has spent a lot of time this winter visiting Joseph Asbury, and even though Joseph is my son, I do not think he would rate that kind of attention from a brother. I am sure I know which girl it is, but I will wait until P.K. lets us know."

The first preaching service after a winter's layoff always brought out the mountain crowd and many others from across the mountain. During the service Ann kept watching a certain young girl who could not have been more than fifteen or sixteen and who could not keep her eyes off Peter Kemp. After the preaching was over Ann watched P.K. as he moved over and talked to the young lady.

Searching for the right moment he brought her over and introduced her to Peter and Ann. "This is Mary Ann Adams."

Alongside P.K., she looked even younger, Ann thought. *He is nearing thirty and she could not be over sixteen.*

On the way home Peter Kemp explained that Mary Ann's father was dead and her mother was having trouble taking care of the children. "All that aside, I would still love her and I would like Pa to be the Bondsman for her."

Ann knew the Adams family that had lived on the eastern slope of the Blue Ridge for many years. "What does her mother have to say about this?" Ann asked.

"Quite frankly, I think she would welcome Mary Ann being married."

Ann looked at Peter and he nodded, "If it is all right with her mother, it is all right with us. You do realize that she is awfully young and you will have to be very gentle with her?"

1847

It was the day before Mary Ann's seventeenth birthday when she gave birth to her first child. As usual, Arissa was around to handle the details. Mary Ann came to Peter and Ann's place for the birthing, as P.K. was tenant farming some of the Lands End property. When the baby finally arrived, Arissa displayed this brand new butterball of a baby. He had both hands up in front of him as he grinned through the baby fat rolls on his face.

Peter uttered the first thought that came to mind. "He looks just like a little toad." And the baby was forever stuck with that nickname.

1848

Was there ever a more beautiful baby born? thought Peter when Arissa passed the newborn around. "What are you going to call her?" Peter asked Mathew.

"We have chased a lot of names around and finally settled on the three we liked best, Louisa Virginia Therese." The baby cooed, as if agreeing that these names, so familiar in Minerva's family, fit her just perfectly.

Arissa looked at Peter's face and laid the baby in Peter's lap, watching a smile flood his seventy-two year-old features.

I wonder what the Lady will say when she sees Louisa, Peter thought as he cuddled the baby between his knees. He had a lot of grandchildren, but there was something special about Mathew's third child.

1850–1860

1851

Peter and Mathew waited for Jo Anderson to clear the ferry before walking their horses aboard. Jo had been back at his ferryman's job for some years now, and it was always good to have him controlling the boat. Jo looked at the two of them, somewhat overdressed, but showing signs of some heavy exertion, thinking that Peter was looking his seventy-four years of age.

"Looks like you have been working mighty hard," Jo ventured as the boat made the short trip across the river.

"Not the work you might be thinking about, but hard work, none the less," Mathew answered. "It is thinking work and that is too much for us mountain men."

"Well, maybe your thinking ain't all the way over," Jo pursued. "Looks like you have a welcoming group waiting for you." He nodded toward the four recognizable figures watching the ferry dock.

Peter and Mathew looked at the four and Peter wondered aloud, "Why would my two daughters and their brother husbands be waiting for us?"

Even before they left the boat the chorus began, "How did it go today in Berryville? Did you get the property?"

"The answer is yes, we got the property. Actually, I got the property, to be exact. But why all the interest now? I sure did not see you when it was going into default, and Will Benson and I were looking around for someone to help."

"Matt, you know we do not have any cash," Hannah said. "But Sam and I would like to talk to you about letting us build a small house on your land, and I think that Fannie and Tom want to talk to you about the same thing."

Fannie chimed in, "Yes, we would like to build a log house near where Hannah and Sam want to build. We have already picked out a place."

"Well now, I will have to talk that over with Minerva," Mathew answered. "You know it was her money that bought the property and we too, are going to build a place."

"Yours is just going to be across the road from Papa's house, actually your house now, since the property you bought includes that house too," Fanny asserted. "The place where we want to build is up Fox Trap Hill near the spring on Ashby's Gap Toll Road."

"Tell me more about the plans. Where are you going to get the logs and the stones for the foundation? I am sure that Minerva will want to know," Mathew Whiting pursued.

Sam and Tom had kept in the background. Now, they both added to the conversation, "There is a good stand of pines just across from where we want to build, and we have already talked to Mr. Green about getting foundation stones from his property around Mount Carmel Church."

"Yes, there is sure a lot of granite around the church, certainly none on our property, where it is all shale. But the pines in that stand on Mocking Bird Hill are pretty big for house logs. In fact they are so big, I am not sure they can be of any use besides firewood, and even difficult to cut for that."

"If we can get them cut, we figure we can quarter them, square them up and they will make great house logs. There are a lot of smaller ones to make up the roof rafters.

Peter smiled, remembering his first look at that stand of pines when he was finding pitch to help Mr. Holker and his canning. *How long ago that seemed to be,* he thought. *Not in years, but in the change of my lifestyle.*

"Give me a few days," Mathew Whiting said, "and I will let you know, after talking it over with Minerva."

Peter passed the news to Ann as they sat on the back porch after supper. He reviewed how, with Minerva's cash, Mathew became just about the only bidder for the same land he had let go into default. "Remember how he thought he was going to make his fortune out of the iron ore off Slatey Ridge? It turns out, there was not enough iron ore there to make a good size skillet. Well, I believe that Will Benson was duped by that assayer fellow,"

Ann responded, "While Will Benson appears to be the one left out on the deal, remember it was Mathew who made all the payments that were made."

"True," Peter said, "but it just does not seem right." Peter's mind turned toward the Lady in the Spring. *She would know how to handle this,* he thought.

Meanwhile, Mathew was trying to explain to Minerva why he should give away some of their property to Hannah and Fanny, just because they were sisters. "Min, it kinda makes some sense. That property is not of much good. You cannot plant on it. There are spring dreens on all sides. There is a marsh just above."

Minerva replied, "It is not the present I am worried about. Who is going to own it when the Grubbs brothers tire of it? They will sell it to some stranger, and we will have neighbors not of our choosing. I cannot say I am too crazy about that."

Mathew searched for an answer. "Why not lease it to them? Let them build on it and when they or their children leave, the land and the building comes back to us. By that time, we may have some children of our own who could use it."

The last part appealed to Minerva. What could be the harm in such a bargain? Aloud she said, "That sounds good, and maybe as a part of the bargain you can get them to cut the trees for our own house across the road. You are going to need some help raising those logs, and I hear the Grubbs boys are pretty good with a broadaxe."

Come Sunday morning Mathew and Minerva were at their usual spot at Mount Carmel. Minerva was always a bit uncomfortable at a Methodist Church, but the only Catholic Church was in Winchester and there was no way she could make that trip, especially that now the two counties were divided up. She loved the hominess of the church, and as she and Ann split from their husbands to sit on the women's side of the aisle she could not help but notice the presence of the two Grubbs brothers. It was normal to have Fanny and Hannah there, but it took almost a revival service to get the brothers to show up.

After church the reason became apparent. They were concerned about the building of the log houses. As Sam would later say, "By then, we each had three or four children and we were all crammed in that small house near Frogtown with Pa and Ma. It is a wonder we survived."

After much discussion, the deal was struck. The Grubbs boys would build the houses on land at the top of Fox Trap hill, near the spring, using pine trees from the hill just north of there. They would also cut trees for Mathew's house, but it would be up to Mathew to pull the logs down the hill. If they moved out, the houses would go to Mathew and Minerva.

"Now, let us get started," Fanny chimed in.

"In due time," husband Tom said. "Since we will be using a crosscut saw we have to wait 'til the sap stops running. Otherwise it would take forever to saw up those trees."

"I have never seen a crosscut saw in the mountains," Mathew said. "Where are you going to get a crosscut saw?"

"Jack Taylor, out around Taylor's Knob, brought one back from Pennsylvania, made by some German fellow named Henry Disston," Sam said. "And he said he would teach us how to use it and how to keep it sharp."

Peter no longer toiled in the fields daily as Mathew and P.K. insisted that he retire from such strenuous work. "Retire," snorted Peter. "I can still work circles around the both of them."

Work had now started on the log houses for the Grubbs Brothers. Both had picked the site they liked and one that Mathew approved. Hannah and Sam laid out some cornerstones for their plot just on the south side of Ashby's Gap Toll Road on the side of the hill as near a spring as possible.

Frances and Thomas picked a spot on the north side of the Toll Road that required a certain amount of preparation before it could be used. The runoff from the wet weather springs to the east made for marshy soil. Finally a ditch was dug around the perimeter of the property that diverted the water from their lot and they were ready for the log cutting. Peter talked it over with Mathew and agreed that if they did not get their logs as the rest were cut, it might be possible that the brothers would turn to the house building part of the project and forget Mathew's logs.

Soon, it was settled that Peter would be responsible for Mathew's logs and he would choose one out of every three as they were cut. He brought a team of horses up Fox Trap Hill and snaked each log down the mountain as they accumulated. It had been an early fall and the sap had dropped so that the cutting went smoothly. Even so, it was necessary to keep a rag saturated with lard nearby to keep the pitch from binding the saw.

By Christmas, there were sufficient logs for everyone to build his own house and again, the three split labor, one day at each house, so that the house building progressed evenly at each location. Sam was the master of the broadaxe and he squared and trued the logs as Thomas and Mathew split the larger ones. As they were finished and notched for the corner ties, they were set in place with the windows and doors to be cut later. Somehow they took on the appearances of stockades as they grew to second story height.

An eye had to be kept open for little Louisa, as the three year old insisted on seeing each bit of progress of Mathew's house. Toward the end, it was Peter who lifted her up into his arms and the two supervised the finishing of the building. Finding a source of shingles for the roof was the hardest task of all. Finally, they found a stand of cedars located on the Green place, which provided the roofing material.

By the end of March, 1852, the houses were ready. Each family worked to bring furnishings to their new home. Mathew brought his from across the road where it had been accumulating, with more coming from Minerva's grandparents at Lands End Farm.

The first fire in each fireplace was always a special occasion and the families gathered around for the ceremonial lighting. There was no question as to who would light the first fire at Mathew's. Louisa's eyes sparkled as she watched the match spring into fire as it scratched along the side of the tin.

With Mathew Whiting moved in across the Toll Road, it was the first time since Peter and Ann were married that they had been alone in any house. Peter thought back, and remembered Philip Earheart pulling away in his wagon, bound for Kentucky. "Wonder how old Earheart is doing these days. Probably is not even alive," Peter wondered out loud.

Ann looked at him. "Are you talking to yourself, Peter Royston?" she teased. "I thought you only did that over at the spring."

Peter blushed, and retorted, "I was just thinking of us thirty years or so ago, when we moved in here. We do not have much more now than we did then, but it has been a lot of enjoyment."

"Well, we have raised a lot of good children and seen many things happen. What more can you ask?"

The words were hardly out of her mouth when there was a rap at the door. Opening it, she was surprised to see her oldest daughter, Mollie, standing there. Mollie had nine children, but none were to be seen.

The grandmother instinct came out in Ann. "Where are the children?"

"James is taking care of them at the moment," Mollie answered. "Can I come in?"

Ann opened the door and apologized for not being more polite. "I am just so surprised at seeing you," she explained. "Come on in."

As Mollie settled down, Ann could see that she had something on her mind. "Out with it, Mollie. You are fidgeting around like you had a good case of the Chiggers."

"Well," said Mollie, "James and I would like to move back across the river. There is just too much goings on over on the valley side. We were wondering if we could move back in with you for a spell until we can find a place over here."

Ann looked over at Peter who was sitting behind Mollie. He rolled his eyes in resignation, thinking that having the house to themselves was very short lived. Besides, he liked having the grandchildren around. Ann looked back at Mollie and said, "Of course you are welcome here. We have the little store going and the Berry's Ferry Post Office, but that does not take up much space. Maybe the children can help with the store."

And so the second honeymoon of Ann and Peter lasted only a few days, and they were shortly treated to the yelling and screaming of nine healthy children and their parents. It was more crowded than it had ever been.

1855

Spring was unseasonably warm, but the evening of March second turned cold and Peter started a fire in the fireplace. *Just enough to take the chill off the night and we will let it go out 'til morning,* he thought. Early in the morning, he awakened to the smell of smoke and the crackle of a fire. "I wonder who got up and started a fire?" he wondered as he pushed his feet over the side of the bed and pulled on a pair of pants and shoes. *It is awfully light outside,* he thought, as he headed toward the living room. Surprised that there was no fire in the living room, he glanced across the road at Mathew's new house.

Flames were coming through the roof and out the front window.

"Ann!" he yelled, as he went out the door and raced across the Toll Road. He beat on the door, and with the same motion, pushed open the door to find Mathew Whiting and Minerva just stirring. "The house is on fire! Get the children and get out! It is bad!" Peter yelled.

Peter grabbed two of the children who were sleeping on a pallet in the living room and raced out of the house.

By now Ann, Mollie, James and all their children were milling around outside. Throwing water on the fire was useless.

Mathew Whiting and Minerva came out of the house with more children and they all gathered on the other side of the road, as the flames consumed their home.

Peter and Mathew looked at each other at the same time and counting heads, shouted, "Where's Louisa?" They shouted more with no answer. Louisa must still have been in the burning house. The two sprang across the Toll Road with James

Doran right behind them. Fighting their way through the flames they found the still body of little Louisa. Peter picked her up and they rushed back through the flames, with their own clothes on fire.

They made for the creek a few yards away and doused the flames. Peter carried the baby girl into the house and shouted for Mathew to take care of the rest of the family. He laid Louisa on the bed and looked for any sign of life. There was none. He was startled for a moment as he glanced up and saw a shadow stirring the curtains, as if something were passing through the window. He turned back to Louisa and pulled her lifeless body toward him. As he did, a blackened tin that once held matches fell from her bedclothes.

It started with a groan, then turned into a moan, as Peter's voice called out to the Heavens for relief. The moan increased in volume until the scream was so loud that it was later said that it scared animals as far away as Millwood. "What kind of God would take Louisa from us? What kind of God would let an invention be made that would kill a little child?" he shouted, cursing the day he had ever seen matches that put him through such Hell.

Finally Ann came into the bedroom and held the shaking Peter. She knew that he not only was suffering the loss, but was also shouldering the blame. She said nothing, just held her man until he finally collapsed in a heap alongside the child's body.

Two days later the procession made its way across the creek to the hillside overlooking the house. It was there that he and Ann had chosen for their burial ground. Little did he know that he would not be the first one to use it. They buried Louisa in a small coffin made up of wood brought by Uriah from Maryland. Peter thought they should use mountain wood but there was no time to prepare it. Inside the coffin, he placed the tin that held the matches that had so delighted Louisa in her life.

Peter sat around listless, as if the world had come to a halt. He responded little when talked to, and Ann was becoming truly concerned about the melancholy she was seeing in her husband. On top of everything, he had not made a trip to the spring since that day that Louisa died.

Finally, she reached outside the door and picking up a bucket, brought it to Peter and said, "We need water. Could you please go and get us some water?"

"Let one of the kids go and get the water. They are plenty big enough," Peter muttered.

"No, Peter Royston, it is you I want to have carry my water. Please go and get me some water!"

Peter picked up the bucket and slowly made his way across Prospect Creek, remembering it was just a few weeks ago that Louisa had come rushing across the bridge yelling to him that she had talked to a lady in the spring. He had cautioned her not to talk about such things, as he was scared to think of what she might say if she had really talked to the Lady.

He carried the bucket to the spring, and as the water began to fill the container, he sat at the white oak tree and began to sob.

After what appeared to be an eternity, the voice said, "Why are you so sad?"

Peter began to tell her, finally confessing to blaming God for something only he was guilty of.

"Peter, Peter, do not blame yourself. There is a time for everything. Some live for many years and accomplish little. Others live for a few years and accomplish much. I know your problems. Louisa was brought to me as you watched the shadow in the window move. She is here with me now."

"With you now," Peter exploded. "How could she be with you now, and who brought her to you?"

"Peter," the voice soothed, "I must tell you things that are not commonly known by those living. When one leaves the living, it is a winding road they travel before they reach their final destination. First they must spend some time near where they lived and while they cannot talk to you, they can hear everything you say. Sometimes people say good things and sometimes they say things that are not so good. They must endure the good with the bad until they are sufficiently humble to take the next steps. Sometimes it takes many years to go through this stage. Sometimes, as it will be in Louisa's case, it will only take a moment of eternity."

"You mean that when I die, I may spend some time here with you before I am sent off somewhere else?"

"Most likely you will spend a lot of time here," the voice teased, "as there are probably many things you need to hear from those who knew you. It might even stretch into some future generations. But if you want to talk to Louisa, remember she may not be here long, and not even I can tell you when she leaves."

Peter turned his attention to Louisa, telling her how much he loved her and how much he missed her. While there was no answer, somehow he knew things were all right. He picked up his bucket that had been overflowing for most of his stay there and made his way across the creek. He was even humming a tune when he entered the back door.

How I wish I could have that effect on him, Ann thought, not taking any credit for her forcefulness that carried him across that creek a few minutes before.

1855

It is been a long spring, Ann thought. *Peter still has periods of grief. Maybe it is time to get the family together. He needs to see that the rest of the family needs him also.* She passed on these thoughts to Minerva, who, herself, was still mourning the loss of Louisa. It was agreed that July fourth was probably the best day. Just about everyone had the day off, even though it came on a Wednesday. They passed the word to all the family and they started showing up early in the morning.

It was a time for reflection, a time to think of the country, its past and its future. While it was normal to have the ferry closed on holidays such as this, Jo Anderson volunteered to man a boat and bring across any visitors from the Valley. Uriah was there with Hannah and their three children, Lydia, George Riddle and nineteen year old Mathew Thomas. Joseph Asbury, now living in Marshall, and his wife Harriet, who was nursing a late arrival, had managed to get all eleven of their large family together. Mollie and James still lived with Peter and Ann, even though Mathew and Minerva had to move back in after their new house burned. Frances and Tom Grubbs came with their six, Hannah and Sam Grubbs and their eight. Mathew and Minerva and their four seemed like such a small family without Louisa. Showing up together were Anna Maria and Washington and her sister Emily and husband Lewis. Neither of the two couples had children. Last to show was P.K. and Mary Ann. By now they had three, including eight year-old Thomas, who could never shake that nickname given him by Peter at his birth. He would always be Toad.

The conversations were as varied as the dispersion of the family. Uriah talked of the changes in travel. Surprisingly enough, there had been a railroad built to the south, crossing the Potomac at Harpers Ferry. Many times, he now hauled freight from Winchester, and trips to Harpers Ferry were becoming rare. He thought he would hardly recognize Baltimore. It was his son, Mathew Thomas, who was the new long distance freight hauler and the one most likely to make those special trips to Harpers Ferry and Baltimore. He would return and report a sense of political change in the atmosphere that sent shivers down his back. He was a quiet lad and one who said little but listened a lot.

The talk turned to the holiday they were celebrating, and Mathew brought out a newspaper clipping from September of the previous year. Minerva had saved it, as it was a report on her cousin, Commodore Perry, and his opening of Japan to trade with America. "Who would have thought that someone who came to our wedding would be this famous?" he bragged.

Peter considered and said, "Do you mean that fellow with a cocked hat with all the plumes that looked like a peacock going backwards in a stiff wind?"

"That is the chap," Mathew answered.

"Well, if I was the Japanese big boss, and someone showed up looking like that, I would greet him royally," Peter commented.

"The country started on the Fourth of July and it is now seventy-nine years old," Joseph added.

Yes, just as old as I am, thought Peter, as he listened to the conversation, as it turned towards the wars that the country had fought over those years.

"We fought the British—twice, the Mexicans, almost the French. Who else is left to fight? Maybe those Japanese fellows," the talk rambled on.

Sam Grubbs answered, "Maybe it will be us. I hear talk of the divisions between the North and the South that has some people talking of the country breaking up."

"No way," was the thought of most. "They will talk a lot, but there is too much blood between us."

Some of the boys began to play a new game that involved throwing a ball, and having a person try to hit the ball with a piece of wood. They began by tossing the ball from one to another, and then one would hit the ball out to the others. Peter wondered what the purpose of the game was.

One of Uriah's boys explained it to him. "There are two teams which are called sides. One side goes out in the field and one of them tries to throw the ball so that one of the other side cannot hit it. If he does, then he runs around the field stopping at places called bases, which are safe areas. If they have the ball and catch him before he reaches one of the bases, he is out. Three of these outs and the other side comes in from the field and they repeat the process."

"Enough of this," Peter said. "I will never understand it. I will bet it was invented in the same state that came up with that poem about Saint Nicholas. It is just another way to take the children's minds off work."

"Aw, Grandpa, you are getting cranky in your old age," complained one.

"Well, it is the truth. I will wager that in a few years, chores will be forgotten and all you will want to do is play that game."

As the members of the family gathered together for good-byes, Ann thought, *it did get us all together, but it did not seem to do much to improve the Constable's disposition.*

The next day Peter worked his way to the spring. He talked of the family and his life. "There was some talk that was worrisome to me," he said. "Fighting amongst ourselves, that does not sound good at all. Do you think that will happen?" he asked the Lady.

There was a pause and the voice came back, "Remember the sounds of the wagons that told of the people going West and how the noise was such a bother. I hear the same wagon sounds, but added to that, the sounds of sabers clanking and men cursing. I hear even gunfire in the distance."

Peter went back across the creek as despondent as when he took over the empty pails. He was so engrossed that he forgot to say hello to Louisa. He hoped she was still in the spring.

It was a cold December morning with the rain almost sleet, as Peter made his way across the creek to the spring. It had been almost two years since Louisa died and always he was drawn to the spring, hoping that this time the Lady would let Louisa cross the bar that separated them. He cried to know if Louisa was still at the spring.

The crotch in the white oak tree gave him some respite from the rain and he hunched forward to catch any words the Lady might say. "Please tell me if Louisa is still here," he implored, as he had so many times.

"You know that I can not tell you that," came the voice of the Lady. "There is only one way that you can find out and that is to come and join us. Why do you hesitate? There is no cold rain or sleet here. There are no cares."

Peter felt the coldness of the rain pass from him and the warmth of a glow he could not describe. He slumped forward and the last words escaped his mouth, "Louisa, I am glad you are still here."

"Me too, Grandpa."

Epilogue

"Ma, how did you ever meet the old man?" Mathew wanted to know.

Ann shook her head, as if to bring old events into focus. "Well, first he saved me from a runaway horse," she offered.

"Ma, was it true the first words he said to you were 'Will you marry me?'"

Her voice softened as she thought back over the years. "That is true," she said. "And then he did not talk to me for three months. What was a girl to think about a beau that was so forward and yet so backward?"

"Ma, why did you marry someone you hardly knew?"

"What do you mean 'hardly knew'? He squired me proper for almost a year, maybe eighteen months, and every time we met, his first words were 'Will you marry me?' Not only did he win me over, but my pa too. He came down to the Crossing so many times that Pa finally said, 'Marry that lad before John Holker fires him for missing so much time at Springsbury.'"

"Tell us about the wedding," Minerva chimed in. "Is it true you were married at the spring?"

"Indeed it is true, and to this day I am not sure why I said yes to such foolishness. But he was insistent, said it was a cathedral and not just the old mission church at Briggs Junction. The Bishop came and performed the ceremony, probably because he did not want to lose two good Episcopals to John Holker's church."

She leaned back in her rocker and considered her life with Peter Royston. "He was a gentle but single-minded man and it did not set well with him to be crossed. Toward the end at our time at Springsbury, the son and wife of John Holker made

Peter ready to give up his job. John Holker was a prince of a fellow. I could not say the same for those who followed."

"Did Pa ever get his money?" Mathew wanted to know.

"Yes, most of it, except the lawyer got more than he did. Getting that money cost us the land that my Pa had given us. We had counted on it to pay off the pledge on the land. We spent so much on the lawyer and then all the bottomland flooded in '23. No crops at all," she muttered. "And he had pledged the land to Bill Berry. Now there is a heartless man," she said almost to herself. Ann settled back in the chair and closed her eyes. The rest of the story would have to wait for another day.

Two years had passed since they buried the Constable. Ann had aged perceptibly. She glanced at the almost empty bucket of water on the back porch and called one of the children to go and fill it for her. Getting no answer, she picked up the bucket and muttered, "I will go and fill it myself." Crossing the bridge, she looked around, almost expecting Peter to meet her and offer to carry the pail for her. She put the bucket under the Spout Spring and leaned back into the crotch of the white oak tree.

As the bucket filled, she dozed for a moment, only to be awaken by the sound of a voice she had never heard, but which sounded so familiar. "Ann Anderson Royston, why have you been avoiding me?"

If you are interested in reading some actual history of the life of John Holker, please be referred to the Clarke County, Virginia Historical Society and their Proceedings, Volumes XI and XII dated 1951–1953.

If you are interested in reading more of the life of Peter Royston, Ann Anderson Royston and Jo Anderson, so am I.

Mark W. Royston
La Mirada, California
mark@RoystonGroup.com

Too Poor
To
Paint

Too Proud
To
Whitewash

PREFACE

To my grandchildren
and
their grandchildren

Genealogy is a hobby that can easily become an obsession. Finding long lost relatives and making family connections makes one want to shout "Eureka." But once found, the desire to know more about that person is real. Most of the time you are, at best, left with the bare facts about the person. Father, mother, date of birth, children, and date of death can be found. If you have these facts, you can fill in the blanks on the computer and the result becomes a part of the ancestral chart.

But who was this person? What did he or she do? What kind of problems did they have? "Born 1757—Died 1832." How did they react to the political crisis of their times, say, the Revolutionary War? Could they read or write? Once in a great while a letter might be found, most likely between husband and wife or parent to child. How we cherish that fleeting look into that person's life!

Today we have all the tools necessary to leave to our grandkids and their grandkids a picture of who we were. Photographs give a glimpse, but most likely when we turn them over for a few words of written description, the cupboard will be bare. Our written correspondence is almost nonexistent. We communicate with E-mail and the telephone, and it is awfully easy to hit the delete button once the message is read.

Somehow I feel the urge to leave a message to that offspring who some fifty to a hundred years from now might want to know more about that granddad or great granddad.

To that end I write. My wife Doris says, "You still do not tell them how you feel about things." And that is true, I have difficulties expressing that side of me. Maybe, just maybe, a little bit will show through, enough to satisfy your curiosity.

To anyone other than the grandkids and their grandkids who might stumble on this, I encourage you to write. Do not have the only picture of you that is passed on to the succeeding generations be that of a faded memorial card or a few lines in some obituary column.

In the Blue Ridge Mountains of Virginia

On a mountain in Virginia
stands a lonesome pine
Just below is the cabin home
Of a little girl of mine.
Her name is June
and very, very soon
She'll belong to me.
For I know she is waiting for me
'Neath that lone pine tree

In the Blue Ridge Mountains of Virginia
On The Trail of The Lonesome Pine
In the pale moonshine our hearts entwine
Where she carved her name and I carved mine.
Oh! June, Like the mountains I am blue
Like the pine, I am lonesome for you

In the Blue Ridge Mountains of Virginia
On the trail of the Lonesome Pine.

I can hear the tinkling waterfall
Far among the hills
Blue birds each sing so merrily
To his mate in rapture trills.
They seem to say
"Your June is lonesome, too
Longing fills her eyes
She is waiting for you patiently
Where the pine tree sighs"

In the Blue Ridge Mountains of Virginia
On The Trail of the Lonesome Pine
In the pale moonshine our hearts entwine
Where she carved her name and I carved mine.
Oh! June, Like the mountains I am blue
Like the pine, I am lonesome for you
In the Blue Ridge Mountains of Virginia
On the trail of the Lonesome Pine.

Copyright

Mark W. Royston
2003
(The songs are the copyrights of others.)

Memories of a
Time
Not So
Long Ago
By
Mark W. Royston

Ashby's Gap was one of the first trails west out of the Piedmont section of Northern Virginia. Those who felt crowded by the masses living in eastern Virginia in the late 1700s looked to Ashby's Gap as the way to the Promised Land. Located almost directly west of Belvoir and Mount Vernon, its easy eastern ascent through a gap, which had an elevation of only 900 feet, drew first a trickle, then a river of immigrants to the fertile Shenandoah Valley and points west. It has been estimated that some 200,000 persons took this route west in the early migration. The ease of the eastern slope lulled the traveler, and he found himself facing a western slope that was filled with animal and Indian trails that seemed to be endless.

There have been many arguments as to what were the first routes down the mountain and across the Shenandoah River, but by 1750 a master trail had been established and a few structures were beginning to appear along this route. I will leave it to others to define the evolution of the trail from path to wagon road to paved highway. My only desire is to record that the area changed little from the late 1700s to the early 1900s. My life in the area began in the 1930s, but the wonderful memory of my mother brought alive years back to the turn of the century. The families living from the top of the mountain to the Shenandoah River were the ones who first settled the area in the late 1700s and the early 1800s. Some ownership of land is still in the same family names even to this time.

My immediate ancestors (Roystons, Smallwoods, Elseas, and Lees) all were in the mountains well before the Civil War. Mom's mother was an Elsea. Mom would talk of her Uncle Newt and it was only after I became interested in genealogy, that I found that Uncle Newt's real name was Isaac Newton Elsea. Further research showed that it was a popular trait in the Elsea family to name their children after famous persons. How about James Decatur Elsea, Jefferson Davis Elsea, Andrew Jackson Elsea?

My dad was born in 1871 and had raised a family of five boys (and a daughter who died young) by his first wife. Along the way he built a house on a hill about 200 yards north of what is now Route 50, a mile or so from the Spout Spring, our source of water in drought times. The road went up a fairly steep hill, to a level area encompassing the house site, two large gardens and some pastureland. The house was weather boarded on the outside, unfinished on the inside and never painted. No foundation was used, and the house sat on a number of piles of rocks. Dad built the house around 1905 with the help of Mr. Shipe, who in turn built a smaller house with the same layout down on one corner of Dad's property. When I say smaller, I mean smaller in every detail. It was a real scale model, with shorter doors and ceilings. Mr. Shipe also was not too confident in his building abilities so he built it between two outcroppings of shale. To insure the stability of the structure he bored a large hole in each of the rocks and using long cables, anchored the top of the chimneys to the rocks at each end of the house. I guess this took care of the stability, but the guy wires were excellent lightning conductors. After a few electrical storms, the "Mountain Ben Franklin" decided that the wires weren't such a good idea, and down they came. When we were kids growing up in the '30s the only proof of the story were the holes that still remained in the rocks with some ominous black burn marks around them.

But back to the house on the hill. By the 1930s, the house was truly weathered. Never having been painted, the outside wood showed the effect of some 25 years of neglect. Dad also was not much of a carpenter, allowing many of the board ends to stop at the same studs, so the nails would pull loose and need repeated nailing to keep them attached, to a point where in many places there was nothing left to nail.

Dad's first wife died in 1918, and in 1923 he married my mother, she being 30 years younger. While Mom could not do much about the outside of the house, she did a lot of work inside, scavenging boards from old shipping crates to cover the exposed studs. She wallpapered on an annual basis, sealing up the cracks with narrow strips of cloth torn from old bed sheets. Thus, the inside of the house was very attractive when compared to the outside. As I grew up, it was apparent that we were very poor. Dad had no job, living off the land, so to speak. The house sat on 20 plus acres of mountain land, some steep and timbered, and some grassland, affording food for an old cow or two. Vegetables came from the garden, eggs from chickens, milk from the cow.

Water was carried from a spring located near the Shipe house about a half mile away. In drought times this spring was dry and water had to be carried from the Spout Spring about a mile away. Mom's dad, who had a farm near Berryville (the county seat, some eleven miles away) also provided a "hog on the pole" each year that Mom turned into the usual array of pork products. Mom also went over to Granddad's and worked three or four days a week and that brought in some cash.

Since we had no electricity, light was from kerosene lamps. Kerosene was expensive so we went to bed early to conserve. I did wonder, however, why we could not afford to keep the lamps lit in the evening, but could at 4:00 a.m. as we arose early in the morning. One of the kerosene lamps was an "Aladdin" brand, which was the only mantle type kerosene light I have ever seen. It was much more efficient than the others and the one preferred for reading.

Heat in the living room came from a Woodlawn wood stove, and in the cold winters, would fairly glow red, as we attempted to keep the cold away in an un-insulated house. Mom cooked on a Majestic wood cook stove that was one of her prized possessions. I am not sure where it came from (Granddad most likely), but there was no question who owned that Majestic. It was cleaned and polished and stood proudly in the kitchen providing heat as well as food. In the summertime, the doors stood open to try and get rid of the heat that we so valued in the winter. The wide open and unscreened doors let in hordes of flies which were chased out with tea towels just before dinner was put on the table. Of course, the ever-present fly swatter and fly tapes helped also to curtail their population.

The house had cedar shingles for a roof. In the wintertime, the burning of pine wood in the Woodlawn stove would leave soot deposits that in time would catch on fire. The resulting chimney blaze would blast some three or four feet above the chimney. The roar of this blaze was unmistakable and we all would rush outside to watch it burn itself out. Since no water was available, the only fire-fighting weapon we had was prayer. Mom was a champion prayer, against which the devil and his flames had no power. The chimney fire over, Mom would go calmly back into the house, while I found a reason to stay outside a while longer, not understanding the power of mom's prayer at my tender age. I did realize the danger of the chimney fire, and it instilled such a fear in me that the second money that I ever earned went to buying tin to put a tin roof on the house. While Mom was quite comfortable with her power of prayer, I kind of remembered something the preacher said about God helping those who helped themselves.

I did say, the second money I ever earned. You have to understand that while my fear of the fire was extreme, it was not in the same league as my desire to own a .22 rifle. The first summer I was old enough to work (I think I was 11) I picked apples for eight cents a bushel at Harry F. Byrd's apple orchards. There was an old school bus that had been painted blue that came through the mountains to pick up workers at about five in the morning. After making numerous stops, we would end up in the orchards near Berryville by seven, work a ten hour day and get home around 7 p.m. This was the fall after dad died and Mom had ventured out into the world of employment with her first cash job of working in the apples. Dad was a very proud person and no wife would be allowed to work at a job where it was obvious who was bringing in the earnings.

My brother, who was almost fourteen and large for his age, possessed great strength. He also worked in the apples, and was able to lift the crates full of apples, loading them on the trucks to be transported into the packing sheds. I was envious of this older brother, since I had no such abilities. I was resigned to working alongside my mother, picking the early apples that ripened during the summer.

I had my own tickets, which were placed in the apple crates to identify the picker, and there was no thrill compared to standing in line to receive my first pay. The unreadable signature of Harry F. Byrd on the bottom of that paycheck is still vivid in my mind. An hour later found me at Coiner's department store in Berryville cashing the check and buying my first rifle: a single shot J. R. Stevens .22 caliber which would shoot "shorts," "longs," and "long rifle" cartridges. My pay was almost enough to complete the purchase and Mom put up the remaining three dollars, for a total of sixteen, which not only bought the rifle but also included a box of long rifle bullets. The squirrels in the woods around home were in deep trouble. The blue bus ride home on that Saturday afternoon was most probably the longest ride in my life.

The road up the hill to our house was enough to tax the best of vehicles. It originally started from the old Route 50 road, ran across a marsh, up a steep slope to a level area, then up a short side-hill-run to the house area. By the time I came along, Route 50 had been cut through which eliminated the marsh from the problem. The steep slope across the outcroppings of shale taxed the ability of any driver and car. Using pickaxe and hand shovel, we attempted to keep the ruts under control, particularly after rainstorms, which created their own miniature version of the Grand Canyon. It took a hearty visitor to make the trip up the hill. We kids wondered why we cared, seeing as how we did not own a car and a smooth road did not make the walking any easier.

We went to church at Mount Carmel, a Methodist church built in the mid to late 1700s. It was a part of the "White Post" charge and had one minister to serve seven churches. Thus we had preaching every other Sunday and Sunday school run by the members every Sunday. In the summer time, they would have all-day services on specially selected Sundays. It was not uncommon to have a visiting minister preach in the morning and the regular minister in the afternoon. This sequence was always followed and I suspect was done so that any doctrinal errors brought in by the visitor could be corrected in the afternoon sermon. The mountain people had a firm idea of true doctrine, and beware the minister who did not adhere to these local tenets. Mount Carmel had been around since about 1760 and had seen the likes of Bishop Asbury as a circuit rider. Legend had it that George Washington had been the surveyor of the land (which was donated by Lord Fairfax) on which the church sat.

Mount Carmel was nestled in a spot with granite boulders all around. The kids loved playing on, around and behind these rocks and turned their Sunday clothes into tatters. The church had originally been built of logs and later covered by weather-boarding. The inside of the church was plastered and an open loft had been sealed off to make an upstairs room used on extraordinarily busy Sundays to teach Sunday school. Dad was Superintendent of Sunday school and tended to long and tortuous prayers; boring to my youthful mind and most others, I suppose. Dad was crippled and had difficulty getting down on his knees. The thought of having to get back up may have contributed to the length of his prayers.

The children's day services in the summer and the Christmas programs were comprised of pantomimes to hymns and poetry recited by the young children. My early ulcers most probably came from stage fright and the fear of forgetting the words I had studied so hard to memorize. "Tell me not in mournful numbers; life is but an empty dream" was indelibly stamped in my mind for all my early years.

Every family brought their lunch, which was spread out on blankets on the grass. There was a lot of movement between families with everyone having a taste of everyone else's food. The sincerity of the eaters in expounding the cook's abilities was appreciated and could make or break the entire all day service. The Christmas programs were similar to the children's day services but with a Christmas focus, a focus that also included some Christmas cheer in the presence of a supply of oranges and sacks of candy that were donated by Ender's funeral parlor.

We kids appreciated this thoughtfulness at Christmas as much as the ladies appreciated their gifts of personalized fans given by Enders during the heat of summer. Since no one family was singled out in the giving of these gifts of oranges and candy, it was acceptable to Dad that we take them. We were cautioned to take only one to insure that no one would think that we actually needed the food. Of course we had to wait until we got home before eating—first the orange—then the candy. My brother, Linton, and I only had thoughts of these treats that we could not afford to buy and we noticed not at all the loss of pride suffered by Dad.

Dad was born only six years after the Civil War ended. In 1895 he married Nota Elsea, (my mom's much older first cousin) and had five boys, Marshall, Luther, Joe, Richard and Irvin. Marshall and Luther lived in the Washington, DC area. Joe moved around a bit, living in the Valley, the Washington, DC area, and the mountains (in the log house across the highway from the road to our house). Joe had four children. The two oldest (Jean and Joyce) were about the same age as Linton and I. We were great buddies for the few years they lived there, and it left a great void in our lives when they moved. Jean was a couple of years older than I, and the most beautiful person I ever met. She was a tomboy with a vivaciousness that made her a joy to be around. Joyce was a bit younger and a bit quieter in demeanor. The only bad memory was the geese owned by Joe. It was almost impossible to play outside without being attacked by one or more of the geese. If I'd only been old enough to own that J.R. Stevens .22 at that time!!

Richard married a girl from Front Royal and had one daughter before dying at an early age in 1936. My only memory of Richard (besides his death) was a visit to our house when he wanted something from Dad. I recall the somberness that was enough to register in my memory even though I was only three or four years old. I believe it had something to do with Richard trying to get into the CCC (Civilian Conservation Corps) camp and needing to use Dad as a home address and Dad to certify that he was not married as was needed to qualify. I do not know how it came out but I know where Dad would have stood on the question.

Irvin never married and died at home at the age of 24, also in 1936, from an unknown disease. I remember Mom taking care of Irvin and the smell of a bed-ridden person in a house with no indoor plumbing or water.

1936 was a long year for Mom. Along with the deaths of Richard and Irvin, 1936 seemed to bring death and affliction at every turn. Mom also had TB in 1936 and spent a lot of time in bed. Mom's sister, Aunt Letitia, died in August of 1936. September of 1936 was my first year of school at Mount Carmel, and I guess an event such as this helped to keep Mom on the road of daily reality.

I remember well the Christmas of 1936. Now, Christmas was always a time of anticipation, even though the presents were sparse. To make sure that we knew that Santa had been there, it was a custom that the Christmas tree be put up and left bare and Santa, himself, trimmed the tree after we kids went to bed. Thus the surprise of Christmas morning centered on the Christmas tree, rather than what was under it. It was a time for receiving clothes and an occasional toy. But 1936 brought presents from a couple of ladies who were friends of Irvin and who had gotten to know us during Irvin's illness. These presents were trucks; complete heavy-duty 1936 scale model Chevrolet trucks. Linton and I spent untold hours building roads around and through the lilac bushes on the west side of the house. We would drive those trucks, filling them with dirt at one point and unloading them at another, repeating the process, time after time. Mom, I guess, bit her tongue, when the presents were delivered, but she saw the generous hearts that were a part of it.

My brother, Linton, and I both were born at home; he in 1927, and I in 1930. We were far enough apart in age for him to disdain my being around and many fights were resolved by my yelling for Mom. Linton was never afraid to say what came into his head, whereas I was always reluctant to let anyone get too close to my mind, probably, because of something that embarrassed me in those early years. Do not remember what it was, but I remember embarrassing easily. Most of our training came from Mom. Dad was around, but not very close. He was a strict person combining his Methodist religion, his pride, and his ever-present cane to present a force with which to be reckoned. Since he was crippled and could barely get around with a cane, we learned his range and so managed to avoid the swift punishment that came from transgressions.

Dad was an imposing figure. While the injuries of the legs had left him somewhat stooped, in his early life he was around six-foot-eight, and his breadth was enough to literally fill a doorway. With this size as a father one might ask how I ended up only six feet tall. Maybe my mom's size had something to do with it, she, being only five-foot-four. Dad had strict rules for us boys, which Mom would enforce, but she had a way of tempering them to make them passable. One of the rules had to do with clothing, the normal wear being bib overalls with denim shirts. The sleeves could be rolled up when we were working but had to be left rolled down if any people were around or if we went down on the road for any reason. Sins were real easy to come by. For instance, movies were a sin, so we weren't allowed to go to the movies. I saw my first movie shortly after Dad died, but that is another story.

In the late '30s we had a couple of cows. Linton learned how to milk them, but I never did. Guess I was too young. The fields at that time were starting to convert from grass to brush and finding the cows early in the morning was sometime near impossible. We had a persimmon tree in one part of the field that was a problem when the persimmons were ripe.

The cows would eat the persimmons and the milk would have a taste from the persimmons. It was my job to keep the cows out of the persimmons. Now I was young but logic told me that if we did not have a persimmon tree, the problem would go away. Since we did not eat the persimmons and they filled no other useful function, I was all for cutting down that tree. For some reason beyond my comprehension, the tree was never cut down and the persimmons outlasted the cows, with the problem only going away when the cows left.

I do not remember how Dad felt about us going to school since he had only a fifth grade education. Mom, however, made sure we went to school—no matter what the rest of the world did. Sickness was only an excuse to miss school if we were sick enough to take a dose of castor oil, and there were few times that I was ever that sick. So off we went to a one room school, called Slabtown by the mountain folks, which officially was known as Mount Carmel School—not because of any religious affiliation, but because the church (about a mile away) was the closest landmark. We walked, taking a shortcut through Uncle Walter's place. A creek or two had to be crossed which only gave us trouble during wet weather. I am not sure how long Mount Carmel School had been there. I do know that Mom had been a teacher there in 1922–1923 after she graduated from high school. I went there for my first five grades. (In 1938, for one semester I went to Berryville School when we went to live at Granddad's home outside of Berryville.)

My first grade teacher was Miss Wagner and I remember mostly the unending hours that we spent making page after page of Os and Ls. Fourth grade was a great year at school. The teacher was Mrs. Riggans who came from Southern Virginia and was around for only one year. She rented the small stone house just across the Shenandoah. I picked up a new friend by the name of Claude Fox and we dreamed of becoming airplane pilots. Claude was much wiser in the ways of the world than I, doing such things as writing to Piper Cub Aircraft in New Haven, PA for bulletins on their airplanes. Hours were spent poring over these bright shiny pictures and memorizing the specifications.

When Mrs. Riggans came back from Christmas vacation she brought a small bag of unroasted peanuts for each of us, explaining that we could roast them and eat them now or save them till spring, plant them and have a crop of peanuts. Linton and I elected to plant ours and did harvest about a basketful of peanuts. This, in spite of being planted in the shale soil that made gardening of any kind a very haphazard affair.

It was about this time that I found the importance of going to school on a regular basis. (My kids were to suffer from this, years later, as I insisted that they go to school every day, including driving in from camping at the beach.) We were learning fractions. The first day we were introduced to them, all the questions had halves as the fraction. Hey, this was easy. You divided the numbers into each other and if the answer was not an even number, you wrote a designator off to the right (1/2) to signify that there was something left over.

For some reason I missed the next day of school, where such things as "thirds," "fourths," etc. were discussed. Back to school the next day and guess what? An exam! Armed with my two-day-old logic I tackled the problems, dividing them correctly and leaving my "½" notation as I had thought to be the methodology. We had maybe ten problems, with only a couple having "two" as the divisor. The paper came back the next day with all but the lucky couple marked wrong. Now do you see the reason why I made the kids go to school every day?

My introduction to patriotism came at Mount Carmel School. Every once in a while, Miss Rose McDonald would show up unannounced, bringing with her a supply of small U.S. flags, a wind up Victrola and some John Philip Sousa records. The flags would be passed out and we would all march around the room to the scratchy but stirring Sousa marches. Miss Rose would tell us great patriotic tales and generally took over the school when she was there. I believe she was on the school board or something that gave her sufficient power to disrupt the teacher's plans for that day. Maybe her size had something to do with it, as she was an extremely large lady. She also believed in evolution and made that a part of her curriculum.

Our regular school teacher was somewhat leery of the mountain people and certainly did not want us going home and repeating what Miss Rose had espoused, so we were always told that "If Miss Rose wants to believe that she sprang from an ape, that is ok, but you do not have to believe that you did."

While many outsiders were leery of the mountain people, I enjoyed very much being one of them. The families were close knit and would help each other through any problem. We did have some interesting personalities and a few are worth mentioning. While some of the stories might, at first light be taken as poking fun at them, I can assure you, my love for them is deep and constant.

One who comes to mind is Bad Eye. Bad Eye earned his nickname from an errant eye that went in a different direction from the other. It was so bad that one could never tell who was the object of his attention. While this may have been a distraction to those talking to him, let me tell you that Bad Eye was probably the best rifle shot in the county. To make things more complicated, he aimed with his off eye (that being the left eye for a right-handed shooter). He had a short stock .22 rifle that would allow him to crane his neck over the stock and sight with his left eye. This usually cleared a wide swath of spectators who might be watching him shoot, what with the contortion of the head and the right eye staring off in to the upper four o'clock position. I did say he could shoot. How about hitting a bumblebee in flight? Saw him do it a number of times. Many years later, Mom sent me an obituary and it was the first time that I realized that his name was Elmos and not Bad Eye. And I wonder how many people read that obituary and still never knew that Bad Eye had died.

Another family having a great impact on the mountain folk was the Reese and Ollie Wiley Family. Mrs. Wiley had taught school at Providence Chapel School and also at Mount Carmel in the early 1900s. She had two children, Irvin and Elwood. Irvin stayed in the mountains and was one of the better known characters. Elwood enlisted in the Army Air Corps sometime before Pearl Harbor and stayed for his twenty-year career. I remember the Wiley's lived in the Shipe place, then at Uncle Walter's Place, before finally buying the log house from Mom.

Most probably the first meeting of Mom and Mrs. Wiley was when Mom was about five years old. Mom's older brothers were going to Providence Chapel School where Mrs. Wiley was teaching. One day they took Mom along to school. They told Mrs. Wiley that Mom knew her alphabet and that she would be glad to recite it for her. The only little detail missing in the scenario was that Mrs. Wiley did not know that the older brothers taught Mom to say the alphabet backwards. When called upon, Mom stood up and recited, "ZYX…" The classroom shook with laughter. Mrs. Wiley was not amused. She called on Mom to say the alphabet correctly. Mom, thinking she had missed a letter, repeated the alphabet the only way she knew, "ZYX…" They went about three rounds to the classroom's total enjoyment. Finally Mom and her older brothers were sent home for the day. Mom recalled that it took a long time before Mrs. Wiley forgave a five-year-old for ruining her day.

Mrs. Wiley had a penchant for poetry and would make up poems about people. She would never write them down, but had them committed to memory. We would talk her into reciting the poetry for us, and we would sit and listen as the rhymes would flow out from her. I do not recall the exact words but she had her husband, Reese, and Tom Willingham in one that used to infuriate Mr. Wiley.

Mr. Wiley liked his beer and Mr. Willingham ran the combination filling station and grocery store in Millwood that was the source of the beer. As the poem went, when Mr. Wiley and Mr. Willingham died, they met down in Hell and fought a furious battle, each blaming the other for his predicament. Every time Mr. Wiley would hear the poem, he would go into a tirade, and Mrs. Wiley would smile a sly little smile, knowing that she had hit home.

I was the subject of one of her poems and again I do not remember most of it. I do remember how it ended: "He is very smart, but it is sad to say, he'd starve to death before he'd work a day." She did know how to nail a person down.

Irvin was born in 1901 and quit school in about the fifth grade. He did have the knack for making money and he became the unofficial banker in the mountains. He also ran a small grocery store (the type referred to by Lum and Abner as a Jot-em-Down store). The more precise name was a Cash and Carry store. It was the carry part that got the mountain families through hard times, because carry meant credit.

Most of the families in the mountains were on credit and without Irvin, would have seen harder times. In some cases the breadwinner was working but it was not bread he was buying. Irvin would give the family groceries on credit and if the cash went to a bootlegger, he would quietly see the employer and unofficially garnishee his wages.

Irvin was also the bank. In his pocket he carried a roll of bills and when the families needed cash, he was there to peel off enough cash to meet the need. The start of school and Christmas time seemed to increase the need for loans. Now just in case you think Irvin was an altruistic sort that went around playing Santa Claus, Irvin had a simple formula. You paid him ten percent whether the money was borrowed for a day or a year. You borrowed ten, you paid him back eleven. Those were figures that anyone in the mountains could understand.

Rules were not made for Irvin. He went through life with little regard for the law, although he was not a lawbreaker. Laws just weren't written for him. He needed to carry a gun so that he was not robbed while gambling or at the store. He did not apply for a license. He just got a job across the mountain carrying the mail between the two small towns of Delaplane and Upperville. The carrier of bulk mail automatically had the right to carry a gun. It might have been frightful to strangers, but we thought nothing of jumping in Irvin's pickup truck and moving the loaded .45 Automatic over from where we wanted to sit. I do not think that I ever saw Irvin that the .45 was not within sight.

Irvin died in 1969, shortly after rules and regulations begin to surface for the common folks. In 1966, we built a home for Mom not far from where the old house was. Irvin had a phone in his house and we used it to make many of the arrangements with the subcontractors who were doing the work on the house.

One of the subs came and put in the drain field for the septic tank. Irvin saw the results, an indoor toilet.

A short while later, Irvin wanted to know who had done the digging? "Buckley Contracting, from White Post," was the answer. Irvin called Buckley over and told him that he wanted a drain field just like ours. Buckley agreed and told Irvin to take care of all the details of county permits. In time, Irvin had the trench dug under the house by hand to carry the sewer line, a well drilled and water brought in to the house. Buckley dug the drain field and installed the leach lines. One day Irvin came back from carrying the mail and Buckley was waiting impatiently. "What'cha waiting for?" Irvin wanted to know.

"I am waiting for you to get the inspector over here and inspect this drain field," Buckley replied.

"Cover it up," Irvin ordered.

"Cover it up?" Buckley questioned.

"Cover it up," Irvin repeated.

"You're the boss," Buckley muttered and cover it up, he did.

About six months later Irvin had a surprise visit from the building inspector. "I hear you put in a drain field," the inspector announced officiously.

Irvin nodded pointing to an area west of the house. "Over there," he directed and continued. "Why do you want to know?"

"I need to inspect it," was the reply.

"Inspect away," Irvin said.

The inspector looked at the weed-covered area and said, "You have to uncover the drain field so that I can see it."

Now Irvin was not about to uncover any drain field, so he inquired, "Why do you want to inspect it?

"To make sure it is sanitary," was the response.

To this, Irvin had an irrefutable answer, "You see that old outhouse standing over there. It has been there forty years and no one ever came to inspect it. Now this drain field has got to be more sanitary than that." Faced with this logic, the inspector got into his car and headed back across the river to a place where rules replaced logic and the question never came up again. The house was finally torn down in the widening of Route 50, and the drain field functioned well but illegally until then.

A few years ago the county, or state, or country, passed a law that anyone in the mountains who wished to cut a tree over a certain diameter had to get permission from some agency in Winchester before doing so. My thoughts went back to Irvin and thought how lucky that agency was to have delayed passing such a law until Irvin was no longer with us. If Irvin were still around, the inspector would have a stump to sit on while discussing the question.

The other son, Elwood, graduated from Boyce High School and entered the Army Air Force. To say that Elwood drank a little bit would have been a serious understatement. Elwood drank a lot. In later years, I asked him where he was when Pearl Harbor happened—a favorite question to anyone of that age. Elwood responded that he was as drunk as a skunk in a bar in New Orleans. After the war years he spent most of his time as a Master Sergeant in California at the Muroc Air Force Base, now Edwards.

By the time he retired in the late fifties and returned to live at Irvin's, he had given up on the hard stuff and concentrated solely on beer. He would be up around four in the morning, and if you wanted a completely lucid response from Elwood, the question would have to be posed before 5:30 a.m.

The beer cans would collect at the back door of Irvin's house and after a period, Irvin would hire one of the locals to get a wheelbarrow and haul the empties down past the drain field. There the pile grew and became a monument to one man's attempt to drink more than the brewery could produce. With the new Route 50 passing over that spot, I often wonder how secure the road foundation is, as its primary support is most likely that supply of beer cans.

When the new road was imminent, and Irvin's house was to become history, Irvin made a deal with us to allow him to build a small home on our property just across the road from his old log house. The agreement was that he would build it and pay the taxes and when he and Elwood died, the house would become Mom's property. And that is how we became owners of a second house.

Irvin died of natural causes in 1969 and Elwood followed him some ten to twelve years later, dying of unnatural causes. A robber at his house killed Elwood. No one was ever arrested for the murder.

One of my favorites and one who gets a weekly thought from me was Harvey. Harvey, as the story goes, was a well-educated man who fell in love with a mountain lass and to the chagrin of his family moved into the mountains. He was to spend the rest of his life there with his beloved and raise a number of children. Harvey was a lover of Saturday Westerns and many of his children were named after western movie heroes. To this day if anyone in the hills asks, "Where's Gene Autry?" the question has to do with Harvey's son.

Harvey was a very tall person with giant strides. To my knowledge, he never rode in a car. If anyone would stop and ask if he wanted a ride, the answer would always be in the negative. But it was his ability to turn a phrase that gained him his mountain fame. People would enjoy telling what "Harvey said." If any clever quip came up from any source it was popular to attribute it to Harvey. If "Harvey said" everything for which he was credited, he would not have had time to do anything else.

Another of the great mountaineers was John Kelly Lloyd. John Kelly had been blinded by a posthole digging accident when he was a teenager. (He had been dynamiting postholes and one charge went off while he was checking on it.) He was a great coon hunter and knew the mountain trails like no sighted person could. With his nephew, Donald Wiley, as his second sight, you could run into them any place in the mountain. He recognized everyone by their voices or a verbal mannerism. During World War II, John Kelly gave more blood in blood drives than anyone in the county. He had a great singing voice and was at Mount Carmel much of the time.

In 1940–1941 the decision was made to bring in electricity to the mountains. The two electrical utilities involved were Virginia Electric and Power Company (VEPCO) and Potomac Power and Electric (PEPCO). I suspect that neither wanted the territory, as it would be a lot of wires for a little bit of revenue. The winner of the dubious task was VEPCO, but before it could get started, World War II came along and no copper was available for such a project. After the war, Mrs. John Lee delayed the implementation until 1952 as she fought the idea of power lines passing through her property. (I believe her words went something like "My Daddy did not have any electricity going cross his house, and there is none going to cross mine, either.")

Mount Carmel School had kerosene lamps and a wood stove. In the winter Linton and I were hired to come to school early and start the fire. I am sure that Mom making sure that we were at school every day got us the job because it took about an hour to get the room heated and the teacher sure did not want everyone showing up to a cold school. It was hard enough to get the mountain kids to walk the many miles that they had to travel to get to school in warm weather. Most of the parents had limited education (grade school or less) and they were unenthusiastic about this education thing.

The quality of the teachers was outstanding, particularly that of Miss Jane Gardiner. She was one of three teaching sisters who lived at White Post. Never being married, she dedicated her life to teaching, mostly at Boyce School and at Mount Carmel. The number of students at Mount Carmel was small, maybe fifteen or twenty, but covering five or six grades with one teacher must have been very taxing. Miss Jane taught me in the third and fifth grades.

I have always said that a person only needs one good teacher to make him a student and for me that teacher was Miss Jane. Many years later she told me of the trepidation with which she faced the teaching at Mount Carmel, mostly because of the stories that she had heard about the mountaineers. In spite of this, she daily went about her work, instilling as much knowledge into us as we would allow. Some of the kids resisted any attempts to pry open their minds, but try she did. My mom had conditioned my brother and me to want to learn so we were willing recipients.

Mount Carmel School closed in June of 1941 as I completed the fifth grade. All of the students attending the various one and two room schools in the county would be going to the consolidated schools in Boyce and Berryville. In those days, Clarke County schools were still segregated with the black schools in the county being in Millwood and at Josephine City, (a black community on the outskirts of Berryville). My grandfather's farm also bordered Josephine City and my first realizations of blacks came from walking through Josephine City to Berryville School during the third grade when we lived at Granddad's for one semester.

I was looking forward to going to Boyce School. Linton had gone there two years before and had many stories to tell about this edifice of learning that covered all eleven grades of school. (This, of course, was before they converted to the more conventional twelve grades. I have often wondered why they now need that extra year—did we learn less then, or is the system less efficient now??)

But back to Mount Carmel, the pay that we received for starting the fire, and which we gave to Mom (three dollars a month as I recall) came out of the teacher's salary. Since cash was hard to come by, I am sure every bit Mom got was well spent, and I am sure that the teacher was hard pressed to give up that amount also.

It was at Mount Carmel that I learned to love to read. I can still remember some of the short stories we read in our literature book. One in particular, *Cousin Roger Goes into Business*, a story of a city kid that spends the summer on the farm and attempts to sell firewood still makes me break up when I think of it. There was a great line where Cousin Roger, while being chased by a snarling dog, dove into the woodpile. The wording: "He went into the woodpile like a cyclone into a knothole" conjured up such visions of both Cousin Roger and the knothole that I was never able to forget them.

Of course, the fact that Cousin Roger was a verbal dead ringer for my nephew, Richard (my half-brother's boy, about a year older than I) may have contributed to my relating to the short story. Richard lived in Washington, DC, and would come "up country" and spend weeks at a time with us during the summer. While he was there he spent considerable time figuring out how he could replace his entrepreneurial income from his city activities, such as begging newspapers and soft drink bottles from the neighborhood and selling them at refuse centers. (I am sure that if Richard were growing up today he would be reversing the operation; picking up products from a central location and peddling them back to the neighborhood.) The chance for a profit came up only once. Mr. John MacDonald, who owned adjoining property to us, hired Linton, Richard and me to thin corn. Using hoes, which we brought along, we would go down the rows of corn, chopping out the extra stalks that were just beginning to grow. Linton and I had experience in this from the garden at home so we knew the process. It took some time, however, to convince Richard that not all the stalks were to be chopped out and that some had to be left to mature. This educational process, plus the fact that we worked some twelve hours, made Richard a less than happy farmer that day and made an awfully long day for us who had to listen to him. The crowning blow came, however, when we were paid, each of us receiving twenty-five cents for our long day's labor. Richard was outraged and threw his quarter as far away as he could. At the same time he taught me some words that I had never heard or had the chance to use until I joined the Navy, many years later.

Linton and I, naturally, turned our quarter over to Mom, so if we were underpaid she was the one who suffered. She, knowing the difficulties of the times and the amount that mountain folks had available, probably thought that we were overpaid. The thought of that thrown away quarter stayed with me for a long time, particularly since I made a number of forays back to try to find it. This was after nephew Richard had gone back to the easier pickings of the big city. But, I digress…

While Cousin Roger gave me my early taste of humor, the poetry to which I was exposed must have also made a profound impression on me. Some of those simple rhymes such as *Rain* are still a part of my repertoire—what, you have never heard of "Raining, raining all day long, sometimes loud, sometimes soft, just like a song…I will sail my boat tomorrow in wonderfully new places, but first I will take the watering pot and wash the pansies' faces." I tell you, such classics are not being taught today. Sometimes I have trouble recalling just when I learned certain things and may attribute later knowledge to earlier days. So forgive me if I credit learning calculus to my fifth grade teacher. I have already said how good a teacher Miss Jane Gardiner was.

Mount Carmel School was on the way to Frogtown, about a mile from Route 50 on a dirt road (now paved and shown on the maps as Route 606). A small triangle of cleared land was the playground, which we ingeniously turned into a baseball diamond. Boys and girls played as teammates, a situation created not only by the lack of numbers but by the athletic abilities of the girls. Most of the equipment was suspect, having found its way into the P.E. department via some castoff route. Baseballs were covered with tar tape, bats were splintered and most likely had no knob on the handle; the first baseman had a glove, the rest did not.

Linton was a good natural athlete. Later at Boyce School, he was to hit numerous home runs off a local un-hittable pitcher. When asked why he was able to do this when no one else could, he answered honestly that, "It was a lot easier to hit a ball that was white and with a bat that had a knob on the end of the handle."

We also had an old soccer ball and used it to play a local rules game that was somewhere between Rugby and Australian rules football. It was co-ed and a lot of piling on was involved, which I think was enjoyed more by the older boys than we younger ones. It would probably qualify as a sex education class by today's standards. Another game we played was "Annie Annie Over." This involved choosing sides and throwing a ball over the roof of the school. If caught by one of the players, all would rush around to the other side and throw the ball at the members of the other team. Any person hit would be out of the game. The name "Annie Annie Over"?? It was required to be shouted by the team as a warning to the other side that a throw was imminent.

Mom was born in the Blue Ridge on Columbus Day, 1901. We always teased her about her "Red Letter day" birthday. When the country abandoned the celebration of noteworthy events by changing them to just an extra day off on Monday, Mom was disappointed that she lost her day on the calendar. Her earlier days were spent on the east side of the Shenandoah, but somewhere along the way her dad and mom split up, and she ended up living with her father over in the Valley near Berryville. Granddad was sheriff of the county for a long period of time, encompassing most of the first half of the 20th century. Granddad had a large three-story brick home on a 100 acre farm just on the outskirts of Berryville, adjacent to the black community called Josephine city. At the end of World War I, Mom contracted measles and the Spanish Flu (the strain that was so devastating in 1918). She ended up spending almost two years in a darkened room trying to protect her eyes from the permanent effects of the measles. As a result she did not graduate from high school until May of 1921. She was one of the two honor students that Berryville High School ever had until they relaxed the standards in later years.

After graduation, she wanted to go into nursing but Granddad was against that, so she got a job teaching school at Mount Carmel. She boarded with Mr. and Mrs. Tom Lee, who lived at the foot of Mount Carmel Lane (where it joined Route 50). Mount Carmel School was only a mile or so from the Lees so she did not need a car. Sometime during her two-year stint at Mount Carmel she met Dad. "Little" Irvin, Dad's youngest son, was one of Mom's students. Mom and Dad were married on May 5th, 1923. In later years, Mom told me of her early married life, particularly having to do with finances. Dad had a tendency to co-sign notes for friends and then have to pay off the note when the person defaulted. It was so bad that he feared losing his land, and as a result it had been put into his first wife's name to be protected.

The land was split into three parcels, which we referred to as the upper place, the lower place and the log house acre. When Dad's first wife died, because of Virginia law, Dad only inherited a "dowers" right to it with the heirs being the children of his first wife. Mom came into this little complication and in an effort to resolve it, the lower place was given outright to the five boys of the first marriage and the upper place was deeded back to Dad with some money passing hands that was supplied by Mom's dad. The log house became a part of the upper place and then was deeded separately to Mom. Had we known that we would have to go through this again when Dad died, I think they would have done it differently.

But, back to the financial problems..... When they got married, Dad was in debt, needing to pay off other people's notes that were in default. I do not know how much it was but it was an astronomical amount compared with his ability to pay. Dad was crippled from an old logging accident and had little or no income. Mom was not allowed to continue her school teaching because of the exclusion of married women from teaching in that era. She spent the next three or four years working at odd jobs, such as thinning, cutting and shucking corn. To this day I have the shucking tool that she used, with its homemade padding to protect against blisters. Most of this work was done on a farm down along the Shenandoah River and that location had more than its share of gnats and mosquitoes.

She also made a deal with some of the dairy farmers in the Valley to take any of the newborn bull calves off their hands, as the farmer only wanted to raise calves for milk cows. She would feed the calf with a baby bottle to get it started, then let it graze in a field near the house, until it was old enough to sell as a veal calf.

Slowly but surely she reduced the debt, all the while keeping an eye on Dad to keep him from falling for the same old story and co-signing yet another note. Why Dad did this was never clear, but it probably had to do with the fear of having someone think he did not have the money. After all, the borrower was supposed to pay it back so it should not have cost Dad anything, but it always did. Mom had a great mind and beautiful artistic talent and she must have wondered what God had in mind for her. It was not until we look back on her life that we could understand what Mom meant to the mountains and what the mountains meant to her.

I soon learned that our house was poor, even compared with mountain standards. I saw that other people had lawn mowers to cut grass; I even got to push one when we visited Granddad's farm. Even Granddad must have been surprised to see someone of my age volunteer to push a lawn mower. Other kids dreamed of toys and candy. I dreamed of having a painted house and my own lawn mower. I worked out a system as far as mowing the lawn. We had a rather large yard, which was between two gardens and woods to the front and back. I learned a technique with a sickle knife, where on the back swing the blade bent the grass backwards and the forward swing would cut the grass as short and as clean as a lawn mower.

But I could never solve the unpainted house issue. It had been unpainted so long that it would have been impossible to buy enough paint to put a finished surface on the outside. I once thought I had the problem solved when I saw someone white washing a shed. Since the white wash dried with a gloss and it appeared to go over anything, I could hardly wait to get home and tell Mom of my discovery. Her simple answer was, "Son, we may be too poor to paint, but we're too proud to white wash."

Our house was on a high knoll, which provided a fine view of the Shenandoah Valley. As a result, it must have been used as a lookout post during the Civil War. The garden to the west provided us with a treasure hunting site, which was encouraged by Mom, as it served a two-fold purpose.

Linton and I dug up many Civil War items, such as harness parts, belt buckles, an occasional bayonet, and a rare find, two projectiles. These were still filled with the powder and were supposed to explode and spread deadly shrapnel. We opened one of the shells and spilled out the powder. Linton got some kitchen matches and while I took refuge behind a tree, he set fire to the powder. The powder burned, but since it was not enclosed, it presented no explosive condition. We lost interest in this great physics experiment and the second shell was thrown under the house. (Our storage spot for anything we wanted to save but had no other place to store). Over the years, it had accumulated many treasures that were worthless then but would be valuable today. I remember, in particular, a broadaxe that was used in a previous age to hew logs. It must have weighed twenty pounds and I marveled at the strength it must have taken to use it. Occasionally used tools, such as briar scythes, found their way under the house. Tools that were used every day, such as axes, were left to face the elements. Every once in a while we would find ourselves trying to find an axe or saw that was left out and which had become buried under a blanket of snow. This created a frantic search by Linton and me to find the lost tools before Dad asked where they were.

The artillery shell that was left under the house was forgotten, only to be a part of a later story. I will relate it now, as it seems to fit. Many years later the old house had been abandoned, and we decided to build a new house for Mom a few hundred feet to the east. After the new house was built, it was decided that the old house had to be destroyed and what better way than to have the fire department burn it, while practicing their skills.

Sometime after the event took place, I was talking to one of the observers of the burning. He described how they would start the fire, put it out and restart it. As the fire grew hotter and hotter, there was a tremendous explosion and parts of the burning house scattered in all directions. The woods started on fire and fire engines from other counties had to come in and assist the Ender's Volunteer Fire Department in dousing the flames. I sagely kept my mouth shut, but realized that the last shot of the Civil War was a lot later than anyone thought.

Mondays—how I hated Mondays—this was long before I had to look an alarm clock in the face to start a new workweek. Monday was "wash day." In the early days it involved Mom washing on a washboard and the smell of Red Seal Lye soap that still haunts me.

Washtubs to hold the wash and rinse water were located next to each other in the kitchen or outside, depending on the weather and the time of year.

Water was heated in the reservoir on the side of the Majestic, or the top, then poured into the three washtubs. One served as the wash water and two as the rinse tubs. In my own devious way, I suggested that one rinse tub should be enough. No, Mom said with a certain amount of pride, it only takes one to wash, and it takes one to rinse, but it takes a second one to get the clothes clean. Somehow I got the message that you washed to have clean clothes, and if it took the third step to finish the job, do not stop part way. Now, I had a vested interest in the amount of water that was needed to wash. All the water needed for the washing (and for all other uses as well) had to be carried up the hill from one of three possible sources.

The nearest source was a branch that ran at the bottom of the hill to the north of us. While the path was steeper, it was only half as far away as was the second source. This could be used for wash water and not for drinking. The next nearest source was a spring about a half a mile away at the corner of our property. This spring had a lot of minerals in it, as its color was a shade of white and in time left deposits on the bottom of the buckets. I always credited that spring for my good teeth because I sure had never heard of flossing. Of course, the lack of candy in the diet may have something to do with it, too. But I digress…. The spring ran well in good weather but failed in a long drought, which made the long trek to the Spout Spring necessary.

Hauling water from the Spout Spring was serious business. Linton, being older, could handle the two buckets a lot better than I and always made the return trip a lot faster. Since he did not want to carry any more water than I, he rested until I made it up the hill, and was raring to make the next trip while I was trying to catch my breath. I do not remember how many trips it took to fill the washtubs, but it was numerous and you can see why I hated Mondays.

I do not suppose Mom was overjoyed about Mondays either, for not only did she have to do the washing in a pretty primitive way, but we kids were not too quiet about the terrible travail to which we were being subjected.

Mom used the washboard through all of the thirties and must have hated it about as much as I hated the shingle roof, for one of the first mechanically operated devices she obtained, after she started working, was a Maytag gasoline engine powered, ringer type washing machine. The washer had a two-cycle engine that required the mixing of the lubricating oil and the gasoline. It had an exhaust pipe of flexible steel to which was attached a muffler which allowed the fumes to be exhausted outside. The noise from the exhaust was evident for a half mile, so anyone within earshot knew that washing was going on. At the end of the wash cycle, the clothes were run through a wringer and deposited into a washtub. The wash water was emptied and the tub refilled with rinse water. Then the process was repeated twice to make sure the clothes were clean. The clothes were then hung on a line to dry.

Rainy days disrupted the cycle and were a matter of conversation between Mom and her God. For some reason it rarely rained on Mondays. Maybe I should have learned the power of prayer earlier in my life and the rain could have shown up in time to have a full rain barrel on Monday morning, rather than my having to make those trips down the hill to fetch those pails of water. Mom used a wringer type washing machine the rest of her life, although she switched to an electric one after power was brought into the mountains in 1951–1952.

Every time I think of carrying the water, I remember one incident in particular. We would make daily runs to the Spout Spring in drought time. This was normally done at around five or six in the morning. Linton and I would walk down our road to Route 50 then down Route 50 through an area called the Fox Trap to the Wildcat Hollow Road. Then we turned up Wildcat Hollow Road past Mrs. Lena Lee's house, a couple hundred yards to the spring path, which led across a stream to the spring.

We had been hearing rumors about an animal that was prowling the mountains. There was a lot of speculation as to what it was. The only thing that people agreed on was that it really stunk and that it had been responsible for killing some pretty big dogs. This particular morning we headed out and as we reached the Fox Trap, we kept hearing something in the leaves in the ditch alongside the road. We would stop and it would stop. We debated about going back home, but somehow, we decided to continue on. We finally reached the Spout Spring and were just filling our buckets from the stream out of the spout, and our greatest fears were realized when an animal scream was heard back on the path we had just passed.

Neither Linton nor I hesitated. Our choices were few. Certainly we could not head home straight at the animal. Behind us was a tall mountain that offered no escape. Our only choice was some white oak trees growing at the spring. In past times we had tried to climb these trees with no success, as the first limbs were about twelve to fifteen feet above the ground. This time we went up those trees so fast we did not stop at the first limbs. All the way to the top we went and as we swayed in the breeze, we wondered, "Now what?" The Lees were within earshot and we yelled as loud as we could for help. Finally Johnny Lee, who was six years older than I, awakened, and lit a lantern and headed toward us. He did not know what our problem was, so he brought both a shotgun and a rifle, thinking that if it were a snake, a shotgun would be the best weapon, otherwise, a rifle would do the best.

He came past where the animal had screamed and did not see anything, so we guessed our yelling had the desired effect and scared the animal away. By this time it was daylight and we carried our buckets home with eyes darting in all directions. Mom was just getting ready to come look for us as we were gone for quite a spell.

We never heard the animal again, although we had a few instances where the hound dogs refused to hunt and a strange odor was smelled in the woods. To this day, no one knows what kind of animal it was, with guesses going toward it being a panther that had somehow found its way into the mountain.

THE
OLD RUGGED CROSS

On a hill far away stood an old rugged cross,
The emblem of suffering and shame;
And I love that old cross where the dearest and best
For a world of lost sinners was slain.
So I will cherish the old rugged cross
Till my trophies at last I lay down;
I will cling to the old rugged cross
And exchange it someday for a crown.

Oh, that old rugged cross so despised by the world
Has a wondrous attraction for me;
for the dear lamb of God left his glory above,
to bear it to dark Calvary,
So I will cherish that old rugged cross
Till my trophies at last I lay down;
I will cling to the old rugged cross
And exchange it someday for a crown.

In the old rugged cross, stained with blood so divine,
A wondrous beauty I see;
For 'twas on that old cross Jesus suffered and died

To pardon and sanctify me,
So I will cherish that old rugged cross
Till my trophies at last I lay down;
I will cling to that old rugged cross
And exchange it someday for a crown.

To the old rugged cross I will ever be true,
Its shame and reproach gladly bear;
Then he'll call me someday to my home far away,
Where his glory forever I will share,
So I will cling to that old rugged cross,
Till my trophies at last I lay down;
I will cling to that old rugged cross
And exchange it someday for a crown.

Mom loved God. She had been raised a Baptist and became a Methodist after marrying Dad. Mount Carmel Methodist church was about a half mile away and afforded the area with the closest church. There was another Methodist church in Frogtown, called Providence Chapel, and located about four miles back in the mountains. Mount Carmel had its preaching service in the morning every other Sunday with Providence Chapel on the same Sunday in the afternoon. These two churches were a part of the White Post charge consisting of a total of seven churches. The larger churches (over in the Valley) had preaching every Sunday with the smaller ones every other Sunday. On the odd Sundays, only Sunday school was held, with the local church superintendent in charge.

Paying out the minister's salary was always a problem, especially during the thirties. Each church was assessed a certain part of his salary and it was necessary that this assessment was paid by the end of the church year in order to be assured of the preacher showing up the next year.

One year I remember, in particular. At the end of the appointed time, Mount Carmel was short of meeting its obligation by some thirty-five dollars. The solution to this dilemma was to keep passing the collection plate until it was paid. On the third time around, Mom put in her last dollar—I do not mean the last dollar she had on her, I mean the last dollar she had. I do not remember how the collection turned out as my attention was on that last dollar, as I was old enough to be aware of how poor we were.

It was awfully quiet on the walk home. As we were going up the path toward the house and just as we reached the brow of the hill, there standing in the middle of the path was a skunk. Not just any old skunk, but a coal black one. All the skunks I had ever seen before (or after, for that matter) had some white on their back and the wider the white stripe, the less valuable the pelt.

Every one knows that a skunk is given the right of way and I started to begin my detour. Mom, on the other hand, picked up a stick and walked directly toward the skunk. I knew what was going to happen next; that skunk was going to turn around and some Sunday clothes were going to have to be buried for a spell to make them wearable again. Not this time. The skunk did not turn or move at all and Mom killed that skunk with the stick. No odor, no mess. I skinned the skunk and Mom sold the uncured hide to the fur buyer for the unheard sum of ten dollars. Mom was sure of the price because God had promised a return of tenfold and this hide had an ecclesiastical price tag on it that no fur buyer could have resisted. The fur buyer would have probably given more, as he too had never seen a coal black skunk, but Mom would not have wanted God to think that she was greedy. Whenever I feel the world sinking in on me, I think of that miracle of the skunk, and the order of the universe is restored.

It was said of early Christians, "See how they love one another." This was their identity. So it is with the Methodists, except their identity is singing. It is said that one does not need to read the sign out front, you just have to listen. Thus, one of the essentials of the church was the organ, and secondly, someone to play it. Mount Carmel went through a period when they did not have an organist. To solve this problem, Mom took a correspondence course and learned how to play the organ. She somehow found the money to purchase an organ at an estate sale so that she could practice at home. When we were growing up, we loved to have Mom play the organ. Today the organ is at our daughter's house in Laguna Niguel, and whenever I see the organ, memories of growing up come flooding back into my mind. (How the organ made a 3000-mile journey is another story.)

I am sure that no one would ever have invited her to give a recital but growing up to mom's organ playing was pure enjoyment. Her favorite hymn was "The Old Rugged Cross" followed closely by "Bringing in the Sheaves." She would never volunteer her services if anyone else was around to play, but could be counted on when needed and since Mom never missed a Sunday, the future of services at Mount Carmel was assured. When Providence Chapel went through the same problem, Mom would start out walking the four miles to their church and be there "just in case they needed someone to play the organ." And as it was normal to have the organist choose one hymn, you can be sure that "The Old Rugged Cross" would be a part of that Sunday service.

Mom never lost her love of God and every Sunday found her and first cousin, Meta Erickson, at Mount Carmel, along with a group of stalwarts that kept the church going. Many years later, I would make my weekly Sunday call to visit with Mom over the phone and I would time it around her getting home from church. Not only would I get to visit with Mom, but also I would get caught up on the weekly news, fresh from the church. No newspaper could have competed with that pipeline. One Sunday I called and the phone rang for quite a while. Mom, all out of breath, finally answered it. She said in a panting voice that she had run all the way home from Mount Carmel because it was pouring down rain. She had tried to wait it out, but since it had been raining for the past 24 hours and did not show signs of stopping, she finally headed home.

After saying that she had never seen it rain so hard, I questioned her sanity of getting out to walk to church. "How many people were at church?" I asked.

"Two" she replied, "Me and Meta."

"How long did you stay?" I persisted. "Well, as long as it takes to have Sunday School," she replied, adding that the two of them had a full-length service.

"Mom, you're out of your mind." I told her. "You will catch your death of cold."

With that she felt compelled to let me know her reasons for wanting to fight the elements to go to church. She reminded me that the area had been going through the most severe drought in recent times and that last Sunday, the entire service was spent praying for rain.

"Now that our prayers were answered," she chided me, "how could I not go and thank Him?"

ON THE TRAIL
OF
THE LONESOME PINE

On a mountain in Virginia
stands a lonesome pine
Just below is the cabin home
Of a little girl of mine.
Her name is June
and very, very soon
She'll belong to me.
For I know she is waiting for me
'Neath that lone pine tree

In the Blue Ridge Mountains of Virginia
On The Trail of the Lonesome Pine
In the pale moonshine our hearts entwine
Where she carved her name and I carved mine.
Oh! June, Like the mountains I am blue
Like the pine, I am lonesome for you
In the Blue Ridge Mountains of Virginia
On the trail of the Lonesome Pine.

I can hear the tinkling waterfall
Far among the hills
Blue birds each sing so merrily
To his mate in rapture trills.
They seem to say
"Your June is lonesome, too
Longing fills her eyes
She is waiting for you patiently
Where the pine tree sighs"

In the Blue Ridge Mountains of Virginia
On The Trail of the Lonesome Pine
In the pale moonshine our hearts entwine
Where she carved her name and I carved mine.
Oh! June, Like the mountains I am blue
Like the pine, I am lonesome for you
In the Blue Ridge Mountains of Virginia
on the trail of the Lonesome Pine.

By the end of the thirties, my world was from the top of the mountains to the Shenandoah River. Just to the east bank, of course, as we were not allowed to swim in the river. The Shenandoah had a well earned reputation that made the most experienced swimmer beware its eddies, whirlpools and rapids. Running along the west slope of the Blue Ridge made it susceptible to fast changes in its character because of the swift runoff from the mountains.

We became intimate with the old roads, paths and shortcuts, and explored all of the hollows (pronounced "hollers" in the mountains). Our house was on top of a hill running east and west on the lower slope of the Blue Ridge. As we looked south, we could see four or five similar but higher ridges, which came alive in the fall and spring with colors indescribable. The Dogwood blossoms were a welcome sign of spring after the winter snows and the spring winds and rains. In the fall, the wide variety of hardwoods turned into a vivid and multi-colored spectacle that left no doubt as to who was the master painter.

In the summer, the thunder storms would bring rain and we would watch the mountains turn to a darker green as the rain storm went through the trees, or to a lighter green as a wind-only storm would turn the leaves over exposing their lighter underside. In drought times, the direction of the storm was watched carefully and hopes were raised or dashed watching the route of the changing leaves and whether they turned lighter or darker.

To the east we watched the sunrise through Ashby's Gap and the haze that gave the mountains their name. The sounds of the woods were a part of us and we learned to recognize most of them. The lack of sounds was just as important, as that told us of something in the woods that had alerted the birds or the squirrels. The sound of a whippoorwill or mourning dove in the late evening or early morning would bring conversations to a halt while the beauty of the moment surrounded us. We kids would chase fireflies in the summer dusk and put the captured ones in a Mason jar to watch them light up. Mom made sure that they were always released to fly off into the grass.

To the north were mostly trees and the only long distant view was the rare northern lights. I remember one time they were so bright that we thought Mr. Macdonald's house, located a couple of ridges away, was on fire.

To the west was the Shenandoah River and Valley. On clear days we could see the smoke and sometimes hear the sound of the whistle of the train as it ran through the Valley. The sound of the train would bring about a certain sadness in Mom, as she remembered the train accident that killed two cousins near Berryville as they crossed the railroad tracks going to Aunt Alma's house.

And the skies—in the winter when the nights had a bite to them, we would brave the cold just to stare at the stars that seemed so close that you could touch them. Cars and trucks going up and down the mountain were an ever-present background noise that one learned to tune out so that we were hardly aware that they were there. We did learn to listen to the shifting of the gears that pronounced how heavy some of the trucks were loaded as they pulled the steep grade at the bottom of our hill.

On rare occasions we would hear a car turn off and head up our hill and we would try to guess as to whom it might be. We learned that Sundays were likely to be a time for visiting and the killing of a chicken to make dinner a treat for us all. In lean times a laying hen might have to be sacrificed, as no one went home on Sunday without staying for dinner.

Visitors that came by automobile during the week were more than likely bringing bad news, so it was with trepidation that we awaited the arrival of the car that worked its way up the hill on a weekday.

At home, for a short period during the late thirties, we had a roomer. Dad's first cousin, "Little" Walter Royston, who was a giant of a man, came to stay while he had a job cutting timber. He would spend the evenings sharpening his axe, while keeping Linton and me entranced with stories of his days working on the railroad. He wore the uniform of a railroad man, bib overalls, denim bill cap and all. But the one true proof of a railroad man was the railroad watch. This he would pull out from his watch pocket with much preamble, snapping open the cover and studying the face with the intensity worthy of the occasion. We would be in awe of such a watch, praying that we too could become owners of a railroad watch, knowing all the while that the chances of this happening ranked right along with the parting of the Red Sea. We never did get the railroad watch, but we came close enough. One Christmas, a short time after, brought us Ingersoll watches. There was no snap cover with a locomotive etched on it, but it was a genuine stem winding time keeping watch that could be heard ticking for great distances. I doubt that one could get through airport security today with such an instrument, but it was just what young lads needed as a part of their growing up in the thirties.

The mountains and woods around us were our friends. Once we left the clearing around our house, we could head in just about any direction and walk as far as we wanted without seeing or hearing another individual. In those days little or no property was posted and it all became our domain. As we learned to hunt, we stayed away from areas near other folk's homes in recognition that the wildlife there belonged to them and their hunting skills. The mountains had an abundance of squirrels, and to many a mountain family that provided the red meat for the table.

Between each ridge was a hollow that had a branch running through it. Only a few were large enough to have to worry about getting wet while being crossed. We would always inspect them for minnows, remembering the good spots that could provide bait for fishing in the river. Since I did not care much for fishing, I left the minnow watching for others. The Shenandoah, once renowned for its bass fishing, had its fish population reduced to carp and mud cats by a polluting chemical plant located near Front Royal.

Some people put out the illegal bush lines which would catch the fish and keep it on the hook until it was tended—usually late in the twilight, in case someone was watching. I think the game warden was much more interested in patrolling the west bank than the east bank so the mountain people had little to fear, or maybe it was the game warden that did the fearing as his trips across the Shenandoah were rare.

Mom was always on a search for flowers that she could transplant to our yard. Her Holy Grail was a rare shrub, which she called the Mountain Arbutus. She would find one and carefully carry it home and try to make it grow. She had a green thumb on just about any other plant or flower, but she never got the Mountain Arbutus to grow.

She knew the locations of the burnt houses that had been abandoned. A lot of these had flowers around them that were now growing wild. We would help her dig them out and carry them back home where she planted them with all the care of a Luther Burbank. Included in this knowledge was the history of the families that had lived in those homes, and she would weave many tales while we were doing the work involved in the flower transplanting. Mom knew the history of the old roads and paths. From her we learned what the country was like before the paved roads were put in that allowed the unconcerned traveler to escape the area as fast as possible.

Many of these roads felt the footprints of the early explorers as well as the Union and Confederate soldiers who met in the many skirmishes through out the area. Mrs. John Lee, who lived at the bottom of the Fox Trap in the original Royston house, told us of the old Indian graves near the side of the road, causing us to give that spot a wide berth as it was her conviction that the area was haunted. Wildcat Hollow was one of my favorite places. It had a wide creek that the road generally followed, each crossing the other a number of times as they worked their way back toward Mr. Pete Cornwall's property. We would walk from its start to its end, a distance of about two miles. Since we were mostly bare-foot, fording the creek was looked forward to. We would keep a wary eye out for the wildcats that must be around someplace, otherwise why the name? An occasional automobile would come through, and we would fade into the woods and they would pass us by without ever knowing of our existence.

A few yards up Wildcat Hollow was the Spout Spring, belonging to Mrs. John Lee. It was located across the branch near the base of the mountain. The actual spring was a distance up the side of the mountain; however, someone had made a small reservoir out of some rocks and ran a length of pipe to the bottom where the water spouted out. In drought times this spring was the only source of water for miles around, and cars would line up on the road to wait their turn to fill their buckets and tubs. The spring was a mile or so walk from our house, so we envied the people from across the river who only had to carry the water from the spring to their cars, some hundred yards distance.

A little farther up Wildcat Hollow lived Mr. Will and Miss Sarah Sillman. Again the branch had to be crossed to get to their log home and in flood times there was some concern for their safety. They were brother and sister and Miss Sarah had dedicated her life to taking care of Mr. Will, who had been shot and gassed in the First World War. The gas had affected Mr. Will's voice so that he talked in a guttural way that was only understandable by someone who had been around him a while. Linton and I cut firewood for them off the side of the mountain behind their house. The hill was very steep and the cutting was probably pretty dangerous as I look back on it, but we never gave it any thought at the time. Mr. Will had a treasure trove of Wild West pulp magazines that I would spend hours reading. I am not sure that Mom approved of my reading material; however, she knew that my wood cutting skills suffered at Mr. Wills' from the time it took me to finish a simple task of cutting some wood. The cutting of the wood was "neighborly" so no money changed hands. At the time I did not appreciate Miss Sarah and her taking care of Mr. Will, but now I always think of her when I hear someone mention selfless dedication.

Proceeding up Wildcat Hollow, there was one more house and barn (owned by Mr. and Mrs. Shaw) and then no human activity until you reached the turn off to the Slack place. This, at one time, was a good farm with lots of flat areas, rather than the ridges and hollows that were prevalent in the mountains. A barn alongside a pond, horses and cows made it a much admired place in the hills. The road ended at Mr. Pete Cornwall's farm, which had land pretty much like the

Slack place. Mr. Cornwell had a reputation of being standoffish, so we did not venture onto his property. It was said that the original trail coming down from Ashby's Gap followed Wildcat Hollow. It was certainly less steep, but would have added miles to the trip.

Another old road took off from Wildcat Hollow, going onto the abandoned "Mac" Cornwall place. We loved to squirrel hunt there. The squirrels would travel along the old rail and stone fences, which were in the process of falling down. If we did not need the meat, we would just sit and watch them as they carried acorns or hickory nuts to some area near their nests.

The woods were filled with dead chestnut oak trees, which had been hit by a chestnut tree blight. Most were still standing, but in the end would be sawed down to provide kindling wood. The woods were filled with many species of hard wood trees—numerous types of Oaks, Maple, Ash, Hemlock, Poplar, Hickory, Locust, and Gum—to name a few. Each was used for their best purpose. I remember Dad making a pull cart with the axle made out of hickory. If you wanted a wood that did not split, use Gum. It grew straight but the grain was twisted like a corkscrew. Locust was the choice for fence posts as it emitted a smell that bugs hated, thus was resistant to rot in the ground. Poplar was a soft hardwood and was cut for barrel staves, as it was easy to work. Dogwood was a gnarly wood not good for any utilitarian purpose, which was probably fortunate as it was the state flower and illegal to cut down. We learned where the good stands of nut bearing trees were located as this would be good locations for squirrel hunting in the fall.

As the older folks died and the young moved out of the mountains, it was not uncommon to find houses and farms abandoned in the mountains. As we wandered through the hills we would come upon them, the houses empty with the doors standing open. The gardens would be in a state of reverting to nature's design with fences falling down and bushes taking over where vegetables and fruit once grew.

The laws in Virginia at that time made it difficult for people to become owners by paying the taxes on the property. Even if the land were sold for taxes, the law allowed that heirs could return and pay the back taxes and reclaim the property and any improvements on it. So they remained a "no man's land" and houses that once were vibrant with the sounds of life, now suffered through their own death throes as they died with no one to minister to them. Invariably there were ghosts involved and not even a transient would stay the night.

Mom was always on the lookout for strawberry patches and she and Meta would guard their locations as best they could. When the berries were ripe, they would take buckets and go "strawberrying." They also did this for blackberries and raspberries, but my love was strawberries.

One of my favorites was strawberry shortcake. The shortcake was real short-cake and not the angel food or pound cake that has become popular in later years. Mom would make a three or four-tiered shortcake and we would make a meal out of it. To this day, I have trouble driving by a commercial patch when straw-berries are in season.

Mom also made something called "chow-chow" pickles. This happened at the end of the growing season when the first frost hit. She would collect all the cucumbers, onions and green tomatoes and would turn those and any other left over vegetables into "chow-chow" pickles. It was a sweet concoction, something like, but completely different from, sweet relish. Mom hated to see winter come, but loved the "chow-chow" pickles and green fried tomatoes that were made pos-sible by that first frost. Talk about mixed emotions.

The forest had its own recycling plan. Clearings left unused would regress to trees, with blueberry bushes the first to appear, then the pines, and after that the hardwoods. One of the last stands of pines in the area was on the south hill of our property, which Dad decided to cut for pulpwood. This was in the summer of 1941 as I was finishing fifth grade.

Dad, being crippled, did mostly supervisory work, along with cutting off the limbs of the trees that Linton and I sawed down. Since we tackled this job during the summer when the pine resin sap was running, a rag that was saturated with lard was a most welcome asset to keep the saw from binding in the saw cut. Lin-ton and I were somewhat accomplished woodsmen by this time in our life so the job was within our capabilities. Being typical growing boys we would have rather spent the summer at other pursuits, but it was not to be. Little did we know how much growing up we would be doing because of the cutting of those pines.

After cutting the trees, they were sawed to length, debarked and then stacked into cord piles. The instrument used as the debarking tools was made from leaf springs taken from an old abandoned Model T Ford. A lot of hours were spent keeping them sharp, so our evenings were occupied also. The days went by and by early July we had an array of trees cut, some waiting to be trimmed, others waiting to be cut to length, a large amount waiting to be debarked and stacked.

The day finally came when the felling part was almost over. At the end of the day only one last lonesome pine was left standing. I was all for getting that tree down before calling it a day, but Linton suggested that we wait until tomorrow and do it with proper ceremony. It was not "Woodsman, spare that tree," but it sure worked out that way. I do not know when that tree ever met its fate, but it was not by our hands.

That night, Dad had a stroke and after a two-week illness, died. The pulp wood project would wait to the end of summer and beyond before being completed. For many years I would look at that old lonesome pine and remember Dad, as he would stand there leaning on his cane giving us directions. In my mind the pine became Dad, and I gave that tree a wide berth to make sure no limb became the cane that reached for me.

Dad was buried at Mount Carmel Cemetery. There were many muted conversations of which I could hear only snatches; mostly having to do with, "What was going to happen to the kids?" The gist of the conversations from Mom's brothers was that no good would come from trying to raise the boys in the hills. Mom gently reminded them that it was not where they were raised, but how they were raised that counted. Thus they got back into their shiny cars and returned to the cities, thankful I believe, that they had offered to do their duty, but hadn't been taken up on it.

After the funeral, we did go away for a week to Washington, DC and visited at my half brother's house. This was a giant step in my education that probably only set me back a few years. Our nephew, Richard, (of the corn thinning fame) was our tutor and we got to see life in the big city. He was adept at begging newspapers, bottles and cans from the neighborhood and selling them to the refuse collecting companies. I can hear him today as he went along the streets, pulling a wagon, yelling, "Any old newspapers, rags, magazines?" Any he collected were deposited in the wagon and sold at the local collection company. We played baseball in the nearby parks, even went swimming in the municipal pool.

One day the entire family went to the zoo and I got to see all the ""wild" animals that I had only read about before. The Washington Monument and many other large buildings became a blur in my mind. But far and away the highlight of the trip and what was to affect my entertainment habits probably to this very day was the viewing of my first movie.

Dad had been absolutely against our seeing movies. I am not sure that he had ever seen a movie, but he was sure that they were a sin of first class ranking. Today I think he was a lot smarter than I gave him credit for, with the films now being shown some fifty to sixty years later.

My first movie could have been some memorable Walt Disney film, and I could have been led gently into this world of make believe. No, they took me to see *"Blood and Sand,"* a movie starring Tyrone Power and, I believe, Linda Darnel, and the meanest bunch of bulls I have ever seen. I did not have any trouble with Tyrone or Linda, but those bulls scared the daylights out of me. There were a lot of shots where the bull came straight at the camera and therefore straight at me. I took refuge behind the seatback in front of me in hope that he would pass me by. They should have called that movie "From Here to Eternity," for that is how long it lasted.

The return home to the mountains was welcome relief from the anxieties of the city and we picked up our world and continued on.

OH SHENANDOAH

Oh Shenandoah, I long to hear you,
Away you rolling river,
Oh Shenandoah, I long to hear you,
Away I am bound to go, 'cross the wide Missouri.

Oh Shenandoah, I love your daughter,
Away you rolling river.
Oh Shenandoah, I love your daughter,
Away, I am bound to go, 'cross the wide Missouri.

Oh Shenandoah, I am bound to leave you,
Away, you rolling river.
Oh Shenandoah, I will not deceive you,
Away I am bound to go, 'cross the wide Missouri.

Oh Shenandoah, I long to hear you,
Away, you rolling river.
Oh Shenandoah, I long to hear you,
Away I am bound to go, 'cross the wide Missouri.

1941 continued on its way to being the momentous year not only for the world, but also for my own expanding environment. Until this time my life was limited to the Blue Ridge, except for a short period of time spent living at Grand-dad's farm near Berryville during the fall of 1938. (During this time we went to the elementary school at Berryville and had learned some of the ways of the big schools.) Now I was ready for the big time.

The decision to close the one-room schools in the summer of 1941 was apparently done in haste. As a part of the process, the large school in Boyce was inspected and, lo and behold, it was condemned. What to do now? After some head scratching, it was decided to allow the school to remain open for high school students only and to find some other place for the grade schoolers.

This dilemma was partially solved by a lady who owned a farm about two miles west of Boyce. She gave the use of her home to the school board for an entire school year while she left for an extended trip to Europe. What she did when the war broke out, I do not know, but I spent my sixth grade going to school at the "Duck Pond" farm. Just for the record, the farm was owned by Mrs. L.J. Langbien, and I wonder if she could have anticipated the wear and tear on the premises brought on by an active group of kids. There were other buildings used in other locations, but they were of no interest to me as an eleven-year-old, who was trying to cope with my new surroundings.

My schoolteacher that year was Miss Jesse Carpenter who also taught me the following year in the seventh grade in the new school. My memories of that year include being called to the phone to get a message of a relative dying. I do not remember whom, but I recall the incident because the phone was one of those modern ones with a single piece to both hear and speak. My embarrassment was complete when I tried talking into the earpiece. Why could not it have been the two-piece variety that I had seen at Mrs. Tom Lee's? (the only one in the mountain at that time).

Fall dragged on, and as I recall it was filled with a lot of cold blustery weather. Mom found a buyer for the pulpwood that we had been cutting when Dad died, using the most of the proceeds to pay off Dad's funeral expenses.

Of course, this was before any electricity or modern communications were in the mountains, and we paid no heed to the outside world that was bringing us all to the brink of war. I remember precisely December 7th, although I was not to find out about Pearl Harbor until the following day at school. Sunday morning always meant church at Mount Carmel. It was one of those days where the wind just tore through any clothes you had on. There had been a slight snow mixed with sleet and no one wanted to be outside. But after church, outside I had to be, as wood had to be cut for the following week.

Kindling was an essential part of the wood cutting routine. Good kindling was getting harder to find as the normal source (the dead but still standing chestnut oak trees) was getting scarce. This particular day, I remembered a chestnut oak tree that had been hit by lightning, whose splintered stump was still unused. On that day, it was my choice as a source of kindling. As I chopped down on the stump, one of the vertical splinters caught the skin on the back of my hand, making a wound that did no serious damage, but left me with a perfect "V" scar on my left hand. Since this turned out to be Pearl Harbor day, I claimed this "V" as my "V—for victory" signal. The scar was to help in 1944 and 1945 to cheer up Mom as my brother, Linton, fought in the South Pacific. I would remind her on those down days that nothing would happen to Linton because of my visible "V" sign. In reality, I now know that it was Mom's prayers that brought him back safely.

Winter and spring came and went. Trips to Winchester on Saturday, while not quite routine in their happenings, were avidly looked forward to. We typically hitched a ride with Bill Erickson on his lumber truck. Most of the time the sawmill would work Saturday morning and then Bill would deliver a load of lumber on the way to Winchester. To unload the lumber, Bill had a method of backing up the truck and by a sudden braking movement, start the load to slide off the back of the truck. Three or four of these sequences would normally be sufficient to drop off the entire load, untouched by human hands. On certain occasions it had to be unloaded by hand, either at the desire of the buyer or if the load had to be split at different destinations. At these times we all would help with the unloading, so naturally our hopes were always for the automated method.

Winchester was the only "large" city in the area having a population of about 10,000 to 12,000. Downtown was Main Street, which was about four blocks long. Some businesses were on side streets running perpendicular to Main Street. It was not long before we knew the downtown and the eastern part of Winchester as well as we knew the mountains. What was on the west side of town, I do not know to this day.

Bill would park the truck on a side street and announce the departure time in no uncertain terms. Whether he would have left without us I do not know, but we were not about to find out. Normally we had time to take in a movie and wander around town a bit. Bill's wife, Meta (my first cousin) would do her grocery shopping at the A&P or at the Safeway store and then do other shopping. She was a great window shopper and this helped us to keep from being left behind by Bill, who could have bought out all the stores in Winchester in about thirty minutes.

Movies for me meant the Saturday western at the Palace or if playing, a musical at the Capitol. Linton preferred the ghoulish or the sci-fi that, if playing, would be at the Capitol. Depending on the number of persons who had ridden with Bill, we would either ride in the cab of the truck or if filled, on the back of the truck. Doing that today would get the driver a ticket before he cleared the outskirts of town. Being a lumber truck, there was no bed to stand on. We stood on the cross braces, held onto the cab for protection and off we went, as we watched the pavement roll below us. I am sure we kept our guardian angel busy, but we thought nothing of the potential dangers.

During the spring and summer of 1942, the war was far away for a twelve-year-old. Linton had turned 14 in October of 1941 and was feeling the juices of manhood and soon talked of being in the war. The closest the war got to me was the fear of not having the apple blossom festival, something I had been looking forward to since I had heard others talk about it. Just my luck to have it canceled just because of some war many miles away. (It is funny, I remember the talk of it being canceled, but do not remember whether or not it was. So much for the important things in your life.)

As the war started to take its toll on the manpower supply in the county, the depression went away in a hurry. Anybody that was able to work had a job waiting. Mom first took a job in Front Royal, a hard 15 miles away. It meant her boarding in Front Royal during the week and coming home on the weekends. We were "latch key" children!! Meta Erickson kept an eye on us and made sure we had a certain amount of variety in our diet. Linton became a better than average cook. As I recall this was the spring of '42. After some months of this, Mom came back, and then spent most of the war years working in the apples and at Mr. Sechrist's stave mill. This mill made barrel staves that were used to make nail kegs and other small barrels. The job Mom had in Front Royal was in a chicken slaughterhouse, and it was not one that she looked forward to.

The economy of Clarke County centered on the apple orchards. Before the war, the men did most of the outside work, which was almost a year-round job. The process started in January or February with trimming and pruning. Spraying was a never-ending job. The buds were sprayed, then the blossoms, and the small apples and the large apples all got their dose. As soon as the apples were "set" and about the size of a marble, the thinning process began, involving reducing the clumps of three or four apples to one apple. This was done with pruning clippers and today would be an exercise regiment that would tax the best in shape at the health spa. Workdays were ten hours long and involved carrying and setting 18 to 30 foot tall wooden ladders.

Most of the apple orchards were owned by Senator Harry Flood Byrd, who also had a bridge crossing the Shenandoah River named after him. (I have often wondered if his middle name had any thing to do with the naming of the bridge.)

The many varieties of apples led to overlapping of tasks, with picking of the early varieties (Golden Delicious) starting in June, to the final ground hogging of the latest (York) around Christmas time. Ground hogging was the name given to the picking up of apples that had fallen to the ground. On large trees this could be a substantial amount, upward of 40 to 50 bushels per tree. Any apple that fell off the tree would start to rot. Since ground hogging could not start until after the final picking was done, the final array was a medley of "all rot" to "bruised" apples.

Ground hogging consisted of judging the amount of rot and then picking up those apples that met the standards of the cannery. Once the collected apples hit the canning process, workers would cut out the rot and the remaining "good" apple became applesauce. To this day I can taste applesauce and tell the quality of the preparation of the apples that made it into the sauce.

By the summer of '42, most of the mountain people were getting onto the old blue school bus, owned by Byrd, and heading to the packing shed in Berryville. Arriving there, they would disperse to the various locations where they worked the day. Before picking began, all the work was outside, including the cutting of saplings to be used for props that were needed as the apples matured and the limbs began to sag. The more experienced workers gravitated toward the jobs that were piecework, as these were the higher paying jobs. The picking and packing normally were the select piece work jobs, where as the propping, spraying and thinning were the hourly jobs. Mom worked first as a picker and in later years as a picker and a packer. As a picker she had to do the ground hogging during the months of November and December. On Saturdays and school holidays, I worked with her. Pickers had their own identifying tickets, which were placed, in every basket. There was always the fear that some one would substitute someone else's ticket and every one kept their own count to check against the paycheck that came at Saturday noon.

In 1942 there were still enough men around to do the extra heavy work, but by 1943 most of the draftable men were gone. The older boys took over the men's jobs, such as loading the trucks and operating the sprayers. The trucks would go down through the orchard between the trees with two sprayers on each side, one spraying high and one spraying low. Linton worked as a sprayer and you could tell which side of the truck he worked from as his trousers had a different color from one side to the other. I often wondered how his lungs survived the effects of the spray.

As the picking began, he went on to loading trucks. He and his buddy, Walter Johnson, would vie for who could pick up the highest stack of apple crates and hoist them on to the truck bed. The pay was 40 cents an hour and the days were ten hours long. No wonder we did not have time or the energy to get into trouble.

Of course, I was a runt of a kid with no muscles, looking like something out of the National Geographic. No way could I make it in the world of the big boys. It was decided, however, that the younger boys would work as a team with a woman, picking apples. In their wisdom, it was decreed that the lady, being of the fairer sex, would get to handle the short ladder and pick the lower branches, while we striplings would carry the longer ladder and pick the top branches.

In some ways it made sense, in that the woman was the breadwinner and needed the highest return on her energy and the lad was a bit more agile than their female partner was. The part that did not make sense was that the tall ladder weighed two or three times as much as the shorter one and most of the ladies could carry the shorter ladder in one hand while adjusting their bandana with the other. The youth, on the other hand, staggered down the row, weighed down with the system that prevailed. The secret, of course, was to stand the ladder at the beginning of the day with a little help from a friend, then to carry it in that elevated position the rest of the day. I learned to stand the ladder against the tree almost vertical, so that it would be easy to return it to a vertical position as it was moved around the tree and down the row.

A part of the learning curve was to make sure there were no limbs in the way or tall grass to snag the bottom as you attempted to move it around the trees. Otherwise you were pressing your luck to get someone to help you re-stand the ladder.

As the 1943 school year approached, it was obvious that the kids were still needed in the orchards, so we were allowed to stay out of school for a period of time to help with the bulk of the picking. My partner for a couple of years was Mrs. Freeland Kent. We worked well together and were friends for many years. Her husband Mr. Kent drove the school bus on our route all through my high school years.

In 1943, I was in my first year of high school and Linton starting in his third year. Linton turned 16 in October and announced that he was joining the Navy. His threat to Mom, that he would quit school and go to work if she did not sign for him, finally wore her down. Armed with a doctored family bible to show he was seventeen and had Mom's permission, he headed off into the Navy within a month after he was sixteen. He went through boot camp at Bainbridge, MD, came home for boot leave, was sent to gunner's mate school, then to the South Pacific on an LST. His boot leave was the last we saw of him until July of 1945, when he came home on a 30-day leave. He had been through the battles of Saipan, Tinian, Palau and Okinawa and others that I do not remember. At Okinawa, he saw the USS Franklin take the Kamikaze hit, not realizing until later that his cousin, Conrad, was one of the marines killed in that attack.

He had finished his leave in July of 1945 and was heading back to Portland, Oregon to pick up a new LST when the A-bombs were dropped on Japan, bringing the war to a close. There was great rejoicing at home as we knew his new LST was going to be a part of the invasion of Japan. Linton got out of the Navy in January of 1946 at the age of eighteen but with the heart of a 40-year-old. The war took its toll, even though he did not have a physical mark on him, unless you count the tattoos.

The Sechrist family moved into the mountains from West Virginia during the thirties. Mr. Sechrist owned a sawmill and a stave mill, which was located on the way to the top of the mountain, about a mile from home. They lived in a house that had seen previous duty as a filling station and store. I remember their front door entrance was under the canopy where cars used to get gasoline, so it served as a porch. There were a number of Sechrist children. Harold (known as "Buckshot") and Iona were about my age and went to school with me. Wilma was about Linton's age.

Mr. Sechrist and his mills brought much needed cash into the mountains and employed many of the mountain people. One son, Trumont, was much older and ran the mill when his dad was absent. Calvin, the next youngest, did everything around the mill from cutting timber to driving truck. Shirley and Mary were younger than I was. Later Shirley became the driving force behind the operations along with Trumont, but this was long after I left the mountains.

Mom started to work for Mr. Sechrist and was the off-bearer at the stave mill for a number of years. Barrel staves are cut with a special saw which I can best describe as a giant hole saw. The timber was cut to stave lengths, mounted in a securing device, which was then fed into the saw where stave shapes were cut. The piece of wood was turned numerous times so that the width of the staves ended in two general sizes. It was Mom's job to catch the stave when it was sawed and while it was still inside the saw. Mr. Sechrist was a true artisan with the stave saw, and Mom was his first choice as off-bearer.

The staves were stacked in special piles, crisscrossing each other with one wide stave and one narrow stave making up each row. They were stacked about five to six feet high and anchored with a heavy object such as a rock, and left to dry for a period of time. After drying was completed, they were then baled in a set manner, again with the wide and narrow staves forming alternate rows.

A device with a long handle to create leverage was used to compress the bale so that they could be tied off with binder twine. The staves were then ready to be sold to the cooperage for the making of barrels. Mom also worked stacking and baling staves. On Saturdays, I would help Mom at this job, but she made sure I never got close to the stave saw. Mr. Sechrist, of course, did not cut staves all the time as he also had a sawmill to operate.

Since the stave mill was partially covered, it afforded some protection from the elements, and I am sure scheduling of the mill was tied in with the weather. Winter brought the necessity of wearing coats and gloves, which added an increased element of danger to the operation, as there was always the chance of clothes being caught in the machinery. The Sechrists were great neighbors. One of the many things we could count on was a Sechrist truck to make some runs up the hill to our house after a deep snow to make it easier for us to get in and out.

Fig Newtons: Today the taste still brings back memories. One Saturday, I was hitchhiking back home from Winchester. It was one of those days when no one picked me up. I would walk and put my thumb out, then walk some more. I must have walked three or four miles outside of Winchester, when finally Calvin Sechrist drove by in his lumber truck and stopped to pick me up. By this time the hour was way past noon and my stomach was letting me know that it needed some attention.

On the seat beside Calvin was a carton of Fig Newtons. I had never seen Fig Newtons before, much less eaten any. Calvin saw me eyeing the box and asked if I wanted one. I did not know what it was supposed to taste like but the stomach put in a strong affirmative vote. I tried one and hunger took over. Before it was through, I had eaten the entire box. To this day, Fig Newtons are a great tasting food, all because they were introduced to me at the right time…when I was hungry enough to eat anything.

Another sawmill in the mountain also came in during the thirties. The patriarch of the family owning that sawmill was Mr. Elmer Erickson. He had operated a sawmill in the state of New York and had moved it to our mountains, chosen through some process of elimination. The sawmill along with the oxen that were used to pull the logs out of the woods were brought in on the train that unloaded in Boyce.

The event was before my memory, but it must have been quite a sight to see the oxen pulling the wagon loads of sawmill machinery from Boyce, some six miles across the Shenandoah to a sawmill location about five miles back off Route 50 past Frogtown. Mr. Erickson had purchased 800 plus acres of mountain land that still contained virgin timber. The sawmill was located in the middle of this timber so as to shorten the distance the oxen had to pull the logs. Sometime during the thirties the oxen were replaced by the now commonplace crawler tractor and the sawmill was moved to a location on our property alongside of the Shipe place, occupied by Bill and Meta Erickson.

Bill and Meta had moved into the Shipe place around 1938. I remember the first time I met Bill and for some reason his first words to me, "Do you live around here or ride a bicycle?" Now why in the world would I remember something like that? I went home and reported the meeting to Mom, who told me the relationship of the new neighbors. Meta was my first cousin and Bill was Elmer Erickson's son. Bill went on to become the best sawmill operator and timber handler in the area and inherited the mill when Mr. Erickson died in the forties.

Bill and Meta had five children, Elene, Ken, David, Harold and Dora Lee. All became a part of our family as we grew up together. Elene was six years younger than I was, with Ken a year or so behind her. David was a couple of years younger than Ken. Harold and Dora Lee were younger still and weren't as much a part of my growing up buddies.

Linton worked some at Erickson's sawmill, while I only tagged along. I occasionally did some work, such as off-bearing the slab wood that was only useful to be cut up for firewood. A John Deere stationary engine, through a flat belt, powered the sawmill. The sawdust was taken away by a drag conveyor that, in time, made a large sawdust pile on the downhill side of the mill. The logs to be sawed were dumped on the high side of the hill where they could be rolled onto the carriage using "peaveys" and "cant hooks."

The saw doing the cutting was a circular saw, which needed continual attention. This consisted of sharpening the teeth with a file and setting the teeth to cut a wide enough path to keep the blade from binding. Many years later, I had the opportunity to visit some sawmills in the Northwest and was astonished at their size and automated features.

Most of the workers around the sawmills had paid the price for being too familiar with the machinery, and Bill had a couple of fingers missing on one hand. Occasionally, someone would violate some basic rules and pay the penalty. The trip to the doctor or hospital was made in a car or truck as this was, of course, before the days of paramedics or ambulances. I remember Bill suffering serious back burns when the engine boiled over as he was working under it. It was at times like this that Mom was called and she seemed to know how to treat such injuries.

In 1946, timber cutting progress came to the mountains. The Erickson's bought a Continental Red Annie chain saw that drew a crowd every time it was fired up. The saw would draw laughter today, but in 1946, it was a giant step for the lumberjack. The crosscut saw was a thing of the past.

Of course, the saw still took two men to operate. The engine needed to remain in a somewhat level plane and changes in the saw's attitude was accomplished by rotating the saw blade section, while leaving the engine section stationary. The chain saw was somewhat unwieldy and could not be used to cut off branches, so the axe still had a use in the mountains.

Somewhere in here, I have to get in a sled-riding story. Some of our winters were heavy with snow, and others were so light we kids were praying for snow. If the snow was heavy, the schools closed and we stayed home. Then, as now, staying home meant, among other things, sled-riding. We did a lot on Mount Carmel Hill, down past the graveyard. Sometimes there would be eight or nine sleds and probably twice as many kids as there were never enough sleds to go around. The snow would start to melt during the day and at night would form a crust that you could almost sled-ride on. If you shifted the weight forward, the runners would break through the snow; the sled would stop; you would not. As a result your front side (most likely your cheek) would turn to an area full of blood. When this happened to me, I would head home crying and breaking up Linton's sled-riding, as he was sort of responsible for me.

Later, I did a shot on my own that most probably could have cost my life. We had a good sleet storm, which coated everything with about an inch of ice. For some reason I decided to sled-ride down our road toward Route 50. The hill was very steep as it approached the highway and my speed was well beyond my control.

Normally, I would ditch the ride by running the sled off the road before it hit the highway. But for some reason I did not, or could not, and I hit the highway at a high rate of speed. Directly across from our road was the Wiley's road and if everything went well, I could go across the highway and end up at the Wiley's. This time there was a minor problem; there was a loaded semi-trailer crawling ever so slowly up the mountain. As I hit the highway, he was directly in my path. What to do?? The sled would not steer too well because of the ice, and there was a sure-fire danger of turning into the wheels of the trailer. Since I did not have a lot of time to think about it, instinct took over, and I decided to go under the trailer, between the front and rear wheels. Fortunately the trailer height was such that I could go under it, and I quickly went from one side to the other and into Wiley's road. I had a good case of the shakes when I considered the dumb thing I had just done. For some reason I had trouble telling Mom about the episode. I think it was probably sometime during the next summer when I got around to letting the cat out of the bag.

I had mentioned that God must have had a reason for Mom to return to the mountains after her high school days. I was told that during the twenties and thirties, although she had no formal nursing training, it was not unusual for her to be called when sickness hit any of the mountain families. When the doctor came to visit the mountains, he would stop and pick up Mom to take along on the visit. Mom would then be entrusted with the medicine and instructed on the dosage. She would then take over the care, as doctors were not regularly seen in the hills. Mom seemed to be particularly in demand when kids were sick and high temperatures needed to be brought down. This was before the days of wonder drugs or even sulfa, when measles, diphtheria and such took a deadly toll on children.

One of the fears in the mountains was snakebite, particularly with the deadly Cottonmouth Moccasin. It was Mom who was called on when a kid was bitten near Mount Carmel Church. She used a razor blade and oral suction to undoubtedly save the child's life. Snakes were always a potential menace and we were trained young how to watch for them and avoid or kill when we had to.

Mom had a very healthy fear of snakes. On one occasion, she put some blankets out on the fence to air on a warm March day. In late afternoon, she went out and bundled up the blankets and carried them upstairs to put back on the bed, not realizing that a rattler had crawled onto the blanket during the day. As she flipped open the blanket, out came the snake in a coil on the bed.

When we came home that evening, the snake, missing its head was laying outside the kitchen door. Mom told us the story and reported on her dilemma. The snake was between her and the door, and she did not want to leave the room and have the snake find a place to hide. Remembering that there was a .32 caliber revolver in a bureau drawer, she dispatched the snake with a single shot.

"Mom," we said, "you very seldom shoot a pistol, how did you manage to hit it?" She replied, "I wanted to make sure that I did not miss so I got the gun so close that I could not miss and I did not." Of course, having faith in the knowledge that a snake will not strike until you are within its length helped. At times like this, I wonder if the snake was aware of that limitation.

As we grew older, the Shenandoah River became more of an attraction. We learned how to swim and spent a lot of hours in the river.

The Byrd bridge was the second bridge built across the river at Berry's Ferry and one of the supports for the old bridge was still in the river. It had been left standing, but had fallen over during one of the floods. We would swim out to this support and sun ourselves on it. The only problem was the capriciousness of the river and depending on its mood, it could surprise you with small whirlpools and eddies. What last week was three or four feet deep was now eight or ten feet deep, especially around the old bridge. We learned to be extra careful and never swim alone as the reputation of the Shenandoah was well earned.

Some people fished the river, catching mostly catfish. I did not care much for fishing and it was only under duress that I ended up as a fisherman. One such time was at the urging of a cousin, George Smallwood. George was probably ten or fifteen years older than I and had spent his time in the Army during World War II. He prevailed upon me to join him in a fishing trip where I was to pole the boat and he was going to take care of the fishing. Turns out his idea of fishing was to toss half sticks of dynamite into the river and catch the stunned fish as they came to the surface.

Add to this, George showed up somewhat under the influence. Somehow, I was more afraid of the wrath of George than the danger of the adventure, so I joined him, poled the boat, and George stood amidships tossing dynamite in the water. I followed George's orders, which made about as much sense then as they do on retelling. I poled upstream, he tossed the dynamite further upstream. Of course, the dynamite floated downstream, back toward the boat. As a result, it was not only the fish that were being stunned. The adventure ended with me abandoning the boat as George, with unerring aim gave a mighty heave, slipped, and the stick of dynamite landed in bow of the boat. The front end of the boat disappeared and the fishing was done. The boat was left as a derelict in the shallow water alongside of Burwell's Island, and I went home using the most remote route I could find.

One fall, a relative who owned a farm over in the Valley showed up and talked to Mom about my helping with his wheat harvest. Before I knew it, I was in his car and off on a week's tour to help him cut and harvest his wheat. In those days, the state of the art was about one step beyond McCormick's reaper. For three or four days I rode a binder behind the horses, as my relative cut the wheat. The binder gathered the grain stalks and bundled them into sheathes. They would accumulate out on the end of some tines and when a set number were collected, I was supposed to let loose my foot petal and allow the sheaves to drop off. If done correctly, the sheaves would end up in a row and would be stacked for drying in a shock.

The farm was typical of the area and consisted of many hills and dales. I doubt that even a proficient farmer could have kept those rows aligned. I did pretty well on the level ground, but unfortunately, there was more not level than level. I left sheaves scattered all over the farm, but since help was hard to find, the relative was forced to stay with me. Finally we got the job done, this after sunburning my legs to the point of blisters and all my muscles aching as I attempted to accomplish my biblical task of "Bringing in the Sheaves."

I had some experience with farming from our visits to Granddad's farm in our early years. During our trips to Granddad's farm, Linton and I used to pester our older cousin, Clifton Lee, the hired hand, to let us plow. We would follow him through the fields and watch him as the large plow turned over the soil. The pair of horses, Tom and Bill, pulled the plow, each trying to get a half step on the other, so as to throw the extra load on the other horse. I guess the horses understood physics better than many humans did. The only difficulty in plowing, besides keeping the furrow straight, was the occasional rock that could catch the leading edge of the plow and bring everything to a halt.

Granddad had spent a lot of money and energy in dynamiting and removing the rocks, but some survived the effort and Clifton was always on the lookout for those remaining. We would pester Clifton until he let us plow a furrow. Of course, I was not big enough to control the plow, but I would get between the handles which were above my shoulders and with a "Gitty-up," we would be on our way.

One of the horses would walk in the furrow of the previous round, so keeping the row straight was not much of a problem. My biggest problem was keeping the blade in the proper depth. If I lifted up on the handles the blade tended to go deeper and the horses did not like the extra load. If I pulled down too hard the blade would come up out of the ground. When this happened and the load lessened, Tom and Bill knew that feeling. Plowing was over and they could head for the barn. Clifton would have to grab the reins and take the controls. It did not take too long before I ran out of energy, and Clifton would retake the handles and we would return to our position of following behind Clifton, walking in the freshly plowed furrows. At the end of the day, Clifton would throw us up on the back of the horse, and we would get a ride back to the barn.

The farm got to be our playground and we would run through the barn and jump out on the straw stack that was the remnant of last season's threshing. This was before the days of the combines, and the threshing machine would be set up in the barn in between the haymows. The sheaves of grain would be loaded onto wagons in the fields and brought into the barn where they would be thrown into the thresher. The wheat would be sacked off, and the straw would be blown out through the open back doors of the barn,

Barns were typically of a two level variety, called a bank barn. This allowed the horses to be kept in stalls on a lower level, which exited to the rear of the barn. The straw pile would form on this lower level and be used to provide the stalls with a material to absorb the manure from the horses.

We kids were allowed to clean out the stalls and put in fresh straw. We would learn which horses were trouble and how to keep out of their way as we did the chores. Granddad always had extra horses that he was doctoring and one was not sure of their temperament. We learned to get in and shove them around in the stalls, so that the old straw and manure could get thrown out and the new straw put in.

The farm was a very self-sufficient unit. The manure and straw mixture was tossed into a pile to become the fertilizer for the spring plowing and planting. Certain fields were planted in hays, such as alfalfa. This provided the feed for the cattle and horses. The hay was stored on the top level on the hay mows and was thrown out the back doors to feed the cattle or down a chute to the stalls of the horses.

There were hen houses to hold the chickens and we were given the chore of collecting the eggs. Other out buildings provided storage for the machinery. The threshing machine was brought in on contract when harvest time came around. The farmers would help each other do the threshing, along with a number of out-side hired hands.

To a youngster like myself, threshing was a very frightening affair. The noise of the threshing machine and the stories of past accidents where someone had slipped and fallen into the opening were enough for me to keep a wide berth. The whinny of the horses added to the melee, as they had to pull up alongside the thresher and stand quiet while the load was forked off by the unloaders. A good driver with a tight hand on the reins was a necessity, as the horses did not seem to care anymore about the environment than I did.

Dinnertime (noon) brought everything to a halt and all headed to the house for food. The women of the house had spent the morning getting ready for a bunch of starving men. At Granddad's, a long table was set up in the upstairs hall and food was carried up from the basement kitchen. The kids were allowed to sit with the men, and while we could not work like they could, we could sure eat as much. There were second, third and fourth helpings of ham and fried chicken. Mashed potatoes, gravy, apple butter, and a variety of vegetables were in abundance.

The kids ran chores such as bringing drinking water to the workers. As we grew older we worked in the field, driving the horses or stacking the sheaves, as they were loaded on the wagon.

A lot of my memories of harvesting are mixed with Granddad's farm and Uncle Cap's farm. They had adjoining farms. As I grew older I spent more time at Uncle Cap's. He and Aunt Alma had five children, two older girls and three younger boys. All were older than I, except for Glenn. Bill was the oldest boy and seemed to work all the time. Wanless was the next boy, and he tried to mix athletics and farm work together. Glenn was the youngest and tried to do as little as possible and was the one with whom I spent the most time. I spent a lot of summer time there, showing up without announcement. I learned enough about farm work to know that it was not for me.

Aunt Alma treated me like a son and I joined in with the boys as they worked and played. They went to Berryville School, while I went to Boyce, so we did not see each other at school. Janice, the oldest girl had eloped in 1939, and was not around as I made my visits to Uncle Cap's and Aunt Alma's. I did get to know Garnet quite well as she was around the farm for most of that time. Both Janice and Garnet were beautiful girls, each winning the Miss Northern Virginia beauty contests.

The war years seemed to go on forever. Linton was in the South Pacific from January of 1944 until the war's end. Each news report, whether radio, newspaper or the Movietone News was watched with Linton in mind. Mom spent a lot of time praying, and you could almost see her aging as the war wore on. Rationing was in force although it did not affect us much. We did not have a car, so gasoline or tires were no problem. Sugar and shoes had their own stamps. The sugar rationing was by far the one that hit the hardest. Jams and jellies had to be put up for the following winter and sugar was an essential ingredient, which could not be home grown. Somehow, Mom would find enough to get by. The garden supplied us with the where-with-all and we did not need a lot of outside help.

During the latter part of the war we got a radio that ran off a car battery. It did not take too long to run down, so we would prevail on someone to take it to a service station to have it recharged. I think the radio came from Granddad when he got a new Philco. I remember Granddad always listening to Amos and Andy.

He did not have electricity at the farm. (Why, I do not know, as electricity was only a few hundred yards away at Josephine City.) I do recall that Granddad was mightily upset if anyone called him during Amos and Andy. Since he was the sheriff, I guess all crime came to a halt during that time.

The radio we had was equipped with a "Tiger eye" tube that had a signal seeker that would narrow or widen as the station was tuned in. As night came on and the stations came in more clearly, we would try and tune in the far away stations such as KDKA, Pittsburgh or WLS, New Orleans.

Before we had our own radio, Linton and I would go down to Bill and Meta's and listen to the fifteen-minute serials that came on every evening. These included "Jack Armstrong," "Sky King," "Green Hornet," and "Inner Sanctum." The latter was the one that normally concluded the evening, and we headed home with our adrenaline flowing as we imagined the witches and goblins after us.

Our local station was WINC, Winchester. Other stations included WTOP, Washington and WBAL, Baltimore. After a while, I found myself gravitating toward the popular music stations and on Sunday the Lucky Strike "Hit Parade" came on. Every week the top twenty songs were played as measured on the number of records sold. We did not have a Victrola at that time, so my only sources of pop music were the radio and the Wurlitzer coin machines located at the Greyhound Bus Station. They were also at the diners, but it was not until late high school years that I ventured into a diner.

My hunting experiences were limited mainly to squirrel hunting. I knew all the best nearby spots in the mountains and spent a lot of my time from late September to January pursuing squirrels. I mostly hunted alone, and enjoyed the quietness of the woods early in the morning as I strained to differentiate between the water dripping off the leaves and the squirrels dropping their "cuttings" as they ate the acorns or hickory nuts.

One of the great thrills of squirrel hunting was the return home, still early in the morning. Mom seemed to know when to start breakfast and the aroma as I turned the corner of the house was the greatest. Breakfast consisted of a menu that would be guaranteed to clog the arteries of an elephant.

First there were corn cakes, not corn pone, but corn cakes. Corn cakes were made from corn meal batter with a small amount of wheat flour added for smoothness. They were then cooked on a griddle, like pancakes. Mom then made a "water" gravy made out of ham fat, a little condensed milk and water. The gravy was poured over the corn cakes and topped with apple butter. A slice of fried ham topped off the plate. What a breakfast! When we were working on the woods, this breakfast, many times served at four or five in the morning was guaranteed to stay with you until (and probably after) lunch time.

There were no deer in the mountains then, and some of us would talk of going deer hunting. At the end of the war, I did get a chance to go to a county near the West Virginia line and try my luck at deer hunting. The trip was organized by Irvin Wiley and George Smallwood, who had recently returned from the war. The three of us were armed with makeshift weapons. I had a double-barreled shotgun, with one barrel loaded with buckshot and the other with a "rifled" slug. Irvin had a Browning semi-automatic shotgun and George, a war surplus rifle, probably an '03 Springfield.

During deer season, you could not hunt squirrels (probably a rule put in to keep mountain people from hunting deer with .22s. Actually the mountain hunter was probably more deadly with the underpowered .22 than with the unfamiliar high powered weapon). The only other game that was legal during deer season were bear and turkeys.

Irvin and George went, equipped with a turkey caller, each extolling his abilities to call a turkey from as far away as a farmer's yard just outside of Winchester. Well, we did not see any deer or bear, but the turkey callers were hard at work, showing their skills. Since Irvin was a bit overweight, he did not like to venture too far from the truck. Finding a sunny side of a hill, he sat on a downed tree and waited for the deer to come to him.

As time wore on, the only chance to get game depended on his ability as a turkey caller. Out came the caller and "scraaatch, screeech" went the sound out through the woods. I was pretty sure this was a futile attempt. After about an hour of this sound that sounded more like fingernails on the blackboard than a real live turkey, I was surprised to hear a turkey return the call. We all came alive at the sound of the turkey in the distance and weapons were put at the ready. I pulled the rifled slug out of one barrel, and now had two barrels waiting with buckshot. The calling went on for an eternity, as it was obvious that this was a wily old "tom" who was not about to be taken in by some amateur from across the Shenandoah. Irvin would call, then wait him out. Finally the turkey would answer and be a little closer. Irvin would wait and then call again, adding his "pièce de résistance," by scratching in the ground with a dry twig. Finally the object of our attention was so close that we could see the bushes moving. With guns at the cock, we waited for the turkey to come into a clearing some twenty yards away. It finally appeared. Guns came quickly down and expletives came out of our mouths when we realized that the turkey was another hunter, who was stalking us. Irvin said later on that he should have known, as the smell of a cigarette was in the air and while he had seen a lot of smoked turkey, he had never seen a turkey smoking.

Coon hunting was a second sport that took a lot of our time in the fall. There were four of us who ventured out two, maybe three times a week. George Estep, Peaty Weir, Burchell Wiley and I would head out with the dogs and spend the nights following the dogs as they trailed the coons. We would vary our areas, from Wildcat Hollow to Fent Wiley Hollow and end up wet and cold, trudging back to the car, at around two in the morning. Since there was no reprieve from school, I would hope for an easy study day. Since we had no ability to shower and clean up after the hunt, I am sure it was no secret what we had been doing, especially when the dogs would sometimes take on a skunk.

Peaty had two hounds. One, Old Blue, had only three legs as a result of an encounter with a barbed wire fence. Old Blue was quite the hunter and would trail until he could not walk. One of us would then carry the dog back to the car. (Did I mention that the teachers and other students probably knew that we had been hunting the night before?)

The car was not really a car at all. It was an old Model A station wagon with most of the wood trim gone and many of its accessories, such as one headlight, missing. One missing piece that became an essential part of one night's episode was the driver's side window.

About midnight, the dogs came upon a hot trail and were on the coon so fast that he did not have time to make it up the tree. It took refuge in a hollow log and the dogs were trying to tear that log to pieces as we came upon the scene.

Burchell, always the guy with the wild ideas, said that he had heard that raccoons could be tamed and made into pets. He prevailed upon us not to kill the coon, but capture him. Burchell would take him home and make a pet out of him.

Burchell pulled off his leather jacket and tied the sleeves together. Some more tying and the top and bottom were pronounced secure. He zipped down the front of the jacket and we proceeded to chase the coon from out of the hollow log and into the leather jacket. We collared the dogs, who were a might disturbed by this animal that was sequestered in the jacket. We headed back for the car and Burchell sat in the front right hand seat with a most active leather jacket on his lap. I ended up in the back seat area of the wagon (the rear seats had long been history). We headed out of the remote area on Mac Cornwall's place toward the Wildcat Hollow road, with the leather jacket jumping up and down and the hounds baying as if they were still "treed."

The story was not to end well. About a half mile from the road, the coon somehow got out of the leather jacket and sprang for freedom, this being through the missing driver's side window. Over Peaty's neck and head he went, clawing all the way. As he exited the window, the dogs, realizing that their quarry was no longer "treed," took off after the coon, following the same trail up Peaty's neck and over his head, both hitting the window at the same time. They managed to get out of the window, having Peaty's head and shoulders as a launching pad. Peaty lost control of the car and it smashed into a large granite rock and the water came gushing out of the radiator. The coon was gone and the dogs after him. Burchell went after the dogs (which took a couple of hours to retrieve), while George and I tried to find cloth sufficient to stem the blood coming from all over Peaty's face, neck and shoulders. We finally got back to my house around four or five in the morning and Mom provided the best patching up of Peaty's wounds that she could. All the while, Peaty was on me for letting the dogs loose. I did not think that it was the time to tell him how lucky he was that Old Blue only had three legs to scratch him.

Somewhere along the line, I began subscribing to outdoor magazines, such as "Outdoor Life" and "Field and Stream." They had great stories about hunting and fishing all over the country and I "lived" the tales of hunting in the Rockies or Alaska. They had lots of advertisements and one in particular got my attention. "Learn how to be a taxidermist." screamed the ad. "Big money can be earned" was the bait. "Anyone can learn it" was the clincher. Since terms were available, I filled out the form and certified that I was sixteen. (I was, barely.) The anticipated booklets started to come, but it soon became obvious that a lot more was needed than a dead critter. It went in to great detail about the skinning and preparation of the hide. That much I followed pretty well, as we had skinned a lot of dead animals before and prepared their pelts for sale to the fur man. When they got into the papier-mâché and the alum and the glass eyes, I knew I was lost. I took the entire course, saved the booklets, but never went beyond that. Mom was probably glad I did not, as I would have left for the Navy with her having a bunch of squirrels to dust.

There was another ad that caught my attention. Seagram's Whiskeys had a promotion for a set of dinner plates. Each was hand painted with fish or wild animals. I dearly wanted that set of plates. Even if I could have afforded them, they were limited to persons over the age of twenty-one. Mom did not think much of me looking at whiskey ads, as there were few things in the world that Mom hated, but whiskey was one.

While I spent a lot of time admiring the plates, I knew how Mom felt about it, so the idea was dismissed from my mind. Imagine my surprise when Christmas came around and my present from Mom was this set of plates. She had somehow concluded that her love for me outweighed the hatred she had for the whiskey merchants. As I write this, I look at my office wall and the four plates left of the set, and think of Mom and what she must have gone through that December of my sixteenth year, as she pondered the decision to sign her name to a form of a whiskey company.

We moved into the new school building as I went into the seventh grade. All eleven grades were in the same building and the transition into high school in the eighth grade meant we moved into a "home room" a little closer to the front of the building. By the end of our eleventh year, our class totaled twenty, including two brothers returning from the war.

Many of the teachers were young and unmarried, recently out of college. One, Ginny Armstrong, had graduated from college at the very young age of eighteen and ended up marrying Dave Longerbeam, who was two grades ahead of me.

Miss Ann Mason taught shorthand and played the piano. Boogie-Woogie was the rage and Miss Mason was a delight to be around, as she would entertain us with her playing. She also was an accomplished basketball player and could outshoot anyone at the school. Added to that, she was a beautiful person and one could understand why the boys were all trying to get into the shorthand and typing classes. (I forgot to mention that she held the state typing speed record.)

The school had been the recipient of a collection of trophy animal heads that had been bagged by General Billy Mitchell, the former chief of the American Air Service. These heads, mounted on the wall on either end of the corridors, presented a continuing surprise as you turned the corners of the halls.

The war came close to us as Amory Sommaripa, in the class ahead of me, was called out of school one day upon the death of his father. Mr. Alec Sommaripa, who spoke German, was killed as he stood on the top of a tank as a civilian, exhorting the Germans to surrender.

The school bus would make its rounds, picking up mountain kids all the way to Frogtown. After it crossed the Shenandoah, it made a turn north and made pickups along the farms that fronted the Shenandoah. There were two or three other bus routes that fed the school. We were on the first run and arrived at school some time before school opened, which gave us time to complete homework before the bell. I was the doer of the homework and many leaned over my shoulder as they raced to finish before school started.

I began my love of crossword puzzles in high school. They were introduced to me by Miss Richards during the study period in the library. She knew I always had my homework done, so she would bring in the daily crossword puzzle for me to attempt.

Sports were a big part of high school activities, although I did not get involved too much. I did learn to play tennis on a makeshift court alongside the school building. It was a rough asphalt court, paved only long enough to reach the backcourt lines. The area behind the lines was dirt and weeds. One developed a certain kind of game trying to take advantage of the paved areas. The principal of the school, Mr. C.E. Miley, not only had his administrative duties, but taught the history class and (in his spare time) coached the boys' football, basketball, baseball and track teams. The football team played in a six-man league. There were special rules for six-man football, which as I recall, involved a smaller field and rules where the ball had to be hiked back to the quarterback. Hand offs were not allowed and the ball had to be tossed. There was one rule, which few knew about, that the team used to win the regional championship. You could throw forward passes anywhere on the field and as many times as you wanted. While I did not play in high school, I did understand the rules, and had trouble adjusting to the eleven man rules I encountered later.

I had my first taste of writing as the editor of the school newspaper. The principal and I had running battles over some of my ideas for articles. He, of course, prevailed, except for a few occasions when I could sneak something in. My only claim to fame was getting the paper printed by a professional printer, rather than the mimeographed editions of the past. This was accomplished in part by my letting the owner of the printing company think that I was going to work for him after graduation.

During my senior year, Granddad decided to sell his farm in the Valley and come live with us. Along with him came my first cousin, Richard. I envied two of Granddad's possessions and looked forward to those coming with him. The first was his Model A sedan, and the second was his "reel" type push mower. He ended up selling the Model A when he sold the farm, but I did get the use of his lawn mower. Now many of you think that this was no prize, but after cutting the lawn for many years with a hand sickle, that lawn mower represented a giant leap forward.

I was not too happy with Richard as a part of the baggage, as I had to share my bedroom with him. He was about my age and wanted to join me in everything I did, so I had a pretty strong resentment built up to his presence.

Mom managed to buy Granddad's old piano and that ended up being shoe-horned into her downstairs bedroom. The piano had a long history as it was from the old country and I believe was one of the first style pianos built. The strings were one continuous wire that went from small to large, as it made its way from high to low notes. Someone said that it was a harpsichord that had been laid flat for the hammers to hit. Its history was not limited to manufacture by someone named Stein, but had a bit added while occupying a prominent location in Granddad's bedroom. Granddad always had a lot of freeloading visitors, who would come and stay and stay and stay. When Mom was a kid, one particular visitor not only would overstay his welcome, but he loved to think of himself as a pianist. The only trouble was that he knew only one song, which he would play continuously. This drove Uncle Dan to think of devious ways to get rid of the visitor or, if this was not possible to stop the infernal noise, his ultimate solution was to take a pair of wire cutters and cut the piano wire. This ruined the piano as an instrument, and did not achieve the desired effect of driving away the unwanted visitor. He continued to play on the instrument, and the completely out of tune piano raised the level of the torture.

The piano had spent many of its last years as a place to store the weekly editions of the "Clarke Courier," and I wondered why Mom bought the piano. She most probably paid little for it, as most interested parties would recognize that it was unplayable. It did have an effect on the old house. It was so heavy that the end of the house started sinking as the piano hastened its demise. Mom finally sold the piano to a cousin from New York. I often wonder what happened to that old (and most probably valuable) piano.

I guess this is as good a time as any to talk about Granddad's house. It was a large all brick house on a 100-acre farm just outside of Berryville. When I say all brick, I mean the inside walls and all. It had hardwood floors and French windows that were floor to ceiling.

Most of the cooking and eating were in the basement, and the entrance to the main floor was up steps, both in the back and the front. There was a long hallway from front to rear, and entrances from it to the rooms. A large stairwell led to the second floor and the rooms were duplicated there.

Of course, the house was haunted. And it had every right to be. One of the rooms had a throw rug that was located in a particular spot to cover the bloodstains of one of the visitors, who had taken his own life. I do not think it was the piano player, but that is entirely possible.

There was a later visitor who withstood all efforts to get him to leave in a reasonable time. Mom and Uncle Dan decided to help him along by telling him of the ghost, which came back to that room of his demise. Did not scare him a bit. Finally Mom and Uncle Dan figured a way. They secretly tied some silk thread to the covers and passed the threads out through the window and down to a reachable spot. They then proceeded to tell the visitor how the ghost hated to sleep with covers on. That night they awaited his going to bed, and gave him enough time to fall asleep. They crept outside and, using the thread, ever so slowly pulled down the covers. They would be jerked back up, and again they would slowly repeat the process. It had the desired effect! The visitor left the next morning, after sitting up all night. According to Mom, he never returned.

So you might think this haunted house bit is a made-up scenario. Well maybe, but I went through a couple of things that still leave me with the shivers. When I was very young and Mom went to visit and work during the week at Granddad's, she would alternate taking Linton or me with her. One of my joys was to be able to sleep with Granddad. His bedroom was on the main floor just next to his office (and what I suppose was the living or "setting" room). The living room had a large fireplace, as did every room in the house. The fireplace had been covered up and a more efficient, wood burning stove had replaced it to supply the wintertime heat. In the summer, the stove would be removed and stored in the pantry just off the living room.

One night, as I slept alongside Granddad, I was awakened by a noise. Someone was opening the front of a stove and rattling the inside of the stove as they attempted to stoke the fire. This went on for a good part of the night, as I crept closer and closer to Granddad. I was no dummy. I knew it was summertime and there was no stove in the living room. Granddad slept on, and I lay there with my eyes on the door connecting the two rooms. I did not have the faintest idea what I would do if that door opened. I probably would have fainted.

The next morning I ventured into the living room and confirmed the absence of the stove, and then told Granddad of the night visitor. "Confound it," he uttered (using his most severe cuss word), "I thought Will Shipe was long gone." Granddad then told me about one of his frequent visitors, who was long dead, but while living never got warm. He would continually open the stove door, and stoke the fire in an attempt to increase its heating effect. Now, if anyone wants to consider that maybe Mom and Uncle Dan were up to their old tricks, this was some twenty years after the "covers" episode. Uncle Dan was long gone from Granddad's. Say, do you suppose Mom would have done...nah! No way.

One last story about the strange goings-on at Granddad's house. "Aunt Alice" was Granddad's second wife and was pretty well crippled when she died. She walked with a cane, dragging one foot in an unmistakable walk. When Aunt Alice died, we all assembled at Granddad's. It was late in the evening, and we were in the living room (without the presence of Mr. Shipe, I hope). As we sat there and talked of Aunt Alice, we heard the back door open, and the shuffling of someone as they came down the hall. It sounded just like Aunt Alice. We looked toward the open door that led into the hall waiting for someone to reach the door and turn in. But no, the walk went past the open door, on down the hall; the front door was heard to open and close and the sound was gone. Somebody spoke up, "Well, I suppose she is gone now for good." I think I was the only one who thought this happening was strange. The older persons seem to take these spiritual events in stride.

Granddad Smallwood was sheriff of Clarke County from 1896 until 1944, with a two-year period somewhere in between where he left the duties to someone else. In those days, he was the only law in the county. If he needed a deputy, he would deputize one of his sons, Uncle Cap, and off they would go in the Model A sedan. He never carried a gun, nor needed one. As he took weapons off persons, they were tossed in his office drawer and in time became the focus of my wanting to own them. He promised them to me, but after the sale of his belongings most of them disappeared as his sons cleaned up the leftovers.

Granddad suffered through one experience that many said changed him forever. There was a murder in the county and Granddad had to go to Pennsylvania to bring back the prisoner. After the trial, the prisoner, Mr. Benjamin Lipjin, was sentenced to die by hanging. It was Granddad's duty to spring the trap at the execution. He did. It was said that Granddad was never the same person afterwards.

Maybe this is the place to insert some information that was written about Granddad that is part of his biography in the "History of Virginia." The date is about 1922–1923, as it indicates that Mom is a schoolteacher. It is printed in small print and is here only to record details that might be lost otherwise. (It should also be noted that the biography somehow misses one of Granddad's children. This was Aunt Josie and she was between Aunt Letitia and Aunt Omega.)

"William Walton Smallwood, Sheriff of Clarke County, is a native of this county and a representative of one of its old and honored families, his birth having occurred on the old home farm on the Shenandoah River, east of Berryville, October 16, 1863. His loyalty to his home county has never wavered, and is shown not only in effective official service, but also in his successful alliance with the farm industry, as the owner of a well-improved farm near the county seat.

Sheriff Smallwood is a son of Sylvester and Sarah Margaret (Thompson) Smallwood, both natives of the Blue Ridge Mountain District of Clarke County, where the former was born in 1839. Sylvester Smallwood became a member of the Virginia militia, but he was not called into military service, though he gave loyal support to the cause of the Confederacy. He became one of the extensive and successful farmers of Clarke County. He passed the closing period of his life at Paris, Fauquier County, where he died in 1887, his wife surviving him by about three years and the remains of both resting in the cemetery of the old home district in Clarke County. Mrs. Smallwood was a daughter of Benjamin Thompson, and the family name of her mother was Blake. The Thompson farm was on the top of the Blue Ridge, in Loudoun and Clarke Counties. Of the eleven children of Mr. and Mrs. Sylvester Smallwood eight attained to maturity; William W. of this review, is the eldest; Julia is the wife of John F. Royston and Virginia became the wife of Walter S. Royston, a brother of John F., and she is now deceased. Emma May is the wife of T.C. Carroll, a farmer near Berryville; Nannie, who became the wife of George Coffman is now deceased; Margaret is the wife of Ira Fewell, of Loudoun County; Charles Henry died in 1922; and Benjamin F. Died in 1921.

Bourbon Smallwood, grandfather of the present sheriff of Clarke County, was a native of this county and here passed his life as a farmer near the summit of Blue Ridge Mountain, where his father, James Smallwood, settled upon coming from the district near Norfolk. James Smallwood was a patriot soldier during the Revolution, and for his service, he was granted a tract of land in Hancock County, Illinois, the present City of Carthage is said to occupy a part of this tract, of which Mr. Smallwood never took possession. Bourbon Smallwood married Eliza Tomblin, and of the children of this union, Rebecca married her first cousin, James Tomblin, her life being passed near the old family homestead;

Sylvester was the next in order of birth; Arrissa became the wife of Robert Drish; Mary married Charles Lloyd; Amanda became the wife of Samuel Lanham; Lucy married Everett Fowler; Bushrod owns the old home farm and there resides; John F. is a farmer in Clarke County, as is also Thomas; George, now deceased, was the only Confederate soldier, thus representing the family in the Civil War.

William W. Smallwood gained his early education in the rural schools, and after leaving school, when about nineteen years of age, he remained with his father until the latter's death. Thereafter he rented and remained fifteen years on the Lewis farm near Berryville, and in 1916 he purchased the David McGuire farm of 100 acres, the fine old brick house on this place constituting the home of the family and having been erected many generations ago by David McGuire.

In 1898, Mr. Smallwood was elected sheriff of Clarke County, and thereafter he was twice re-elected, without opposition. He resigned near the close of his third term, but in 1915, he was appointed to fill out the unexpired term of Sheriff Levi, his incumbency of this office having continued through regular elections since that time. One of the disagreeable duties that devolved upon Mr. Smallwood in his administration of sheriff was the execution of Benjamin Lipjin, convicted of murder. He is unfaltering in his loyalty to his official charge, and this has been significantly shown in his firm stand in upholding the provisions of the national prohibition law. By virtue of his office he was chairman of the Clarke County Draft Board in the World War period. It is to the credit of the county that only four men in Clarke County evaded the draft, and they are still listed as "slackers."

December 2, 1882 recorded the marriage of Mr. Smallwood and Mary. E. Elsea, who was born and reared in Clarke County, a daughter of Albert Elsea. Mrs. Smallwood, one of the younger of a large family of twelve children; Lillian, wife of H. W. Lloyd; Dora, wife of Clifton Lee, Sylvester, who married Elizabeth King; Albert, who married Maggie Appell; Nellie, the wife of T.M. Reed; Letitia, wife of Ernest Carroll; Omega, wife of George Coffman; William Walton, Jr.; Nathaniel, who married May Elsea; Rudolph; Alma, a teacher in the public schools; and Daniel."

When high school graduation came, and it was my duty to give a speech, I used the identical valedictory speech that Mom had given in 1921. Nothing had changed in the challenges of the world, even though a world war had been fought between the times.

As we graduated, and our thoughts looked toward the future, I had a dream of becoming a Forest Ranger; a dream that was out of any realm of possibility as no local colleges offered a degree in forestry. The only ones I could find on the East Coast were Duke and Penn State, both of which were out of my league. In addition, advantages were being given to returning veterans.

So after graduation, I went to work for Joe Hough in his construction business. Joe had himself, his brother, a nephew and myself (and sometimes, Linton) as his total force. We built some new homes, re-roofed others, added garages, and painted others. All of which gave me the tools I needed to be a homeowner many years later. (That, of course, was not in my mind at the time.) We went to work in Joe's old '33 Plymouth sedan, which was showing the ravages of time. It had a steering wheel with a "Lover's Knob" on it, which was necessary, not for any amatory reasons, but because the steering wheel had about a full turn play in it. Driving that car was almost like watching little kids pretend to drive cars, as they busily spin the steering wheel back and forth and nothing happens.

The Plymouth was also equipped with a flat belt pulley attached to one of its rear wheels, which gave it kind of an ungainly look as it went down the road. (The flat belt pulley was used to supply "on site" power for such tools as cut off saws. By jacking up the rear wheel and setting the throttle on the car, the wheel would turn and supply the power through the "flat" belt to a saw that had been towed behind.) The car did have one feature that made it the place to be on a cold morning. It was equipped with a "South Wind" heater, which burned gasoline and was by far the most efficient heating device I have ever seen.

We had jobs in Upperville, up the Shenandoah, Paris, and one as far away as Fairfax. The last one made for a long day as we added the 50 plus miles each way to the day's work. I remember that one well. It involved attaching a new garage to the existing house. As we finished putting up the roof rafters, Joe showed up and cast a critical eye on the job and noticed that the rafters had a different pitch than the original house and they needed to be matched. So down they had to come. The chore was given to me, as I was tall enough to stand on a board laying on the ceiling joists and reach the top of the rafters with the hammer. I was never known for brains, but what little I had I almost lost as I swung the hammer back towards me to knock down the rafter and catch it at the same time. Yeah, you guessed it. I missed the rafter and hit myself directly in the forehead with the hammer. My compatriots on the ground were torn between concern for my condition and the hilarity of watching me weave and wander on the "one by twelve" plank that was my safety net. I finally slumped down on the board and supported by that and the cross joists, I kept from falling to the concrete some distance below. I was rapidly taking on the appearance of a unicorn as a knot popped out about an inch or so long. I do not remember how they got me down, but everyone called it a day, and with me in the back seat they headed home.

The next morning, the swelling had gone down; I had no headache, and I headed back to work. No one was happy with me, as Joe not only docked me for the time off the afternoon before, but included the other two, who had taken off early to get me home.

By fall, I had enough spending cash to buy a new Mossberg semi-automatic .22 rifle with a telescope on it. I bought it on a Saturday just before Christmas. The following morning, I set up some targets in the yard to the west of the house and started to sight it in. Mom called me for breakfast; I put the rifle in the corner of the room after making sure it was on safe. During breakfast, Ken and David Erickson showed up, probably after hearing the shooting. Ken was nine or ten and pretty familiar with guns, so when he picked it up, I was not too concerned (after all it was "on safe"). The pop of the gun going off and six-year-old David slumping over is a memory still stamped in my mind. Dave had been shot in the abdomen. Mom picked him up and carried him to Bill and Meta's. Bill was out cutting a Christmas tree and Mom found Irvin Wiley at his store a short distance away.

Mom and Irvin took Dave to the Winchester Hospital, and I was left standing around wondering how Bill was going to treat me when he found out what my rifle had done. Of course, Bill had little concern for me, as he headed for Winchester to check on Dave. The bullet had entered the abdomen in the front, and exited his thigh in the rear. It missed bones and vital organs. He was operated on and thanks to the new sulfa drugs, which came out of World War II, any infection was stopped. Dave was home in time for Christmas. At the age of seventeen, I had been responsible for a near fatal accident and the process of aging had begun.

On a Saturday in late January 1948, I went to Winchester and as usual went to the movies. I do not remember what the movie was about, but apparently it had something to do with the Navy. Before the afternoon was out, I found myself at a Navy recruiter's office and I was seriously talking about joining the Navy. With Linton having been in the Navy, I never thought of any other branch of the service. Linton and I had discussed me and the Navy and his only advice to me was, "Make sure you get a rate designation assigned to you before you sign up, as they have a way of forgetting unwritten promises once you're in." I wanted electronics and Navy Air and now I found myself saying that I would join if they would give me that rate. The recruiter looked at his manuals and confided that I was lucky, as normally they required the recruit to have a prior history of electronics, confirmed by an "EDDY" test, whatever that was.

For a 90-day period, they were suspending the test to see what kind of recruits they would get as a result. (This was the beginning of a series of flukes that seemed to follow me through my Navy life.) All I had to do was score well on their general tests and I was in. After agreeing to come back the following Monday for a physical and the battery of tests, I headed home to give Mom the "good" news.

I told myself that Mom would be okay. She really would not be alone, as Granddad Smallwood and Cousin Richard (Uncle Rudolph's boy) were staying with us. Mom was not overjoyed at my decision, but after some persuasion, agreed to sign for me for a three-year enlistment. I told her of the great things I could learn in the Navy, especially electronics, which would be a start on a new life after I got out. To top it off, I told her of one of the sales point as given me by the recruiter. "Every year they take up to 160 sailors from the Navy and send them to the Naval Academy," whatever that was. After a day of testing on the following Monday, I was pronounced physically fit for the Navy and mentally fit for the Naval Aviation Electronics school.

On February second, 1948, I found myself standing down on the highway, satchel in hand, awaiting a station wagon to pick me up and take me to Washington, DC to be sworn into the Navy. It was three months plus before my eighteenth birthday and it was time to leave the protection of home and the mountains to see what the world had to offer.

0-595-30187-8

CPSIA information can be obtained at www.ICGtesting.com
Printed in the USA
LVOW06s0711270813

349674LV00003B/236/A